THE
WELL

THE WELL

by Jack Cady

ARBOR
HOUSE
NEW YORK

For Frank and Bev

PHOEBE *Why have you not thrown open the doors,*
and called in witnesses? It is terrible
to be here alone.
THE HOUSE OF THE SEVEN GABLES

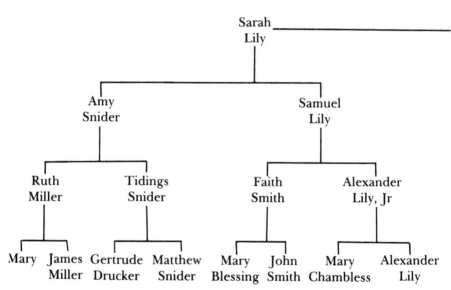

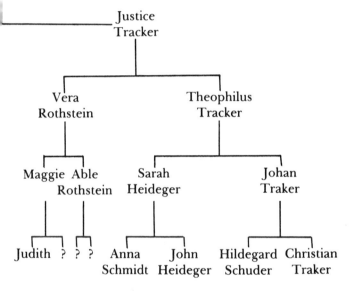

CHAPTER 1

There are Things that do not love the sun. They weep and curse their own creation.

Sometimes on earth a cruel shift takes place. Time splits.

Corpses possessed at the moment of their death rise from tombs. The dark ages of history flow mindless from stagnant wells and lime-dripping cellars. The corpses, those creatures of possession, walk through ancient halls and rooms.

The house of the Trackers stands. It was begun by Johan Traker, father of Theophilus Tracker, grandfather of Justice Tracker, and great grandfather of John Tracker.

Through endless halls are dusks gathering like the memory of screams. There is a concatenation. Presences drift toward combination. Darkness rises and takes shape behind the sound of footsteps. The house prepares.

Autumn rains followed the river, and the construction crews made a final effort. Men slogged through slick clay that stained the weeds blown dead by powerful chemicals. Grasses and leaves fell to decay.

Fungus grew between the toes of men, with boots greasy with clay that dried overnight like well-fired pottery. The storm-thrown rain drove operators from high seats on machines that stood hefty in the puddling soil;

1

the yellow compactors, the tough orange graders and the green buckets.

The new highway stretched raw along the bottoms. It jumped creeks and cut hillsides. It drove a plumb line through the rolling country. For miles it was enclosed by burr and acid-loving weeds which insinuated seed into the soil of the sprayed ditches. In the third heavy frost all of the plants were dead, but the men were gone by then.

The road ran in spurts like extended humps over mass graves. One section ran to the edge of an industrial city where stack flame and sulphur hung over the crowded population. Another section leap-frogged the Ohio River on the bluffs of southern Indiana. All sections were joined by a scheme on blueprints, and all were actually to be joined in the coming year.

After the rain came arctic cold. The mud froze. As the winter turned into one of the worst ever recorded in Indiana, the highway became a mound of white. Storm followed storm. The new year opened with ferocious wind. Then, in the third week of the new year, there was a lull. The highway stretched toward the horizon, unmarked except by an occasional track of a fox or rabbit, a stain of blood when the tracks met.

That is how John Tracker first saw the highway that cut him from property he had not seen since he was twenty, a house where he had not lived since he was ten. During his teens, when his father was normal, John had visited his father here. He had tried to push these years from his mind. Failing that, he had tried to press them into his memory and hide them. It was almost like those memories lived in a well of fear; and he had tried to cover that well. Now it seemed about to burst its cover. Tracker cursed the circumstances that brought him here.

The mound of highway stood like a wall. Beyond that wall, the house of the Trackers.

Fear. His spine felt numb, a contradiction, but true. It

2

was as uncontrolled as a hanged man's kicking. His shoulders were tight. The back of his neck felt like it was in a clamp.

He had avoided thinking about this place. He had avoided dreaming of it. Usually John Tracker worked so hard that he believed the absorption of work kept him from dreaming. For years he had fought memory and believed it was whipped. Now he was finding that some of his memories were present like the events of yesterday. He told himself that of all men in the world he was best equipped to handle this place. While he thought it, he also thought that he might not be able to handle it at all. Memory pressed. He could nearly hear his own childish voice questioning:

"What's in the well?"

"Nothin' in that one, boy." His grandfather, tall, gray-haired, blue-jeaned and with tools at his belt. "Nothin' in that one, atall. Don't get nowhere near that other'n."

"Where is the other one?"

"If you don't know, then you got no troubles."

"What's in the well?"

"Water. Don't fall in. Don't go near any well." His father was usually preoccupied, his brown hair curly and uncombed, his head bent over ledgers or old and crackling books.

"What's in the well?"

"Fall in there and you'll see, all right. Look in there and it'll grab you." His grandmother knew and was not telling. She was sharp-tongued and had no time for little boys, unless she was scaring them into silence.

John Tracker sat in his car and watched the snowy grade. He was forty years old. For the last twenty years, since the last time he saw this place, he had admitted that there were at least two minds in his head. There was the business and decision-making mind. It was the mind that ruled him. It caused a little laughter, a lot of money-making and lately it was beginning to accept and enjoy pleasure.

He thought of the girl. Amy seemed a long way off, which was not true. She was in the hotel in Indianapolis. He had slept beside her last night. Something beyond casual sex was happening between him and Amy. When he thought of it, it made him shake his head and concentrate on business.

The other mind that lived in his head came from the past. It once lived in the passages of that house beyond the freeway. He controlled it pretty well, but now it seemed ready to make demands. Tracker knew enough of himself to know he was at least partly depraved. He knew enough about the world to believe that most other people were too, but he figured he was, somehow, a special case. He shook his head. Except for the girl, who was really a woman but who thought of herself as a girl, he was alone too much. Either that, or he was in the company of businessmen.

He wished he were back in the hotel with Amy instead of sitting in his car looking at the snow-covered mound. She was a tall woman who showed a strange combination of sensuality, grace and sexual desire, mixed with prudishness. Tracker knew enough about women to understand that Amy sometimes worked under a lot of pressure that seemed unnecessary. It was like she made pressure so she would seem important when she solved the problem. She was still the best woman he had ever met, though she did not seem to have had much experience with men.

Amy was his traveling secretary, and had been for three years. They had always slept in separate rooms until this last week. Tracker again wished she were with him, right now, and the wish did not have much to do with sex. He slouched in his car and stared at the grade. The few automobiles that traveled this side road held farmers and small-townspeople who looked at his foreign car and were

4

always talking as they passed. Talking in the stores, or on the courthouse lawn or in the churchyards on Sunday. Talk was the most plentiful commodity in the world. By evening the whole county would know that John Tracker had returned to the house of the Trackers.

A low rumble vibrated in the back of his throat. His lower jaw dropped, and he felt his hands curling. A feral sound seemed to rise from his throat. It sounded to him like the warning of a cornered animal.

He was shocked by it, he thought it was long past. He'd worked so hard to get rid of it. He knew that other people did not hear it; at least he was pretty sure they did not. But now, here in the presence of the house of the Trackers, it had returned, and even if others did not hear it, he did. Once again, he did.

The story going around the county might say that John Tracker was eight feet tall and had the blood of babies on his breath. For a shocking moment he wished it were true. Actually he was 5' 11" and muscular. His teeth were clean and even and unbloodied. He kept from fat by constant work and exercise. His face was weathered from the years before the first big money, and he had dark eyes that sometimes announced decisions well ahead of his voice. On this visit to the house he was dressed in wool shirt, work pants and boots. Usually he wore business suits.

His Mercedes was out of its element. Snow melted on the windshield and wind gusted against the car. It responded with shudders like his own. He stopped the engine and continued to look beyond the freeway. He could not name his fear, but he could name its source.

Immense and towering beyond the mound was the house, rising like twisted battlements on the bluff above the river. Coarse, cankered, its spires and points faded in and out of Tracker's vision as low clouds ran through the snow-blown sky—a sky that seemed a funnel of gloom. A well of despair? The house reached high, weatherbeaten.

It looked like the last castle of defense in a chess game against civilization-striding forces. Yet Tracker knew that the house was, in its fashion, as contemporary as himself.

Beneath the cold sky the house seemed luminous. Its brown and yellow mosaics, the Stars of David in purple, blue and green, the silver crosses, the umber and gold birds, black octagons, russet circles, white moon crescents and multicolored triangles. Rusted iron railings on tiered balconies held carved satyr's masks, sea beasts. There were griffins and Biblical renderings of Jonah and Goliath and the Fall. Because of the light and distance, Tracker could not make out the figure on the enormous stained glass window that wove the face of the house into an imitation of a medieval cathedral.

Rusted, cracked, faded, the designs swirled and beckoned, as sure as the Book of Revelations, as obscure. Some balconies were tumbled. Carvings that decorated them stood singly on posts like chopped heads displayed as some stern lesson. Ancient fecundity figures with oversized bellies dwelt beside satanic forms. From eaves sprouted faces of forgotten gods that seemed struck dumb by surrounding gargoyles. The wind pressed against closed shutters. The house bore the injury of time and weather, yet at no place did it seem weak. Only the shrill tumbling of its symbols was affected.

Nothing so huge could be just a house. It was more a trap, a disaster visited on Trackers for over a century. Man after man, and woman after woman, they added their share: predestined, it seemed, to pour into the monster the best of each individual genius.

And they were, in their fashion, geniuses:

Johan the builder. In Johan's middle age the theme of the house emerged. Johan began to worry about his soul. He built the first trap in his already enormous house. It was a trap to capture the Devil. Johan's wife was named Sarah. Her genius was sainthood, if tales about her were to be believed. Sarah was a saint of patience and forbearance.

Their son Theophilus was the designer and primitive artist. Theophilus was also a builder. His wife's name was Vera, and her genius was to inflict mental and emotional pain. If John Tracker, their grandson, could not remember his great grandparents Johan and Sarah, he could remember his grandparents Theophilus and Vera too well.

Justice, John's father, was considered by many to be out of his mind, but in his rational moments he was a theologian and historian. Justice's wife was also named Sarah. John Tracker did not know what his father Justice had built into this house, but it had to be something huge; when Justice was all right he was truly brilliant. John's mother, the second Sarah, ran away from this house, and John figured that no matter how frenzied his mother's later life was, she gave this house its proper name. Sarah never called it the house of the Trackers, she spoke of it as "that hideous place."

As for himself, John Tracker had no wife. He also, he was sure, had no genius. Right now his job was to destroy, and you did not need genius to do that. You also did not need a wife. This was a job best done alone.

The house had to be destroyed because of the new freeway. Actually that was only one reason. There were other considerations. If it was only a matter of destruction then the state could do the job. He smiled and tried a low laugh, and this time the laugh came. He would think of the other considerations later.

The house dominated his view, and he plotted its destruction while wondering at its size. There would be more than two hundred and fifty rooms, not counting the towers, not counting the darkened plain of the cellar nor the subcellar, which he considered a true nether-region.

He paused. There was one decent thing in that house

his father, Justice, once built a greenhouse on a third floor terrace, which was the sole retreat for John as a child.

He smoothed his hair, rubbed at his eyes, was surprised by the rough wool shirtsleeves. He raised his hands. They were strong, not trembling. Dark hair on the backs of his hands contrasted with the brightly colored wool shirt

It was past time to get moving, but he remained seated to watch the scud of clouds between the towers. High gables gave onto areas of flat roofs, wide porches; first floor, second, third, and now there was a porch on fourth. That was new in the past twenty years. Roof to subcellar the house stood railed, bannistered, balconied of oak, pine, teak, mahogany, walnut, elm, poplar, cherry, gum, rosewood and maple. It was foundationed in rock with rock underfootings cut from the bones of the land.

Tracker thought of his grandfather Theophilus and of his eyes that sometimes flared with new ideas, that at other times were cold, flat like the eyes of a reptile. No doubt Theophilus was dead by now, his eyes blank, slatelike. The corded arms of Theophilus, the white, Methuselah hair . . . dead, kicked out of Hell, if John Tracker was any judge.

Wind buffeted the car and whirled snow along the top of the grade. The snow danced formless. Tracker shuddered. It seemed like there were memories that were going to come no matter how he tried to hold them back. He had visited his father here more than once. Those years between ages ten and twenty had been bad ones. Maybe they'd also been bad for his father.

Tracker turned from the memories. Snow whirled on the grade. Time to get moving. He was, after all, John Tracker; a millionaire businessman who did not put up with foolishness from anything human. This was not, after all, the thirteenth century. A cold draft touched his ankle. Tracker restarted the engine to run the heater. The weather was already dragging on the afternoon light. With

8

this kind of winter, he was sure there would be more snow.

The heater warmed him, and he reluctantly stopped the engine, opened the door and stepped into deep snow, nearly sliding into a shallow ditch along the access road. From the trunk he took a flashlight and a crowbar.

The snow whirled, danced, feathered.

He was sure the place was abandoned. His father was reported missing and presumed dead for more than the required seven years. His grandfather Theophilus was either dead, or in his nineties. His grandmother Vera, the same. Nothing was alive in that house except spiders and rats.

He wished he knew more about his family. If he knew more he would not feel so damned alone, so alien. Those were strange things for a man to feel when that man controlled the kind of business John Tracker owned. Still, he needed facts and his memory mostly fed him emotion. If he had more facts there might emerge some overall *scheme* in his family's history. That scheme might not *be* logical, but at least you could *look* at it logically.

The mound of freeway rose high. The house seemed to stand as a prop for the mound. Thirty-by-thirty rafters. Double-slate roofs. Limestone and granite mazes far beneath the earth. The monster was built and ballasted against winds so incredible they could never blow except in the mind of a demon imagination. He paused and wondered if he was overstating. Demon? Were his grandparents that bad? And he remembered their furious needs, their bizarre compulsions. Yes, his grandparents' lives wove a tapestry of lust and spite and destruction.

The snow whirled in his face and he slid twice before gaining the top of the grade. On the crest he felt saturated with snow. It was down his shirt and coat, his boots were full. He thought of going back to the car and knew he was trying to kid himself.

He looked down the white, snow-dancing grade, then

caught movement in the corner of his eye and looked back at the house. A sliding gray shadow? He saw nothing. Blown snow? If it was a running, sliding gray shadow then it meant . . . he shook his head, there was something he should allow himself to remember.

A door on the right side of the house opened and an angel carrying a large cross emerged and moved, draped and gowned, through the snow to disappear through another door at the left side of the house. The transit was slow. The angel wore gilded wings, was taller by far than a tall man. It made a faint but distinct clicking as it mechanically followed rails. It plowed snow with its carved-wooden robes. The red and silver cross was faded, but before disappearing the angel turned and presented the cross forward, directly at the grade. Some trick of light, some illumination of the dull afternoon magnified the words written on the cross. *Apage Satanis.*

Either it was a trick of the light, or a trick once constructed by John's grandfather Theophilus. John now remembered that there were three basic styles of mechanics that had been built into the house by Theophilus: there were Tricks, there were Traps, there were Warnings.

This mechanical angel, of course, was a Warning, though John did not know whether Theophilus had built the thing to warn the Devil or just to warn everyone, including himself.

The thought of generations pressed in John's mind. He recoiled from the angel, then relaxed. It was exactly the kind of trash-ridden symbol that he needed to get him started. Wooden angels. Magic crosses. He tightened his hold on the crowbar and prepared to slide down the grade, skidding through drifts toward the house of the Trackers, where the voices of generation after generation of the dead were not yet stilled.

10

CHAPTER

2

The generations of voices swirled in the air and snow about John Tracker's face. If he dared to listen he might have heard them.

One voice was Johan Traker's, founder of the house of the Trackers. During the First World War the name was changed from the German Traker to Tracker. Johan was at once the major victim, and villain, of Tracker history. He came to America in the late nineteenth century with cash. He was clever and hardworking and devout. His parents were peasant stock who prospered, but their religious beliefs were medieval.

Johan, living in a rapidly growing modern world, seemed to know nothing about that world. He clung to the god of his father, an authoritarian Protestant being that had changed little since the Reformation. He lived during a time in the history of his adopted nation when theology was essentially dead, and had been since the Civil War. Johan's world was a world of evangelicalism and dogma, and he feared the counterpart of his ferocious deity. Johan feared the Devil.

He bought timbered land and he began to build. The house that grew beyond a house that grew beyond a house was originally shaved slabs. By the time Johan had erected a rambling two stories, he was stopped from building in the direction he desired because of a well, so he decided to build his house over the well and dig a second well. Labor was cheap. Men were practical. If Traker wanted to pay, his neighbors were more interested in wages than reasons. By

11

this time Indiana was no longer frontier territory, but enough legend and memory of siege remained so that no one thought it was impractical to have a well in the subcellar of a house.

Johan's next action reflected one variety of his diabolic fear. He built his first trap to trap the Devil. Then, having built one trap, he felt compelled to build more. The already large house of the Trackers embarked toward immensity.

It may be that Johan eventually found peace, but not in this world. He died of a crushed chest as a machine he was trying to rig broke loose from hoisting tackle.

Johan was not a bad man, according to his lights. His problem was that his lights were pale, medieval lamps.

Approaching the house which Johan Traker had begun enlarging a century before, his great grandson slid to the bottom of the grade, dropped the crowbar and picked it from the deep snow which got inside his gloves. He turned to the house. There were no tracks. Surely the house was abandoned. He looked up, and through a slit in closed shutters on the second floor came what seemed a vaporous, flashing blue light.

He stared and told himself that the light was more shocking than a specter.

Maybe someone *was* alive. Maybe electricity was being generated in the house. He felt dwarfed by the rising façades and symbols, the now-hidden towers and his knowledge that mazes and catacombs lay beneath his feet. He searched as high and wide as he could see. No other light appeared.

An eighty-foot blue spruce rose beside him, brown and dead in the snow-covered garden. It was root-cut by bulldozers. No green appeared anywhere, except for a fringe by the porch where snow blew from branches of low juniper. The soil would be full of sulphuric acid from shooting bedrock for the freeway. Tracker looked with professional knowledge and told himself that if anything could live in hell it would be juniper.

His favorite business, the one that started as a hobby and was now making enormous profits, was industrial landscaping. He figured that the urge to build was natural in his family. Inborn. He liked to carve the face of a mountain and turn that raw face into a park that framed a factory. He landscaped freeways. He would get the contract to landscape this one. The freeway, he knew, was a political hot potato that was not, strictly speaking, needed. In an office at the state capitol, some weeks before, several men including a U.S. senator, gathered and Tracker was told that there must be no publicity in connection with the freeway. He was also told that as the last of the Trackers who could be found, he must get rid of that sideshow of a house before the road was open.

"Eminent domain," they said. "The state could tear it down." "It constitutes a hazard," said a man with state highways. "The feds say so, and I say so. It's the kind of curiosity . . ." The man's belly was paunchy, his mouth tight and his face red. "You can just see a bunch of yahoos crossing that new bridge when it's in. They'll take one look, hit their brakes, and bam; we'll have built the most deadly road in the nation."

"I don't own the place," Tracker said.

"You probably do," a lawyer with the state attorney's office told him. The lawyer was young, thin and seemed worried. He was said to have hopeless political ambitions. "We've been able to make no contact with anyone in the house. Your father is dead."

"Missing."

"Legally, he could be declared dead."

"I like design," Tracker said. "In my business you always work with an architect. Most landscape architects don't know pussywillow from night-shade."

It was a fair price. Every one of the men knew it. Tracker

13

would get to landscape the freeway. More important, no, *most* important, he would get to design the job. It was like he'd always interpreted other men's paintings. Well, with this job he could paint his own.

Now he stood in the cold and snow, looking up at the house. What the men from the state did not say was that the house had them buffaloed. They made no contact with that house for more than one reason. Maybe nobody was alive in there, but the real reason was that the state could find no one who would set foot in the place. The Trackers had a reputation for wildness and perversity, but the house's reputation was even stronger.

In a way he was being given an immense gift exactly when he needed a new shot of energy. When you turned forty it was a big shock. He had always heard that was true, and now he was finding out that it really was true.

He thought of Amy. Tracker knew himself well enough to figure that one. If he was not forty, he would probably not have gone beyond a good business arrangement of three years standing.

He shivered. It was stupid to be standing in deep snow when he could be inside. He tested his reluctance and surveyed the house. There was an immense scrap value. There were truckloads of antique furnishings. There were hundreds of thousands of board feet of hundred-year-old cherry and other furniture woods. Absolutely irreplaceable material. Wood like that was no longer available anyplace in the nation. He had no idea of the scrap value, but he was sure that even after high labor and trucking costs the scrap would net high in the tens of thousands.

He figured he could run a temporary road just east of the cemetery. He stopped, then smiled. He would have to check specs on the road. There was no mention or order for exhumation, but the family cemetery was certainly under the grade or near it. If his grandfather was there then traffic would be thumping across the old man's belly.

"You old bastard," he muttered. He paused to still the first surge of elation that made him want to shout and cheer. He stood with the dead tree like a monument at his side and thought that the state was really in a bind. Newspapers could be emotional. People starved, beat, cheated and pushed each other around, then got emotional over graveyards. Tracker figured he had a greater advantage than he first thought.

"You old son of a bitch," he said, turning in the direction of the grade and the covered cemetery. "You fought Hell. You listened night after night to wind against the windows. You allowed no music because it might hide the movement of evil. Wait until that road is open."

He turned back to the house, flicked the flashlight on and directed the beam into the gloom of the long front porch that was railed like a ship, running narrow like a corridor. There were seven doors on this wing. Two were built to accommodate the angel. Tracker had been away a long time, but he had memory enough when it came to traps. He went to the third door from the east and tested the footing with the crowbar as he advanced. He stood at the side of the door, turned the knob, pushed the door open and quickly moved back.

Nothing happened.

He pounded with the crowbar, the blows muffled as he struck the snow-covered porch. Then he brushed away the snow. Thin, lightly painted-over lines showed the trap. The safety was on. His memory was correct. This was the door he once used as a child. It was also the original trap built by his great grandfather Johan.

He stepped through the doorway, hit the crowbar against the floor in front of the entry. Everything was sound. From this point it should be easy as long as he stayed in remembered areas. Remembering those parts should not be difficult. For a Tracker, learning to walk through the house of the Trackers was as drilled by rote as when other people learned multiplication.

The late afternoon light did not greatly illuminate the hall. The old hex-mark-covered coffin still sat in state at the end of the front hallway—another of the early contrivances of Johan. When the lid was lifted to remove the interred soul, the fake coffin would quickly tilt backward. Concealed hay hooks were set to rise and lift any Devil by his privates. Over the coffin, if memory served, was a picture of old Johan.

Tracker found a light switch. The picture was changed. It was a picture of his father, Justice.

Except for the coffin and the picture, the long hallway was empty. Halfway down the hall a doorway led to the right. Further down another led to the left. There were three concealed passages leading from the hall. Tracker walked the length of the hall to look at the portrait of his father.

The portrait showed his father at about age fifty. Tracker could almost feel, but not see, how such an obese man could represent the lean ascetics of religious theory. Like his son John, Justice Tracker burned away fat and kept in shape, but this picture showed him fat. The face was jowly, the hair long and curling about the ears; the thick lips were relaxed, the eyes were not. There was strength and depth in the eyes that declared the subject was beyond easy fanaticism. No, Justice Tracker was not a crazy man. He was not a fundamentalist preacher either. The hands were not fat. They appeared strong and loosely folded. The subject seemed deliberately attempting to conceal their strength and tension. Tracker's first impression of the picture was that his father, while sane, looked like a man ridden by an obsession.

John turned away, trying to will himself to feel nothing and not making a good job of it. He had avoided seeing his father for years, and then his father had been reported missing, the news coming through a lawyer. John felt regret, loss and guilt, but at the time he did not understand the feelings.

He understood them now. In the whole world, for all his life, only one person never lied to John Tracker. That person was his father Justice. True, there were times when John needed support and Justice could not help—either he had not been present or he was inept—but John always felt that his father loved him, and that he never lied.

Now his father was either dead in one of this house's many traps, or he was a drifting, dying old man along some street of choked gutters.

Who had painted that picture?

He stood in the empty hallway and thought about it. Most likely Theophilus, his father's father. The other possibility was a self-portrait. His grandmother Vera had different talents. John turned back. The painting was unsigned.

A sensation as old as his childhood went through him. Something was different about the portrait. Between his first look and the second, something was changed. He looked closely. The eyes were the same. The position of the hands was the same. The change had something to do with color.

Tracker stood there, stunned. It was happening again. He blinked hard. After all these years, and after the fight against mental darkness, it was happening again.

He could almost hear the voice of the psychiatrist explaining to a child that time did not shift. Still, there were reds in the background of that painting the first time he looked. Now the reds were gone.

"We teach ourselves how we will see," the doctor once told the child. The psychiatrist was a woman of around fifty, and she was kind. He visited her every week when he was age eleven.

"When we are born," she said, "our eyes actually see upside down. After we use our eyes for a while, our minds learn to turn the picture right side up."

To an eleven-year-old it should seem no stranger than anything else. But even at age forty, and understanding a little about optics, he felt what he had felt as a child—disbelief. He had not believed her. At age eleven he believed nothing. His father told the truth, no doubt, but his father was also so removed, so abstracted that John could not understand much of what he said. And every time anyone else told him anything it always turned out to be a lie.

In the house of the Trackers it seemed that time shifted. There were, though, other possibilities. He had to think about them. This was crucial. He did not give much importance to traps. He did not give much importance to history. What he could not bear was to be without control.

He waited for the apparent time shift to be over. From the distance came a low murmur of voices. Light music tinkled somewhere. From a concealed doorway at his back came the joyful laugh of a child. His own childself laughing at some long forgotten joke?

Silence descended like a weight. He could hear himself breathe, hear his belly gurgle. The silence raked his mind. Then the shift ended as quickly as it started. The silence became normal silence.

He looked at the picture. There were no reds in the background. He was seeing an unfinished painting; the work was in an earlier stage of its production.

Several possibilities occurred and he examined them all.

It might well be that time did shift. It was against experience, and maybe it was against science. Time never shifted anywhere else. Or . . . maybe it did shift. For a moment he almost heard his father's explaining voice. At some time or other in the past, his father had given a reason for this. Of course, his father had been strange. . . . Or, it *could* be that he was hallucinating sound and silence. Tracker once had good reason to understand abnormal psychology. He could see how his mind, repressing fear on returning to the house, could be using the outlet of hallucinating old experiences.

It could also be that he had looked too carelessly at the painting in the first place. It was at least fifty percent possible that his eyes saw red where there was no red. Painters knew how to get the eye to cooperate in the composition of a work. Even advertisers knew that.

And it could also be that John Tracker still shared the madness of the Tracker family. He sure as hell did not want to believe that.

"So just stop it," he told himself. "You operate normally in a normal world.

"And you," he said to the picture, "you're dead." He did not know whether he was talking to his father, or his grandfather. The sentence of death seemed surer for his grandfather.

"Remember that you are in a circus," he said to himself so loudly that his voice echoed in the empty hall. "This is a place of low clowns, a sideshow. It's a place where the freaks have genitals for brains." He almost smiled at that.

He ordered himself to be calm. He was in this house for sane reasons. He must make sure it was abandoned. He wanted to see if there was a way to put the house on safety so that a wrecking crew could take it apart.

The third reason was both practical and symbolic.

Trackers made money. They always had. There was more money in this house than John Tracker might ever make in his life.

Did he need money? That was a question he asked himself after his meeting with the state people and the senator. He had a lot. Did he need more?

There were all kinds of answers. He figured none of them were correct, but all of them were a little bit correct.

He was tired of wheeling and dealing. He told himself

that he would not have been attracted to Amy, except that he suspected she felt the same. Money gave power to do whatever you wanted in a world that could be almost as disgusting as this house. Somewhere in these endless rooms was a cache of money that would make his own business fortune look like small change.

This house could not live without money. Destroy the house. Take the money. He grinned. He already knew what he would do with the Tracker fortune when it was found.

He would build parks. He would design them and install them and maintain them until they were established. He would take the hoard of money and turn small parts of the world into green and private places. It would deny everything this house and its people had ever thought valuable.

This house and these people had nearly destroyed his life. For years he spent dark nights, dark thoughts, in a struggle toward understanding. He still did not have this house and the people of this house driven from his mind. There was that damned involuntary snail-like sound. He was afraid that someday other people might actually hear it.

Of course, he would get to design the parks. Maybe that was romantic, he thought, but it was also decent. And prosaic, as compared to the history of the Trackers.

Tracker began to walk down the hall and through the doorway that led to the oldest part of the house. He passed through conventional looking rooms and thought that if you did not know better, you would believe this was just another old house where generations had lived. Of course, if you did not know better, you would find out fast how wrong you were.

At one place it was necessary to step around a section of floor that, when depressed, revealed needle-sharp harpoon heads that would ram through the toughest boots; their hooks would hold the victim in place. In another spot was a pressure-trip that caused the room to fill with gas. Tracker tested the quality of his fear and was pleased to find that the traps and the angel and the ornate coffin had an almost soothing effect. They could be accepted for what they were. It was like being in a madhouse and knowing you were safe because all of the patients were locked in cells.

Sometimes the rooms were staggered. You could only see from one room into the doorway of the next. Sometimes the rooms were in line, and it felt like you were in a partitioned hallway. The rooms were musty and close-smelling. Some held electric lights, others did not. In this oldest part of the house huge beams and rafters were exposed. He felt that he was walking through an enormous cellar, and it was cold like a shallow cellar. The house rose invisible above him, the massive rafters telling of the weight that towered into the scudding clouds.

He saw the unmoving figure well before he could recognize its shape. Three rooms ahead, silent in the dim light, like a figure disappearing into the fading lines of an old daguerreotype, a shape seemed to huddle in a room at the end of one hall. Tracker took a deep breath, told himself that he might have expected this; in fact, did expect it.

She was old. She was older than anyone else he had ever seen. She was old like undisturbed dust, or like the filament of crackling fragility that lies invisible on the surface of ancient books. She was as old as the dreams of presbytery, of necromancy, of praises that had once raised now tumbled spires. She was old like the echoes of pagan chants. John Tracker stood breathless with shock as he realized that he was looking at his grandmother.

CHAPTER

3

John Tracker's grandmother, Vera Tracker, was a woman whose power was inherited from the past. John's memory, nourished on childhood fears, had distorted and strengthened Vera's power. If he had known its source he might have understood it better. Vera's power went back at least three generations.

John Tracker's great great grandmother, on his father's mother's mother's side, was a woman named Judith who was a witch. Judith was the mother of Maggie. Maggie was the mother of Vera.

Witchcraft traditionally dealt in sex and mutilation, and although witch trials disappeared in America during the eighteenth century, witchcraft did not. Judith's skills were rare, but they were not out of place in the south and middle-west. They fitted well with the voodoo traditions of some former slaves, and with the fading ghosts, man-killers and dark haunts of Cherokee, Creek, Iroquois and Huron.

Judith bore the illegitimate Maggie, and kept the girl at her side until Maggie was fourteen and felt old enough to run away. Maggie received enough instruction to later pass on a distorted inheritance of knowledge. Judith died shortly after Maggie left, killed amid fire and steam in a boat explosion on the Mississippi while making passage to New Orleans. Tracker history contained a large number of tough and unique women. Being a Tracker woman had never been easy.

Amy Griffith lay half hugging a pillow as if it might become a dear friend. The pillow blocked a view of anything from her right eye, but with her left she stared critically at snow which whirled before the hotel window. She was not a Tracker woman. She was not even sure that she wanted to become one.

She had never had a house. Not ever. Now John was talking about tearing one down.

She felt pleasantly sore, her muscles stretched from having moved against and with John's weight. When he'd left to attend to the business of the house, about which he seemed awfully close-mouthed, she'd remained in bed for more than an hour. She thought there was nothing wrong with small luxuries as long as you did not make them a habit.

Almost she felt guilty about feeling so good. Tracker was not the very best lover in the world, but he would learn. So few men were in her experience that she really could not set standards. For her, Tracker was best, except one. She rubbed her belly, the inside of her legs; stretched her legs and wiggled her toes. She was glad because her legs really and truly were quite beautiful.

There was work to do. John was not sure how long he would be gone, but there was lots of time. She decided to do the work and then go to a movie. The newspaper was somewhere. She stretched comfortable and happy in the warm bed, then told herself it was time to move. If she stayed any longer the luxury would turn into indulgence.

She rose to walk naked across the room and look from the high window into winter streets. A lot of traffic. A terrible winter. The winter was easier to take because you had an excuse to get all gussied up and dressy. She had a new coat.

She found the newspapers. Plenty of movies, plus the usual war, politics, violence and sporting events. There were Hoosier debutantes, which was pretty funny. There

23

were marriages, divorces, want ads, sales on mattresses and clothing guaranteed to increase men's lust if you followed a particular commercial flag. Amy had been trying to fly her personal banner for a long time, but often admitted to herself that the results were not flamboyant. She was thirty years old, and though she could tell herself with reason that she looked more like twenty-five, even that age was bad enough.

You had to admire John Tracker, whether he was highly skilled as a lover or not. John Tracker was already a success. He was even young. Age was different when you were a man.

Well, she thought, she could have done just as well if she were a man, if there were no bad streaks of luck that came like punishments. As it was, she had a high paying job and she was respectable.

It was nice to be naked. There really and truly had not been many men. This kind of nakedness did not happen often. Thinking of nakedness, Amy did not think of naked expression. Her experience with that was mixed. She figured that experience was best forgotten.

If she wanted a lot of men it would be easy, but it was better to be a little bit lonely than promiscuous. She told herself she did not need a man, and that was proved.

Why then, did she feel so good? She was not even sure she was in love with John Tracker, although she surely did admire him.

She could almost count the reasons, like you added figures in a ledger. First, John Tracker was a good, quiet man and she was used to him. Second, he was respectable. She would not have gone to bed with a bum, because she already tried that and it didn't work. Third, he did not make her afraid. Men, being the way they were, often did make you afraid.

Dictated letters were in the open steno book on the desk. Her shorthand was impeccable. Her skills were complete. She could even read two-day-old, cold notes. When she and John occasionally argued about a letter, it was always his memory that was wrong. It had to be. She did not make mistakes like that.

She stood watching the winter streets, so far away down there, then picked up the steno book and flipped through to estimate work time. They were all pretty standard letters: "J. Lincoln, Manager, Bargain Dist TransAm, Dear Jim—expect two hundred cases of interior paint, seven hundred glazed aluminum sash, assorted kitchen furnitures (322 count) and about two thousand sheets of Jap panel this week. The drivers will be running splits for K.C. Riffle your inventory and top off their loads. Consigner is a construction supply in Medford, Mass. Cost sheets with the inventory. Have you solved your warehousing problem, yet? John Tracker."

She had a reasonably interesting, well-paid job and she did admire John Tracker. When you knew a man's business, you could guess a good deal of his history. When that man hired business managers who loved to talk, you could learn a lot more. It paid to give attention to the way John Tracker had built his business, especially if it looked like something really good was beginning to happen between you and the man.

Men were the worst gossips in the world. Amy recalled talking to the business manager who had worked longest for John Tracker. He'd told her that John had only a few thousand dollars when he left college. His stepfather at that time had been a banker. The banker guaranteed some loans, and then, the gossipy manager said, Tracker avoided the banker and the banking business. He paid back the loans, of course.

The gossip also said that John Tracker had had so many stepfathers that it was hard to keep track of them. By the time the loans were paid back, that banker was no more than a memory. Next, an auctioneer won John's respect—

sometimes John still referred to the man when he was making a business decision—and John got a job with him and watched and learned and worked hard. The auctioneer came and went pretty much as he pleased, selling things for other people, taking title to nothing. His capital risk was small. When times were good his sales were high. When the market was off the price structure broke, but he had more to sell. Another thing John learned was that men made mistakes. Small firm or large corporation, men made overpurchases or bought stock that did not move. There was plenty of insurance stock around . . . Amy smiled and thought of one of their private business jokes. The saying went that sometimes the customers had to bat down the flames of somebody's successful insurance fire before they could buy the goods. Tracker opened a discount consignment house to handle other men's mistakes. He rarely took title, charged a twenty percent commission and business flourished. After a few years of hustling he had established warehouses in eleven cities. That way he could ship back and forth between warehouses to keep the merchandise moving, and could bump the load for shipping charges each time.

She could certainly admire that.

Bananas, paint, potato chips, drums of pickled frogs, china, clothing, furniture, medical instruments, construction supplies, guitars, bulldozers, plumbing, hymn books, office machines, automobile parts—finally all of it came his way; his warehouses were like museums of modern industrial foul-ups.

Then, three years ago, about the time she came to work for him, Tracker went into the landscaping business. That was the part of John Tracker she did not understand. He lied to himself about that business. He never did that about the consignment business. His overhead was high, which was okay if you figured it into your bids. Somehow, though, the landscaping never much more than paid for itself. The lie Tracker told, and believed, was that it made money. The books showed the opposite, showed also that he was putting more material, or higher-priced material, into the jobs than was required by the specs. It was amazing to see someone as sharp as John Tracker fool himself over a business that was only a sideline.

She would have to speak to him. If she dared. When you went to bed with a person, life mostly got better, but in a way it got worse. When you went to bed with a person you could talk about things you would not have talked about before. On the other hand, things like this landscape business might well sound like nagging.

Amy paused, ran her hands across her naked belly, looked at her slender arms and smiled. She was much prettier naked than dressed, if only anybody knew it; well, she guessed John Tracker knew it now. No, she thought again, it really wasn't like him to fool himself. He had a job in Council Bluffs next spring, the biggest landscape job his company had ever done. He was so excited about that job, and planning for it, that he was already wasting time that could be put to other business. Then there was this matter of the house. He shouldn't be so reluctant to talk to her about it. All she knew was that there was a big old house downstate that belonged to his family. Period.

She paused. Her mouth, which had been lax, became a firm, disapproving line. She went to the bathroom and began running water in the tub. Somehow it seemed like a bad sign to make love to somebody, and then start tearing down a house.

The tub filled rapidly, and Amy stood for a moment before entering it. Her worst worry, the one she had not allowed herself to think of yet, splashed over her the way the water splashed in the tub. Was she only a trip mistress? Was that what he wanted? Just somebody to type letters and sleep with but not someone to be a part of his life? That would be bad, that would be really really wrong. She couldn't handle that.

She turned to look in the mirror. When you stood erect and pushed your kind of skinny chest forward it helped draw attention from your big nose. It seemed like she could remember every single one of the naked times. When you had a past that could be told in two minutes, you needed to hang on to all of it.

She was raised in religious schools—her family almost always had enough money for that. She came from the discipline of school to a home where her father was an amiable drunk, though he liked an occasional fist-fight in bars. He went to Mass because, as he said, "They need the money." If her father was an amiable cynic, and alcoholic, it was largely because nothing was ever asked of Jefferson Griffith except that he defend the Pope and the Cincinnati Reds against all comers. Her mother was worse. Her mother was so selfish that when the family broke up, her mother did not even want Amy to live with her. So Amy sought her consolation in the known. What was known in her childhood was the firm regimen of the Church. That pretty well preserved her for the first eighteen years. She spent her time all the way through high school with her father, checking for him in bars as if she were acting in a play written for the temperance league. Sometimes Jefferson Griffith brought a woman home with him. There would be laughter and thumps heard through thin walls. Against this, Amy had church or the streets. Church was more certain.

The first of the naked times was best. Until she was eighteen she'd considered a convent, but then she joined a theater, where the best man in the company was also a fair actor. Jim Randall deceived no one but himself, and seeing this, Amy trusted him and perhaps loved him. The convent was forgotten. They lived together for two years, then parted. Randall wanted to go to Europe to study acting, and Amy refused to go because they didn't have enough money. Randall was not practical, going off in spite of her good arguments.

Then there was the time with the bum. That was at twenty-four when she was so lonesome. His name was not important and she made herself forget it. He was not important, except she got pregnant, quit the theater, and was so nervous that she lost the baby. She had no interest in where the man went when he left.

Jim Randall wondered, though. To him it was important. He felt that he had loved and lost and had to leave. Randall was entranced by memory, and as the years passed, Amy received occasional letters that dropped like faint astonishments into her mail. The envelopes bore stamps from all across Europe. When a hotel was especially bad and the loneliness surfaced, a letter would arrive for Amy. And, impractical or not, Randall's letters were welcome. Her answers were vague, but somehow encouraging. She didn't exactly want Randall, but she didn't want to lose him either. His letters brought fantasies of youth and love. She liked the fantasies, but avoided encouraging reality.

Sometimes Amy felt that she was too practical, not quite realizing that practicality was her defense to protect her innocence. When wrong-doing brushed past her she took a direct approach in her advice: "Sober up. Buy a new suit." Her picture of herself was of a responsible career woman. She held to it as well as she could.

There were other pictures in her history, if not in her memory. They were in her mother's attic in Cincinnati. She told herself that she would not think of the past, and then went right on thinking about it. The picture taken at the time of her first communion was best, her long dress revealing the slight slump of her shoulders and the contrast of thin arms and hands with the overpuffed dress material. She was obviously taller and thinner than most other girls her age, with not a trace of baby fat. Her lips were neither thin nor full. Her cheeks and forehead dominated her face; this and a look of both self-consciousness and quick intelligence. Her hair was abundant, and worn to her shoulders, rich and thick and dark brown.

Two other pictures were important, not only because they showed her, but because they told something of her past. Her family's fortune was not money but tradition. It was the tradition of black Irish poverty. Amy could never, would never, admit that her father was a failed and badly spoiled child who was good at nothing but drinking. Since he had little money the only picture of Amy's graduation was of a group of students, she standing in the back row of uniformed girls, still slumping a bit, and half-obscured by a heavy, grinning girl who displayed the sureness of ignorance. One of her thin shoulders, she recalled, was visible. Her face was still intelligent, but now it held both withdrawal from her surroundings, and confusion. It was a relief to turn to the last important picture. Amy on stage. She was twenty in this photo, working ten hours a day on a job that was advertised as thirty hours a week. Her youth and hope gave her the energy to work and still attend long evening rehearsals and performances of little theater. In the glossy photo she was shown as Miranda, a part she played to considerable acclaim. The performance ran for thirty weeks, a record for both Shakespeare and little theater in Cincinnati. Amy was a great beauty. The dress was long and cut to display the swell of adequate if not large breasts. The curve of the neck accented its length. There was a gentle line of shoulders and arms. Her hair was piled high, which pushed her dramatic cheeks, forehead and nose forward. She mourned that big nose for years, but it was thin and aristocratic, well-suited to the particular play.

Amy at thirty. She toweled down and again passed the mirror. She hesitated, looked for the imperfections that had to be there if you were a woman who was thirty. She looked carefully, searching, testing first for detail and then for overall effect. The age seemed to crawl beneath the smooth skin. Surely she could see it if she looked hard enough. Her high forehead wrinkled with traces of some old confusion, then smoothed above high cheeks. Her hands rose to touch her long hair, worn long because John Tracker at one time indicated that he liked it that way.

She smiled and for the moment imagined that she really was beautiful, although for years it had been her private pain to believe she was not. She dressed and turned to the work. Get it done, and then to the movies to cast herself in parts owned by other actresses.

CHAPTER

John Tracker's great grandfather on his father's mother's side was named Able Rothstein, an immigrant. Able met Maggie, the illegitimate daughter of the witch Judith, when Maggie was fifteen. Maggie bore Vera who would eventually become John's grandmother. Rothstein moved his family west.

Rothstein was not a yielder. He had learned nothing about survival from his Jewish heritage. Within a year he was beaten and drowned. His body floated on a pond in Minnesota for several days before it sank and passing neighbors were able to stop averting their eyes. Rothstein's crime was not recorded, but it was doubtless his religion or his accent. Tracker history does not know, or has conveniently concealed, what eventually happened to Maggie; but Vera stayed with her mother Maggie until age thirteen when she felt old enough to run away. She ran to Chicago, where she lived until the time when she entered the house of the Trackers.

John was sure she was dead. Vera Tracker, a woman who could not possibly be less than eighty, sat with her profile turned to her grandson. She was probably a lot older than eighty. Dead or alive, she still seemed to preside over this ancient house as she sat motionless in the old rocker. She had to be dead, John told himself.

She stared straight ahead. The eyes held the flat, profound and yet expressionless look of a corpse. Her hands and arms extended to the arms of the chair like rigid, brittle sticks. A lap robe of purple and brown velvet fell about ankles that were bone-thin in cracked and faded shoes. There was dust on the shoes.

John nearly stepped backward, and then made himself stand still. Involuntary movement in this house could put you in the mouth of a trap. When he had accepted the fact that he had to come here, he also accepted the possibility of finding the remains of Theophilus or Vera or Justice. He felt he could bear to confront a corpse. He did not expect one that sat and stared at him.

His grandmother's eyes blinked once, snapping; the snap gaining momentum like an unused camera shutter that almost, but not quite, sticks. Her face was tight and loose at the same time. The flesh hung over cheeks and was pulled smooth like thin wattles about her mouth. Her face was like half a death's head with the wings of a dying moth in the eye sockets.

He stepped toward her, relieved. He was also strangely angry. Her eyes did not blink again. The room was not as cold as outside, but it was coat-cold, breath-frosting cold. She was dressed in light clothing.

"Vera," he said. "Old Sis." That had been the name Theophilus called her, when he was not calling her something worse.

She stared at him.

He walked toward her. Her eyes did not track. The thin clothing and lap robe seemed like wrappings for a mummy. He walked through two conventional rooms, found an afghan lying on an antique loveseat and returned. He placed it around her, and as he tucked in the light shawl he found that she was as bald as he knew she would be. A few strands of hair were yellow with age. There was a mole as big as a thumbprint on her head.

He had not known of that mole.

He did not know whether there was more fear than anger hanging just beneath the surface of his mind. The part of him that was Tracker was both unfrightened and angry. She was a double-damned inconvenience. How did you get her out of this place and over that snowy grade? She might die any minute. Part of him wanted to snatch the afghan away and let her freeze, and he had to will himself to be careful when he touched her.

The arms and hands seemed so brittle he feared to move them because they might break. She did not move. The eyes did not blink again. Once more he began to believe she was dead. The veins of her hands were submerged, faint gray lines where there was no flesh to bury them. The hands were skeletal, except for competent nails. She had always been proud of her nails. They were tools that could cut.

He turned to the fireplace. Wood was stacked, but a fire was not laid.

Impossible, he thought, to be unable to tell whether a human being was dead or not. He touched her arm. It was cold, but cold enough?

He felt time shift, and told himself that either time was shifting, or he was separated from his normal senses. If you were in the house of the Trackers, you were, after all, *prima facie* mad. He made his mind switch to indifference. From the distance came the tinkling notes of a piano, but at the moment his mind sought indifference the sounds started to fade.

"I'll get you warm." His voice sounded worse in the silence than the silence itself. The thought crossed his mind that if he thawed her out he was only saving Hell some trouble. Let the Devil thaw her out.

The black, Tracker side of his mind was fighting to gain control. He pressed it downward, back into the depths of his unconscious. He was not going to let this place get him, Vera Tracker, or no.

He laid the fire and lighted it. As he worked with his back toward her he felt movement. The silence intensified. It was like the silence was turning into a void.

"Tracker walks." The voice was dry. Her tongue seemed to grate in a mouth that held no spit. "Walks." The voice was a whisper.

He wheeled and stumbled from his crouch in front of the fire. In spite of his logic, some part of him was still convinced she was dead. He was adding shock on shock. Or she was.

He watched her movement. There was none. Then the fingers of her left hand began to tremble, made feeble, grasping motions. He watched but did not move toward her, and then her words seemed to echo in the vacuum of silence.

"Walks. Who walks?"

He watched her slowly raise her hand, pluck at the robe, apparently trying to pull it closer.

"How long were you without fire?" He knelt to place more kindling under the logs. The wood was dry like old bones. The fire was catching quickly and illuminated the shadowed room. As he worked his hands were red with the glow.

"Good spell."

He turned back. Color was on her cheeks. It was only a trace, and it might be a reflection from the fire. Reflection or not, she no longer looked dead.

"Been ill?" He felt that he was bustling.

"Fits, I reckon."

He assumed that meant epileptic, and was glad to discover any weakness.

"A good thing I arrived. The worst winter, ever. It would have gotten colder."

"Lord save us from a fool."

Her color was coming back. She looked no more than

a worn eighty. She no longer looked like something dragged from a burial cave.

"You haven't changed." He almost admired her. Old. Weak. Helpless. Still calling names. Soon she would start cursing. He decided to try for information before she regained full control.

"What do you mean, walks? Who walks? The old man?"

"Which old man?" Her voice was filled with contempt. "Which dangledy old man do you mean?"

"You said Tracker walks. Which Tracker?"

"Theophilus walks. Cellar, subcellar, woodlot, rooms. Hollers silent-like, mouth wide as a cistern, head fulla scream. Comes of tampering things." She stopped speaking. Her mouth became a rigid line. Her body stiffened. A slight tremble.

"Tampering?"

Her eyes were getting quicker. There was flash in them, movement behind her eyes like sudden awareness. The tremble stopped. Her face went calm. It seemed more fleshy and substantial.

"You knew the old rut. You figger it out."

"Justice?" He watched to see if there was any reaction. "How did he die?"

There was a reaction. A tight smile.

"He aint walkin', sonny, and he aint crawling, neither. Your pa aint goin' nowhere."

"What?"

"Comes of tampering things."

She was crazy. Living alone. Imagination. She was always a woman who drove goads into boys, into men. Now her goads must have reached into herself, her mind twisting and building the images of hate that she threw outward. Destruction, he figured, was bent on its final victory. Self-destruction.

"You're not well. I'm going to get a doctor."

"You're gonna build houses outta cow pies. You aint

leaving. I aint leavin'. Twenty years gone and you aint leavin' until this trouble's laid."

She stood to pull her chair closer to the fire. She seemed younger every minute, and Tracker could swear that she was adding weight. Vera was not tall, her weight always came from her tongue.

"I told the old scut to follow you. Go to him, I said. Thrash out the difference. Lay the dead."

"What dead?" He over-reacted.

She saw it and smiled. "You don't know," she said, "despite it belongs at your feet. Despite they're laying all around you. You run away too soon."

He was amazed to find she still owned her old power to harm. Forgotten feelings of hurt and inferiority were crawling through him like worms.

"I was a kid," he told her. "Between my mother, who was known as a bitch, and my father, who had at least one shot of sanity, I got sprung from this place—"

"And came back, little man. You came back and then left."

"I turned my back on this rat's nest—"

"Run." Her voice was a wellspring of spite. "Coward. You run from a fortune. You could of had it all."

"I've got it all, anyway," he lied. "And damn you."

"To the well, sonny."

Her eyes told him she was winning. The old pattern was re-established. She hit him bare, naked, and he did not understand how she was hitting. He only understood that he was frozen in place. She was gaining weight by making him hate her. He forced himself to breathe.

"This lousy place," he said. "You sorry people." He watched the effect. She was pleased. There was more color in her face.

"Nothin' you say makes a difference," she said. "You run to new things, new people, big ideas . . . but none of 'em are. Just the same old buggers with nary-a-nothing in their heads. I know you." She spat into the fire. Impressive. Now she even had spit.

"I'm hungry." Her voice changed. It was whining.

"So go to the kitchens."

"I et everything there."

"All right. Where is it?"

"Where would it be?"

He was turning to go and stopped. "How should I know? I'm in the middle of a madhouse."

"Lower pantry on the south side. There's cans."

"Any changes before I get there?"

"Don't take nothin' from in front. The old bastard stuffed them with poison."

"Any changes? Tell me or I won't go."

"In twenty years?" She sat thinking. "Nothin' bad. He did most of his tinkering on fourth floor."

Tracker turned and left. Outside, he told himself, the wind was blowing across the snow-filled sky and there were automobiles skidding back and forth. Where it wasn't snowing, like maybe in Bermuda, buildings were being built. There were hospitals, and whorehouses, and banks. There were churches. Women were buying dresses, and men were looking at the legs of women who were wearing their new dresses. There were land deals. There were people cheating each other. There were oceans and forests and bulldozers, and in this house none of it made the least difference.

"You haven't changed." He yelled it at the top of his voice, tasting his own hatred, taking an exact pleasure in breaking the silence of the endless rooms.

The answer came back needle-tongued, mocking. "I kin take care."

He slammed doors to violate the silence, knowing that there was not a door in the house that could be broken unless you used a sledge hammer. Then he remembered his forgotten crowbar and turned back.

The fire brightened as he reentered the room. The woman cast a heavier shadow from its light. She said nothing. Tracker picked up the crowbar, turned, turned back. "What's that? What are you doing?"

She was casting a double shadow.

"Doin' nothing." Her voice was low, unafraid, but the mocking tone was gone. The second shadow lay like light smoke beside the heavier, actual shadow. He did not see how it could be a trick of the light. As he directed the beam of the flashlight the shadow faded, and he could no longer tell if it was real or only illusion. He could almost swear, though, that it was the shadow of a younger woman, and the hair was piled high.

"Who?" The fear was back like frost along the edges of his teeth.

"I'm hungry." She turned. The real shadow turned with her. "Hungry, hungry." The whine was coming back. "I kin take keer."

"Witch yourself something to eat." He headed for the doorway, turned the knob, found it locked.

"Open it."

"No." She stood. The lap robe fell. She threw away the covering afghan. "They's nothin' wrong. It's you. You're as full of beans as the old one ever was." She trembled, moved one faltering pace, then sat back down in the chair. "I'm hungry." She reached to press a lever by the fireplace. The door clicked. He turned the knob, found it open, came back. She looked colder. Her trembling hands were in her lap. She was weak, pathetic. His logic told him he was a fool. His hysteria was hitting him with shadows that ought to be easy to explain. Illusion, delusion . . . still, his rational mind also told him to be careful.

"I'll get you something," he said, acting it out.

He followed a passageway that ran off on a forty-five-degree angle from the third room back. The passage began halfway up the wall. When the steps were folded up, the wall looked like any other wall. Tracker began unwinding twenty years of forgetfulness. His life depended on remembering. As a child he did not think of this as a concealed passage. It was only a hall that you climbed steps to reach.

The passageway was dark. He used the flash and allowed memory to guide him. If he trusted automatic recollection, he told himself, it would be safe; if he tried to plan he would make a wrong turn. The flashlight showed the beginning steps and he switched it off. The steps must be climbed in darkness. In light they would so confuse that he would surely fall.

He began climbing and was startled that the machinery was well-oiled and quiet. The steps wound off-center, rising and falling, twisting and occasionally on a tilt. He had to remember to always keep to the right. As he climbed he felt he was going down. The slight movement of the steps, their great number, and the twisting, alley-like corridor gave him an antique feeling of timelessness. Impossible to climb out this way. He climbed the steps down half a floor. At the bottom was a small room. He flicked the flashlight. There were stacks of canned and dry food, and he filled his jacket pockets from the back of the stacks. Then he turned to a blank wall.

He kicked a baseboard. A small trap door fell open. He reached into the dead space in the wall and found three levers. When they were moved to form a Y, he reached further into the dead space and found a knob. A door fell open at his feet.

He climbed down to a passageway that slanted upward, jogged off to the right, reversed, and at the top entered through a wall panel into a hall on the south side. He looked through a window at another part of the house. From the time of entering the first stairs until the time of entering the hall he had covered a lateral distance of less than a hundred feet. Yet he had been walking, walking.

"Tracker walks . . ." Her voice came back to him. He looked down the empty hallway and cursed because he was afraid. He had forgotten to control his imagination because of his concentration on traps.

"Get back under the grade," he said to the empty hall.

Vera Tracker was the source of some of his worst misery. She was a cut across consciousness. But she represented reasonable movement in this unreasonable and silent house. And for that reason he wanted to get back.

The conventional hall led to a main hall in the south wing that connected with the rest of the house through the kitchens. He started that direction, saw two off-colored boards in the floor, and stopped. Something was different. He turned and walked back in the other direction.

He passed a door. He remembered that if he turned the knob and pushed the right side he would be in trouble. If he pushed the left side he would enter a conventional room. The right side went into a sealed passage that made two wide circles cròssing each other. With no light a person would move until he dropped.

Further down the hall. Press in two places with evenly spaced feet and you dropped quickly but safely below the floor into another hall that was harmless if you went left. Go right and it automatically sealed, to force a man into a passage that apparently went nowhere. Worse, it started wide and narrowed to a point. A triangular tomb if a person stumbled in and did not know that three paces from the beginning of the point a panel could be slid in a zig-zag. Both hands had to press the panel and describe a streak of lightning. That panel opened a door into a conventional staircase, except for the third and fourth step which had to be jumped; otherwise the steps would collapse the unlucky body into a forty-foot drop ending in the subcellar. Except for that the stairs were safe, and led a winding circuit to the third floor greenhouse, the one decent thing in this place.

John was remembering more than he believed he knew.

The house seemed a monstrosity, but at least now it did not seem senseless. It was fantastic, like the tortured shifts and balances of an otherwise well-run, self-determined mind. The obscure routes were clean and sane and purposeful. The designer's mind was sound, granted that his premises were crazy. He felt that the house was a masterwork. Genius designed and built this place. It was only necessary to remember that it was a demonic, bedlam kind of genius.

It was too bad the house could not be defanged and saved. A gigantic museum. A Golgotha of sought-after torment, not hell but purgatory.

John shook his head, feeling the weight of the past.

"You're young, try to remember this, later you'll understand . . ." His father's voice sounded in his memory.

He did not remember his father well. Still, some part of his mind must remember. Golgotha. Purgatory. Those were not his words. He looked down the hallway, heard a sound, turned, looked the other way and nearly screamed.

At the far end of the hall a door swung open, paused in the apparent grip of an invisible hand, and then slammed again. If something moved through the doorway it was in the hall with him.

He could not go forward. To run away in this house was certain destruction. He gripped the crowbar. It might have no value for defense, but at least it was hard and heavy and real.

Down the hall and to the left another door opened, was held, slammed. Something or somebody was passing from one room to another, and they or it ignored him.

Either that or it was another trick. A Tracker trick. He eased off. His relief was as shocking as his fear. A trick. John Tracker congratulated himself on a lesson well-learned but for a time forgotten. His grandfather could be trusted to return all acts, all intentions, with a trick. There was a new technology, this trick must be part of it. Heat switches, electric eyes, solenoids activated by the slightest pressure. He remembered the old-fashioned chemical activators on part of the second floor.

He was no longer afraid as he searched for the loose board or the silent beam that his foot touched to activate the doors. Even when he didn't find it he was not worried. It would be there if he looked long enough.

Ahead of him was tampering. Behind him was tampering. He was in a trap. It did not worry him. What Theophilus could build, his grandson John could unravel.

He returned to the far end of the hall to inch past the new boards. The doorknob was new. He examined the boards and door, then backed away and reached forward with the crowbar to hit the boards. The boards gave a little, then returned to their former position. Whatever happened would happen when the door was opened. He stood to one side, turned the knob and shoved the door.

A silver-bladed sword snapped from the floor on a sixty-degree angle at the right height to catch a man between the shoulders. The point and about six inches of the blade were gone. The metal was shaved, a clean cut.

In the entry, about seven feet high and four feet away, was a rack of flashbulbs. They were already burned out. The trap was simple. A man walked through the doorway, was blinded by the bulbs, jumped back onto the blade. The blade was useless and the bulbs were shot. Why mount a sheared-off sword?

He walked to the kitchens, where it was warm, and he wanted to linger there after being so long in the cold house. Well, at least part of the heating system was working.

He leaned against a counter and thought of what he knew about the logistics of the house. He tested a faucet. Water splashed. Then outside services were still connected, someone was paying utility bills.

There was a generator somewhere. There were wells. He shuddered, looked around, felt a rush of fear. The generator was in the subcellar. At least he seemed to remember it that way. He had never seen the generator, but Theophilus talked about it at times. If there were huge tanks of fuel, then outside services might *not* be getting into the house.

On the other hand, someone would have to maintain the generators. Tracker was annoyed. Shutting down services was one more problem to be taken care of before wrecking this place.

He passed through the warm kitchens knowing that in this territory everything would be safe, and he wondered why his grandmother did not stay in the kitchens, where at least it was warm. Had she been walking and been caught in that cold room by a fit, or stroke?

The woman seemed pathetic. Old, violent and ended in this house of decay. He opened a food cabinet and found it full. He opened others. They held a great variety of canned and dried foods. It was enough to last an old woman for a long time.

His trip through twenty years of memory had come to nothing. His grandmother had not told him of those new traps. She was not in the room when he returned. He looked around. The house was like tinder, the wallpaper dry and faded, crisped at the edges. Here and there were small droppings of plaster dried to powder. He could hear no footsteps.

It was a clear win for Vera unless she could be found. He checked his watch and felt an urge to spread the still burning fire from the fireplace onto the floor. But that would be murder, and he shook his head to push away the thought.

She could not have gotten far in the shape she was in. Tracker started to check rooms.

Pine floors, hardwood floors, parquet floors. The switching beam of the flashlight pierced the darkness as he moved toward the interior. In one location was a maze. He did not even bother to go there. If Vera was in the maze no one could find her.

In the interior of the house, halls wound and disappeared in darkness. When he found light switches he turned them on. Between patches of darkness the bulbs burned like feeble streetlights in a fog, small night-sleeping bulbs that seemed to gather the darkness around them.

He was headed north. Conventional traps lay all around him. He recalled them at the last moment, like the hunchy feeling before the recollection of a dream. Or like, he thought, a part of time slid sideways to let him see what forgetfulness long ago had shunted away.

His flashlight beam searched one room, then another, danced across mohair and carpet and dusty drapes that gave an illusion of windows. A fanciful house. A house of mad fancy. He turned a corner and blue light glowed from an open doorway fifty feet down the hall. He walked, expecting a trick, opening his mind to memory so that no trap would touch him. He reached the open doorway through which the light shone, looked inside the room, was stunned.

Theophilus Tracker stood in a cloud of steam and smoke, open-mouthed, screaming in total silence. An apparition which carried in its hands the full rack of horns from a deer, an apparition that was steady in the rigid beam of the flashlight. Steam rose. The blue, sketchy light began fading to black.

John Tracker, grandson of Theophilus, grandson of a spectre, ran. He was too frightened to scream.

Past rudimentary traps that failed when he tripped them, if he tripped them. Past the picture of his father, Justice. Past the ornate coffin, to leap the trap at the front door and fall into the snow. He ran to the grade and climbed frantically, floundered over the grade and slid to his car. As he disappeared, lights burned on the fourth floor, the angel took another walk past the seven doors in the front of the house. This time its stern injunction was confused. It presented the cross, but the cross was changed in the angel's wooden hands. It challenged the grade, but it was held upside down.

The snow and wind murmured, like the questioning voices of generations of the dead.

CHAPTER

5

John Tracker's mother was Sarah Lily. Sarah, who hated the house of the Trackers, was in some way its spiritual counterpart. In those winding halls and passages, the dwellers often seemed unable to tell which was illusion, which real. In much the same manner Sarah Lily lived her life.

She was born in Andover, Massachusetts, and died at age sixty-one in Indianapolis as she lay beside her fifth husband who was a retired stock broker. He assumed she had a stroke. John Tracker was in St. Louis at the time. He did not return for the funeral. He told himself that he was forever done with his family. Illusion has always been a Tracker specialty.

Sarah was buried with the dignity that her fifth husband's modest fortune could buy, but her casket shivered and stuck against a rock or root as it was being lowered. It was raised, the path cleared, and then it was carefully placed.

In the family of the Trackers, women were traditionally treated in one of two ways. Either they were considered useful property, or they were worshipped. That was one reason Sarah always existed for John's father, Justice, as a silver-laughing, incredibly beautiful haunt that thrilled along the corridors of memory. John's father loved only one woman in his life, although from time to time he tried to love others. He never understood the woman he loved.

Sarah was complex. Her life was one of questions. As a young woman she questioned with her hands—painting, pottery, carving and sculpture. She also played several musical instruments but mastered none of them.

Shortly after her son John was two years old, Sarah began to question with her body, leaving her husband, her son and the house she had always hated. Sarah went to bed with a lot of men, looking for answers to her questions.

At age forty she turned to social functions for a semblance of control. Sarah was not much of a thinker, but she was a talented doer. She had a genius, but little discipline, and she was completely moral. Letters to intimate friends reveal that she probably never did a wrong thing in her life, though some called her actions bad. If she had not acted, she would have offended her search.

Her last words puzzled her husband and brought fearful delusions into the last years of his retirement. She said: "Of course I want to know. But, no, not that much. The price is too high." Sarah was more of a Tracker than she cared to acknowledge. Their answers, however, were more than she could abide, so she searched elsewhere, to save her soul.

When the Mercedes stopped fishtailing on the snowy road John Tracker eased his speed and began looking for a spot to pull over. His forearms were trembling. He drove erratically, telling himself over and over that he had seen a trick. A whole crazy house of tricks.

The road was bad, the shoulders covered with snow. The danger helped cut through his near-hysteria so he could mindlessly point the automobile through hazards that slowly began to demand his attention. The road wound between hills and snowy groves; there were no side roads. Drifted fence rows were like long-running mounds of snow, shadowless in the declining light.

He saw movement in the periphery of his vision, an animal loping over a small crest. It must be in deep snow and yet it ran easily. A large gray dog it was, moving along the crest. It must be hunting. The light was fading, the dog might not be gray at all, it might be white. And a memory stirred. John shuddered, tried to pull it forward in his mind, but the memory would not come.

Sometimes people in shock did not know how unstable they were. He told himself that, and cut his low speed even lower. All right, he thought, take stock. Get a grip on it. He knew the apparition of Theophilus had to be a trick. He knew that because he knew Theophilus. The knowledge was the kind that worked in the world in which you drove cars, ordered steaks and did business. It was not, however, quite enough for the world of the Devil and Theophilus Tracker. Even as a child John had felt something pressing about the house; a gloom, a glowering presence. He'd always told himself it was because his mother hated that house. She had, after all, left his father, and she'd left her son not yet three years old to grow up alone in that house. For a time, these things explained his sense of gloom.

Later, like his mother, he had sought more rational answers. He told himself he'd grown up living with tricks. Even now, he reminded himself, there was that apparition —a trick. It had to have appeared by projection, film on smoke and steam that rose from a jet. Technically it was simple. Combined with expert lighting, it would be far more real than a movie. It would be three-dimensional. That was the kind of patient and exacting work that characterized the productions of Theophilus. The answer did not completely satisfy him, but it at least allowed him to feel some relief.

The sight of the dog was still trying to jar something loose in his memory. He waited, but the memory still would not come.

He turned to his problems. Strictly speaking they were few and not as bad as they looked. Tearing down the house would be easy, and it would not even be difficult to salvage. True, there was a question of ownership with

Vera still alive, but that would be no problem; he had the state on his side.

Vera was no real problem either, once she was found in that house. He planned to bring a four-wheel drive truck across fields and avoid the grade. He could take her to a retirement home or a hospital.

The real problem was himself. It was easy to make money. Once you understood your own system and set it up to work with other systems, business required your time but nothing more. Talent and intelligence and originality were inappropriate. He had nothing against business except that it was boring, and too often conducted by boring people. Still, maybe it wasn't business that bored him. Maybe such feelings were his way of avoiding an issue.

The real issue was that he was forty and was accomplishing nothing special. But a good many men might feel that way, even men who controlled more companies than he would ever control. All right, the real issue was that he knew so little about himself, less about the universe, and was not a creature of the present at all. He was a slicked-down version of diabolic fear who drove through the world in an expensive automobile. He was a Tracker. Face it, he was not free, not even from his family. Especially not from them. Hell and the Devil had been simple for Johan and Theophilus. They were never simple for Justice. Justice may have, as some claimed, been crazy, but he was never unkind. John felt—hoped—that if he dug hard enough he'd find his father's early teaching was in him somewhere.

He could distinguish between myth and legend. Somewhere, deep, was tucked away history about the Inquisition; a haunt resting deep in the subconscious. Devils, druids, Dionysus, demonology and angelology. It was all there and could be studied out. Studied out? A quaint phrase, also of another time. Rural, not natural for a so-

phisticated man of the world like himself. Of the world
. . . Which world?

Maybe such a question was the place to start. It might
bring him to terms with his father Justice, although he
doubted it would ever explain Johan or Theophilus.

Then there was the money. In his world it was valued,
it was a key to freedom. You could do whatever you
wanted if you had enough money—except he knew he was
kidding himself. He wanted to be free, but he did not
know what the word meant.

There was a lot of money in that house, though. And
with Vera alive it was a touchy problem. Vera could not
live forever. It was amazing that the old bat had held on
this long . . .

Fatigue made his mind hazy. A closed filling station was
further along at a crossroads. He drove slowly and made
himself concentrate on the road. When he arrived he
pulled onto the snow-covered lot and stopped. A few minutes rest. He leaned back to drowse, and suddenly came
erect. The gray dog. He did not want to think of what it
meant. Oh, coincidence, surely; but the memory he had
sought now came crashing in. It was overpowering. When
he was little. Eight or nine . . .

Bee stinging, leaf dropping, the buzz of insects over the
hot, corn-crackling fields. It was the summer his grandfather lowered him down a well and also killed a dog. He
sat rigid, remembering the wind moving through nights of
heat and fireflies as it rose from the river and poured over
the bluff. For Easter, Justice had given him eight baby
ducks. Six grew into fat white pekins that rustled in the tall
grass between the house and the woodlot. One died when
it was little. A second swallowed a bee and was stung
inside. His father helped him bury both. At the time he
could not remember his mother, although he would soon
be sent to live with her. His father still had hope in those
days. John could remember Justice saying that maybe the

three of them, he and his father and mother might all be together. His grandfather Theophilus held other opinions, but by the time Theophilus got around to talking, John would not have believed him if he said the direction of the sky was up.

Before the ducks and the well it was different. He believed everything. He believed the old well by the chicken house was a mysterious, horrible place. He believed it possible that everyone loved each other, because their cursing was usually at the world in general.

The ducks caused his grandfather to take an interest. John remembered hot August afternoons when the ducks lay panting in shade while chickens clucked and pecked in their pens. His grandfather would connect a hose, and sometimes in the hot afternoons they would squirt water at the ducks. It made John laugh. The ducks would rise, poke their heads high in the air and take the water in front. The ducks seemed to fear getting their backs wet, and John never decided whether they liked the spraying or not. Sometimes one of the cats, or the small hound, would amble by and catch a sousing.

It was the hound and the big gray dog and his grandfather that caused the trouble. At first it was only funny. Then something in the old man seemed to build. There was a big gray dog roaming the countryside and it was apparently fearless. It had been shot at, trapped, poison-baited. Buckshot must have laid under its pelt like freckles. Yet for over two years the dog took small game, chickens, sucked eggs and made at least as good a living as most people in the county. It also had strong herding instincts, it was known occasionally to hang around the vicinity of a tethered goat. The dog was shrewd. It worked all through the area before it tangled with Theophilus Tracker.

On a morning when his grandmother slept late, as she usually did because of helling around with the old man all night, there was cackling and flutter among the chickens. The chicken house was a hundred yards from the kitchens. The disturbance could barely be heard, and if anyone had been talking it would not have been heard at all.

Theophilus tensed. Listening. Justice, his long hair curling about his ears, a frying pan in one hand, stopped breakfast; standing, mouth half-open, caught in the middle of making more pancakes. In John's memory it was terribly etched and clear.

Theophilus unhunched from above his plate, chomping, his blue eyes brilliant with fury. Jubilant. "Hot damn." He chomped. "Hell 'n breakfast." He jumped from his chair, kicked a panel in the wall which fell open to display weapons, and grabbed a heavy shotgun. He was moving fast. Justice stood there, silent.

Theophilus wheeled, ran from the kitchen, and John followed in spite of the yell from his father.

The old man seemed to gallop. John could still remember sunlight on the blue-clad, gray-haired figure; the bouncing form of the old man as he ran through tall grass, the shotgun carried like a club. The grass was green, green, green, like the very roots of color, like the color tumbled off the blades in shouts, extended into the black earth and yelled from the roots. Theophilus ran and John's short legs could not keep up. Behind him came Justice, and John knew he was going to get caught.

"Come here." His father scooped him on the run, stopped, turned him toward the house. John wiggled, nearly got loose but was caught firm.

Theophilus stopped now, braced, and the gun boomed twice, pounding over the tall grass toward the low buildings that housed the chickens.

The first sight of the gray dog was when he appeared around the far side of the chicken house and lit out for home. A chicken dangled like an afterthought in his mouth; spit red, a little fire of color glowing between the

53

gray head, the green grass and the white chicken. The dog was running seriously but without desperation. His hind quarters were up. His head was high enough to brag about the chicken.

John wiggled loose and ran. His father did not catch him again until he was near the chicken house. He nearly reached Theophilus, who was still braced in the tall grass and swearing at the summer sky. The old man turned, grinned like a man who could kill death itself, and threw the shotgun down. His teeth looked like he could grin and chomp at the same time. "I just kilt ten thousand goddamn chickens." Theophilus seemed proud. John leaned past him to view the destruction and knew that it was not ten thousand, but it was a lot of chickens. White bodies spouting red were scattered and tumbling about the henyard like torn paper. Some were already silent. Some were flopping and spasmodic. As John watched, the unhurt chickens began clucking their way through the bodies and occasionally pecked at the live remains. John was interested, but Justice made him go back to the house.

The next day the dog took another chicken. Theophilus hit him, but only enough to burn the dog's flank. He went off in a low squat, still running seriously, still with a rose in his mouth and flaunting the white chicken.

Theophilus went to town, returned with a thirty-thirty rifle and spent the rest of the day shooting at cans, sparrows, twigs, hawks a half mile in the air, clods, and between the legs of neighbors' cows. Because it was a rifle and not a carbine the kick was bruising. He stove up his shoulder for three days. Justice made worried grunts. Vera scoffed and claimed that his shoulder was in better shape than the rest of his parts.

The dog got two more chickens. Then the scene changed. The defiant dog took one of the ducks. John's little hound watched the snare, made an indifferent sally to run the dog away, then lay down in the shade and seemed to be thinking about it. While John wailed for his duck, picking soft white feathers from the thick grass, Theophilus turned from contest to war.

John Tracker shook his head, trying to dislodge the memory. His car was too warm. He turned down the heater, thought back to his visit to the house, shuddered, and returned to the memory. Forty years old, and it was still vivid.

"Don't go near the well."

His father told him that over and over.

"Don't go near the well." When he went out to play his grandmother would tell him that. His grandmother knew why, he was sure. No doubt there was something in the well, a formless scary blob. It lay dreaming of the crunch of bones from little boys it occasionally got in its mouth.

"What's in the well?"

"Water," his father said.

"What's in the well?"

"Nothin' in that one, boy. Nothin' in that one atall." His grandfather would never tell him the location of the other well. Sometimes in dreams he believed it was hidden under a trap door beneath his bed.

"What's in the well?"

"Fall in there and you'll see. Look in there and it'll grab you."

His grandmother knew. He always walked wide of the well. It was fun, in the sunlight, to circle the chickens, walk through the grass, head out across woodlot or pasture and know that the black spot that was the mouth of the well was like a lid on a pit. Nothing down there could move above the black spot. Sunlight did not touch the blackness. Sometimes in bed and staring into darkness John imagined the mouth of the well, existing as a black spot in the night.

Sure. The Devil was in that well. He must be. According to grandfather Theophilus he was everywhere else. The well had to be the Devil's headquarters. The sun held him under, but on extra dark nights the black went with black and he could get out.

"Hell and business," Justice would say. He was a quiet man, but when he spoke it was often half-humorously. One evening Justice complained of having to make a trip to the city next day. It was a matter that could not be handled in the neighboring towns, and John figured it was because of the library. When his father went to the city he always returned with books.

The kitchen lights were still on against the weak dawn when John fumbled and eye-rubbed his way into the early light of the next morning. Theophilus was half dressed— pants, undershirt, no socks. His gray whiskers were untrimmed. He was stiff and had scratches on his arms; always scratches on his arms. When he was a lot older John would figure who made those scratches. The first time he bedded with a woman who used her nails, the realization about his grandfather and grandmother was more shocking than the bleeding marks on his back.

"What are you doing up?" Theophilus said as he slurped coffee. The rifle lay on the table. Bronze cartridges fanned in front of it like fingers. The flow of the electric light on the black rifle made it look soft. The polished stock was already gouged where Theophilus had banged it against something in anger over a miss.

"Goin' to help get the sumbitchin' dog."

"Goin' to get a lickin' about that mouth." Theophilus was growling, and he was pleased. "Go back to bed."

"It's cold."

"It's August." Theophilus looked at him, grinned, and John once more realized early that any deception was better than none.

His father came in. "What are you doing up?"

"He came down to see you off," Theophilus said. "Sit down."

Justice did, and started rolling the cartridges with his short, accurate fingers. He seemed abstracted as he sipped at the coffee; about ready to speak, he turned to John instead, his hands seemingly nervous. "I'll bring you a present," he said. "Now go back to bed."

"But it's—"

"Early," Justice told him. "I want to speak privately. Boys need a lot of sleep." Justice's hair was so curly his ears were hidden. His hair was brown and combed close but it popped up in places. He was, John noted, dressed in his Sunday suit.

John turned, left and went to his room, went into the big closet, slid through a sectioned corner of the wall that turned like a lazy Susan, and entered a passage that ran left and up to a hallway on second floor. That hall jogged right at a ninety degree angle and dead-ended against a wall. John jumped twice, was not tall enough, and went down the hall to drag a chair from beneath a windowseat. He stood on the chair, reached high, found the pressure point. A ladder hinged from the ceiling, and he climbed to the third floor. The ladder closed behind him as he followed another hall that led onto a stone terrace that had a fountain that did not work. It was a broad terrace, flat limestone laid and cemented, slicked by the weather. This was not the terrace with the greenhouse. This terrace was like a lonesome stone plain—a little paper, a few leaves and some soil trapped in wind corners. Turtles cast in concrete sat on the edge of the fountain. John twisted one of them and a chute opened at his feet.

He climbed into the chute, which descended on a fast slant, turning twice; a large slide through darkness that dropped him one-and-a-half floors to a small cell that automatically lighted as the chute entry sealed. In the cell was a human skeleton that lay on a bunk beside a chair and a table. John wiggled under the bunk, pushed a panel and rolled sideways until he felt a ledge, then climbed down a ladder leading from the ledge, opened another panel, stepped through garlands of dried fruit and was in the pantry next to the kitchen.

"See her and get yourself laid and forget it." That was Theophilus' voice.

"I don't know why I talk to you." That was his father Justice. John figured that his father was finished with the coffee. He was up and moving. His voice was unsteady but it didn't sound afraid.

"I don't care what you do, as long as you take care of business." Clicks, Theophilus was slipping cartridges into the rifle.

"I always take care of business."

"I got to give you that. You're always sober when you're making a deal."

Rustling. Creaks of shoes on feet that were stepping slow. Heavy intake of breath. Pop of knuckles.

"Bring her back," Theophilus said.

"She won't come."

"If you want it, bring it back. Where did you get the idea that what she wants means anything? Tie a sack over her head."

"She has rights."

"She's a woman." Theophilus' voice was heavy with disgust, and John could not figure out who he was disgusted with.

"If I get hit with a custody suit, you'll see that she has rights. More than she deserves."

"So let her. The boy will come back."

Justice's voice betrayed anger. It was lower, and not submissive.

"She's got a point," Justice said. "When you're raised with crazy people, then you're crazy. One of these days I may have to take the boy and leave. I can do something else—"

"You kin be a preacher." The rifle lever locked, the

shell chambered. A careful grunt. Lowering to half-cock. "Anytime, boy, but in the meantime go get drunk and laid. Too long between tussles is bad fer a man."

"Make it three days then. You ought to be able to handle her and the place for three days."

"Or forever." Theophilus' voice was lower. Now he was on the defense.

"If I ever left for good you wouldn't last ten minutes."

"Get outta here."

"I've studied on it for a long time," Justice said. "There are people who act like natural lines of transmission. And you know what she transmits—"

"She's nothin' but a good romp with a sharp tongue, so take your time."

"Our time is running out. All of us."

Click. Crash of the rifle. It filled the room, the explosion grunting and booming through the door, full, heavy, the shatter of glass nearly lost in the reverberations.

"Damn—dammit, see what you made me do."

"That was a perfectly good cabinet."

"Buy a new one. I aint got time to make another." There was a heavy sound as his grandfather hit a chair. "Git."

Justice left.

John huddled, and started to whimper, but being caught would be bad, so he chewed on a dried peach to keep from making any noise.

Yells from another room. Cursing. His grandmother Vera was awake. When his grandfather went outside John moved carefully, willed himself to move, and in a little while felt he'd gained enough control to go outside.

By then the sun was full up but still low across the land. Nearly invisible mist rose from the grass fields, and it felt slick beneath his feet, cool between his toes. The dust where the ducks had knocked down the grass near bushes was also cool. It spurted in little puffs. The ducks stood as he walked toward them, then chased off a few feet to stand peeping privately to each other. And then one started yelling, the loud whack whack to tell that he should have come with bread or corn. As the little hound joined them the drake made a lunge at it, but the hound merely yawned. The ducks talked among themselves. Puffs of cool dust settled on John's ankles.

"Keep it quiet."

He turned. Scared and guilty and ready to lie, but Theophilus didn't notice, which gave John some confidence. He didn't know where Theophilus had come from, but there he was, no mistake, and the rifle hung in his hand.

"He comes from over that way," Theophilus said and pointed toward the far corner of the hill that was fenced in barbed wire. "We'll get over here."

They walked, Theophilus, John and the little hound, past the far corner of the house, across the glistening grass, toward the chicken house. The chicken house and low buildings surrounding it were roofed in galvanized steel, washed pink in the early sunlight. Chickens clucked in the runs. Roosters crowed, pursued hens, fought.

"We'll squinch down here. Keep hold'a the dog and shut up." Theophilus crouched behind the wall, from which position he could cover all areas of the hill, except immediately behind the chicken house. He could cover the flat leading across the grass and toward the ducks. A hundred yards. The ducks looked like small white dots now, and the house looked ungainly from the rear, stark and new and rough.

John did not want to get down, he was too close to the well, but he knelt behind his grandfather and clutched the little hound in both arms. They waited.

The hound struggled, John held tight. The hound licked his face, he giggled.

"Keep it shut."

Silence. Cluck of hens. Ten minutes. Theophilus

shifted position, looked over his shoulder, looked at John and the hound, and whirled back.

The gray dog came then like a smooth-flowing sinuous gray line, sliding across the hill from behind the chicken house. It was not coming especially fast but it moved steady, the motion true and clean-lined. One moment it was not there, the next moment it was there and the straight line pointed toward the ducks.

"Gotcha, bastard. Gotcha." Theophilus thrust the rifle forward, braced and started to lead the dog. His finger tightened, and it was then that the little hound got brave and began to yell. He snarled, barked, struggled in John's arms. The rifle cracked and Theophilus swore. Levered. Fire. Levered. Fire. Now the gray dog was zig-zagging like a combat veteran, crossing in front of the ducks, disappearing around the house. Fire. Splinters flew from a post on one of the porches. Silence. Theophilus levered and shot the goddamn house. Silence.

The hound was whimpering. Theophilus turned, threw down the rifle, picked up the hound, and threw it into the well. It screamed as it fell. Then Theophilus picked up the rifle and started to walk.

Noises were coming from the well and there was distant splashing. In the still morning, with the cluck of chickens, the little hound splashed and gasped for its life.

John sat in the grass, not thinking, not comprehending. And then he started to scream and cry.

Theophilus turned back, death-white. The rifle lever dangled. He closed it up. "It aint but an old hound."

John squalled. The hound gasped and splashed.

"Aint but a well for the chickens. I'll let out his misery." Theophilus pushed the rifle over the edge, searched with the muzzle like he was trying to figure which direction to point in the darkness. The hammer clicked. No loads.

"Time you was growin' up." Theophilus walked toward the house and the new construction that had been going on in the summer. He returned with a rope. "C'mere."

John came, still bawling. When Theophilus tied the rope around his waist, then around and under his arms, he did not figure it out. Then he *did,* and started to scream.

"You want him, go get him."

Theophilus got him over the edge. The hound was maybe down there still struggling. Theophilus maybe lowered him a long way, maybe not. As he entered the black spot John screamed himself beyond panic, and passed out. When he woke up he was in his own room. No one was around. The little hound was maybe still swimming. Maybe not. The gray dog did not come back. His mind would not allow that. Nor in his memory was there a recollection that his ducks finally disappeared one by one.

The engine was still running. The car heater blew so hot that condensation formed inside the car. Melted snow was wet in his clothes. He raised one hand, looked at it, raised the other. Funny how you lived with your hands and did not notice them. One hand seemed older than the other. There were more wrinkles, the veins more prominent.

He rolled down a window and breathed in the cold air. The heater's blast made his boots hot and his feet wet in the wool socks. The dull gleam of the car's dash, the soft leather, the barely heard purr of the engine intruded on unwanted memory. But there was no denying it now. He was into the pit, the well, the great hollow of dark that was longer than his life, that was as long as his life's history. No question. He knew now that he was truly engaged with the house. He must come to terms with the house.

When you were forty you knew you were not going to live forever. When you were forty you pretended that what you did was valuable and moral. Either that, or you learned what the words "valuable" and "moral" really meant. Strange words. Actually they were Justice's words. His so-called crazy father. All right, maybe he was crazy, some people said so, but there was one thing to think about. The ones who called Justice crazy were not so damn rational themselves. You could not exactly call Theophilus or Vera well-adjusted. And John's mother Sarah had not been a great shining example of reason. And if he, John Tracker, was so terribly sane, then what was he doing sitting in this car weak with memory? He should get back to that hotel. Get back to Amy. It was at least three hours of driving. The afternoon light was nearly gone, soon it would be dark.

Maybe the whole world was nuts. If the Tracker family was certifiable, maybe the Tracker Family was only different in its style. Maybe Amy was as whacko as the rest. Tracker did not understand what he feared, or even felt, but he somehow knew that the past made the world. The house said that. He wondered if he could trust Amy. Well, he didn't trust anyone else. He was not even sure why she had to be trusted. What could she do to him, or take from him that mattered?

As soon as his hands felt steady he pulled the car into the road and managed good speed, considering the road condition. His car's headlights turned the feathering snow into silver tunnels through the night.

It was just that the situation between himself and Amy was so recently changed. She had worked for him for so long. They had traveled together, and he had not even much wondered if she had a personal life, or if her personal life amounted to anything.

And then, one night, it was like a decision was made between them without either saying a word. They became lovers, or at least bed partners. It was nice, but when you went to bed with a person it meant you were no longer in the single role of employer or boss. There was change between them, though he did not know how much or what kind.

He did know that he wanted to get back to her and hold her and be held. Like a child, almost.

CHAPTER

6

Mary Blessing was John Tracker's great great grandmother on his mother's father's mother's side. Her knowledges and fears were more ancient than John's rationalization could allow. They were more ancient than Amy's Catholicism. They derived from a dark prehistory.

Mary Blessing deserted her husband before the Civil War, doubtless with good reason, took her daughter Faith and joined a band of religionists who talked of heading west. Tracker family history claims that she followed Mormons.

That is almost surely a lie. Mary was Negro, devout, superstitious and knew at least the rudiments of voodoo. In addition, she was a few years displaced in time for the Mormon migration. Mary lived in a more certain world than did most Trackers. In the presence of evil, she knew enough to seek a balance instead of making a deal.

In the richly carpeted hotel elevator John Tracker's thoughts were surrounded by ranks of muted violins piping from a hidden speaker. His car was parked in the heated garage. He lived in a modern world. The reality of the elevator, of cars and canned music had a way of dispelling ancient ghosts. At the same time those things could bring an unreality of their own. In the streets, cars rode like purple, yellow and red clubs on chain-wrapped wheels that flopped and smacked. The background noise of recorded violins was bothersome, like the buzzing of disembodied insects. He was going to meet Amy. He needed no distractions.

A skeleton danced in his memory like a recurring dream. The skeleton was in a tiny cubicle. He wondered if the skeleton was real or only fantasy. Kids responded the way adults responded. If memory was right the skeleton was real. It had always been taken as a matter of course by Theophilus. But if it was real, who was it? Did it lie dreamless or dreaming? He touched the steel sides of the elevator that were painted in imitation of wood grain. At that moment the elevator seemed as weird as anything he had ever experienced.

Feelings like that worried him. You could not run a business, or a life, by constantly objecting to things that offended you. Besides, what was offensive about an elevator? As you matured you ought to look differently at the world. Here he was, age forty, thinking of skeletons.

The elevator doors slid as smoothly as a habit, and John stepped into a panelled and musically tuned, articulately lighted corridor. He walked to the room, turned the key and Amy got up from a chair and reached to click off the television.

She was simply beautiful. Her familiar face, slender form and accustomed gestures seemed so sane after the day. She moved toward him and looked both eager and hesitant. He felt the same. They still did not have the intimate parts worked out.

"It's late," she said. "I was getting a little worried."

"I'm always careful."

"The storm."

He reached for her hand, drew her to him. He kissed her lightly in a way that he hoped was sort of husbandly; although, having never been a husband, he was not quite sure how such kissing went. He wanted her close, but he had had enough vigorous scenes to last for a while.

"Have you had dinner?" She seemed trying to play the same game. She was subdued, friendly and kind of wifey, he supposed. If he were wearing a business suit instead of the wool shirt she would probably be untying his tie.

"Is something wrong?" He felt suddenly possessive, as though by her quiet reaction she was rejecting him.

"Nothing is wrong." She put her arms around his neck and drew tight against him. "You look tired and you're acting sort of distant."

"It's been one hell of a day." He paused, not quite able to smile at the usage. That also was not what she wanted to hear. "I've not had too much practice at living with someone," he said. "I'm clumsy."

She changed from her quietness almost as though he had flipped a switch. This time when they kissed it was full. Her long fingers were in his hair and across his back, her body pressing to him so that he felt aroused in spite of his fatigue. He moved one of his hands up her side and she moved a little sideways so that he could touch her better. Women were so soft and warm. He wondered why, when there were women in the world, he spent so much time away from them. Or rather, why he spent so much time on business.

To impress women, he supposed.

"I haven't had dinner," he said. "Would you like to go out?" Before they started playing at being lovers he would not have had to ask.

"Shower first," she said. "You'll feel better."

"Is it that bad?" He hoped it was not fear she smelled.

"You always shower. For three years you've showered at the end of every day." Now she was smiling.

"You sat in the next room listening."

"I sat in the next room minding my business and listening to the world's most eclectic baritone." She seemed ready to giggle and he found himself about to do the same. The pressure of the day was disappearing. With practice, he figured that they would both learn.

"Be right back."

The world's most eclectic baritone. This time he would not sing in the shower. He smiled in a way that said he was tired of smiling, and it occured to him that if he were a little bit dumber life would be better. If he was slightly stupid he would be in control of millions, would be buying legislatures, might even be on a political bender.

It was confusing. Ideas were more interesting than business, but business was safer. Academic foolishness bored him. Specialists bored him, although he hired them sometimes. It was a strange mix. The visit to the house told him that the early years with his father must, indeed, be important. And it occurred to him that by the time he was ten he had probably heard more obscure ideas than most people met in a lifetime. As the hot water sprayed over him, it seemed that he heard the echo of his father's explaining voice . . . "world without end . . ." But Justice was not a preacher. Justice had been explaining something, yet those were a preacher's words.

Time. Time was without end. It was more than simply relative. It was constant; and all the time that ever was or ever would be was now. The hot water spattered against his skin, flushed away not only dirt but fatigue, made him feel more vital, as if he had been fifty and was now a refreshed forty. Justice had once tried to tell him something about time, and John felt that he had almost remembered, had almost solved the time shifts. And then he accepted that he had not solved them, yet.

Enough of that. *Time* for dinner. *Time* to make friends with Amy.

Could she be trusted? He wished he would quit thinking that. He wished suspicion would leave him alone. Eventually he would have to tell her something about this day.

They went to the lobby and waited for a cab. John stepped outside of the hotel for a moment. A breath of fresh air. Snow swirled. Wind crashed down building-enclosed streets and rattled the glass in storefronts. Ash and sand and street dirt were gray beneath city lights. Engines revved. He returned to Amy, who remained in the lobby. He tried but he seemed to have nothing to say. Finally the taxicab pulled to the curb.

The restaurant helped. Though in Indianapolis, on Sunday night, the choices tended to be rather limited. A sulky waiter took orders for an Italian dinner that would predictably be breaded veal covered with tomato sauce. The room was large and brightly lit—too big for intimacy, too deserted for whispers.

Amy sat there across from him. Bright smile. Probably acting, but if so it was a very good act. She was dressed in a dark outfit that softened the color of her hair and promoted her brown eyes. It seemed incredible that they were lovers. It was almost like being in high school and finding yourself in love with a teacher. Amy seemed unattainable, even now. In addition to her beauty, that sense of being unattainable was surely one of the most compelling things about her. With the well-styled outfit she wore a nearly transparent blouse, high-necked and buttoned. Her long, near-perfect legs were crossed so that one calf and ankle formed a graceful line that seemed full of promise.

And was, he thought. It certainly was.

"How was the movie?"

"How did you know?"

"You always go to movies," he said. "I'm not yet the world's leading expert on Amy Griffith, but you always go to movies."

"A potboiler," she told him. "First-rate camera work,

over-edited, but with some wonderful scenes." The salad arrived. She plucked a lettuce leaf with her fingers and nibbled at it. "You can cover a lot of bad script with a good set and cameras."

"I've never really learned about those things."

"You've never really had time," she said. "I never really have, either. Now it looks like I won't." Implied sadness made her seem even more sexual.

He felt the remaining fatigue from the day lifting. It was like the time had stepped sideways. It was like the day existed, but it did not exist in the continuum in which he now existed. It was like a scene edited from one of those movies Amy had described.

"What do you mean, you won't have time?"

"You have to be young," she said. "To make it in any kind of theater you have to be really young."

"You are. Besides, not all acting parts are for kids."

"Not young enough." She clearly did not want to talk about it, although she was the one who had brought up the subject. "How was your day?"

"Unbelievable."

"Tell me."

He found himself really wanting to tell her all of it. He felt nearly obsessive. At the same time he knew how crazy the whole thing would sound. You could not, after all, tell the history of a life or a family over dinner. Especially not his life, his family. Even if you knew the whole history you could not impart the sense of time, over a hundred years of it, that existed in that house.

"I want to see."

He pretended to be thinking about it. The problem was that, even now, he just did not know how much of what he had experienced was real. He did not know if the disrupting time shifts were real. He did not know if, overwhelmed by the long repressed sense and memory of his family and his early life, he had somehow hallucinated that specter of Theophilus to bring him back, to confront him but in a way so as not to have to believe in him. *Tricks.* That would have been *his* trick if he did that. And Vera . . . what about her? Could he say for certain that Vera was alive, or had he somehow hallucinated her too? One thing *was* real. The traps. The traps had been there since his earliest memory.

"I want to see," Amy said again.

"It's dangerous. It's stupid and crazy, but it's also truly dangerous, Amy. The house has thousands of traps. Any one of them could kill you."

"If an old woman can live there?" She was prepared to argue for her right to see the house.

"You don't know that old woman. That old woman could scare the horns off the Devil." He told himself that he had never known Vera well enough to understand her. He knew that he would always fear her, even if she were dead.

"I want to go, I insist on it."

He wondered if her life was so boring, if he was so boring, that she so badly needed variety. He tried to stall. "I'm going back day after tomorrow, it'll take a day for a driver to bring a truck here from Cincinnati. We'll talk about it later."

Her look said that she was going. He'd fumbled, if he was going to say no he should already have said it.

"If you do go," he said, "you'll have to do exactly as I say. The place is dangerous beyond belief."

She seemed not to hear. She seemed distant, as though structuring a fantasy about having an adventure. To her it was like a play. He decided not to press the point further about the traps until they got to the house. Once she saw the place she would understand.

He decided that he was glad she had talked him into taking her. He did not really want to go back to that house alone.

CHAPTER

7

As a child, John Tracker's grandmother, Vera Rothstein, learned what her mother Maggie knew. Mostly that was superstition, but much of that superstition came disguised as witchcraft. Maggie also knew primitive methods of contraception and abortion. She knew how it was to be raped by police. She had realistic methods for dealing with ham-handed laborers, who, working a twelve-hour day, brooded in taverns. Maggie knew poultices for bruises, and how to treat rotten meat so that it could be safely eaten. She knew how to steal. Vera learned all of these things, either from Maggie or from the streets, or both.

Vera learned these lessons from her mother Maggie as Maggie had learned from her mother Judith. The difference was that Judith had been a skilled witch. Judith knew that witchcraft and satanism dealt with sex and mutilation. Judith was also sufficiently well-versed to know that witchcraft flowered in medieval times because of the need for revolution. The sky was low in those old centuries. Life crowded close. The silence was profound. The only sounds in the gathering darkness were the lowing of cattle and the clank of the church bell. Travel was nearly unknown. The feudal system, manor and cathedral, struggled toward belief in a world where nearly all were serfs. Plagues swept whole nations. Rotting bodies stripped of their rags lay swollen in the streets. The peasant had no words or the opportunity to use them. Malcontents fought using the only weapon at hand, a figure that was against the manor and the cathedral, against the law and the church. The Devil, summoned, let loose, rose and began to walk.

In her way, John's grandmother Vera Rothstein Tracker represented much of the American experience. She was born from a long line of theology (in her case dark) and emerged into an age of dogma. The development is easily traced. Vera's grandmother Judith was a practiced theorist. She understood her skills, and the source of her power. She was capable of relating herself to that power, and understanding the relationship. Vera's mother, Maggie, daughter of Judith, ran away before she was fully educated. No doubt she had a few skills, but the theory and the dark theology that justified those skills she never acquired. And Vera ran away even before she was able to learn the little that Maggie knew. All Vera had gained was a nearly blind faith in the powers of what she called darkness. Other presumably rival dogmatists arrived on the scene in a similar fashion. The only difference was that they praised the powers of light.

Until she met Theophilus, Vera's life was confused and bitter; as degraded as those of starving horses that were whipped through Chicago's streets. At age thirteen she fled into a society that placed iron deer on its lawns, iron regulations on sex, prosperity in banks, and immigrants in sweatshops. Vera knew more about sweatshops than she knew about banks.

To combat both she turned to sex. Early experience taught her that prostitution was the work of the ignorant, the failed, the lazy and the starving. Sex was only a method. Experience further taught that control through sex could be managed as long as something was withheld. Vera fell in love once, with a man who became bored by love and sexual excess, so Vera decided that to control with sex she would withhold some aspect of love.

At twenty-four she met Theophilus, who was twenty-one and who, for a young man of his time and station, was refreshingly cynical. After World War I, and before the Depression, it paid to be an optimist. Yet Theophilus, hard-working and with money, sneered at nearly everything and everyone he saw. Which touched

Vera's experience. She called it good sense. It was also rather romantic.

Theophilus was a builder, and she recognized that she was also a builder. When she arrived at the house of the Trackers it seemed that the darkness of her past was actually an illumination. In this house ranks and ranks of violent ideas were ranged against the dreams of a steadily cheapening world. Vera decided that in a world of lies, she had found a refuge of truth. She spent the next fifty-six years in company with Theophilus in the house of the Trackers, which was her spiritual creation, as it was his artistic creation.

Vera bore one child, Justice, John's father, when she was twenty-five. She died at seventy-four as she was seated before the dying embers of a fireplace. Her son Justice was forty-nine when she died. Her grandson John was twenty-three. He returned to his grandmother when he was forty.

Arctic winds blew the midwinter snow for two days causing drifts to mount against the windward side of the house. The house was wrapped in a New England kind of cold. The cold penetrated the thick walls and lay in deserted corridors. It was life-stilling cold. The room where John had seen Vera sitting was like an ice chamber. At night the temperature fell further, plummeting on the river wind like a hammer dropped from a ship into hundreds of fathoms.

John and Amy came across the fields, and this time John felt prepared. They rounded the far side of the woodlot, approaching in a dark green four-by-four which had TRACKER AND ASSOCIATES painted on the door, the truck a new piece of equipment belonging to the landscape company. Purchased especially for the coming job in Council Bluffs, it was rigged with a heavy winch and dump bed. The four-wheel drive and off-the-road tires discarded snow in loud whirls as the truck jarred back and forth. John held the wheel too tightly, the truck skidded even at five miles per hour.

He wondered and worried about Amy. If you loved somebody, or thought you did, then it seemed wrong to expose her to this. He fought the wheel and tried to understand what he saw in Amy's behavior. She was different, though he couldn't say exactly how. Her literal-mindedness was the same, he'd always known about that. Her innocence about business seemed too innocent to be real. He had known about that too. It was as though she had some childish faith in the rightness of the universe and the naturalness of what they did . . . not what they did in bed, sometimes she was still uneasy about that. The faith was in the naturalness of the current *order*. She assumed that he was good, and that what he did was worthwhile. The most noticeable new thing about her was her discontent. In the past it had been hidden. He was sure she wanted to come on this visit for the sheer adventure of it. If she'd wanted to come because of him, or because of the house, then surely she would have asked more questions.

Now she sat quiet beside him, gazing across the snow, and as they rounded the woodlot she got her first sight of the house. She gasped.

"I told you." Tracker heard the grimness in his voice. He over-corrected. The truck skidded, pulled back, wobbled at an unsteady five miles per hour.

"No wonder you left." She reached to touch his shoulder, and her expression said that a man as smart as John Tracker could never come from this bizarre-looking place of rising towers.

"We can still go back. Maybe we should—"

"Of course we can't go back," she said. "Not after all the trouble and expense—"

"It hasn't been much."

"Of course it has. You lost Sunday. We've lost two business days already. You paid a driver's wages to transport the truck."

"You have to do *exactly* as I tell you. It's dangerous. I mean it."

She kept silent and looked rather resentful. He supposed it was because he was talking like the Boss.

"I'm sorry, Amy, but it's beyond any experience you could ever possibly have had."

"I've not exactly been living in a convent, you know." The resentment in her voice was clear. Now she thought he was being paternal.

"It's beyond any experience anyone ever had."

"I'll do as you tell me." But she sounded like a petulant child obliquely saying she would do anything she wanted.

There was, then, no answer except to show her the house. She would change her mind. He drove and was pleased with the way the truck handled. Damn few vehicles of any kind could manage this depth of snow. "I want to get in and then away before the storm."

She looked at the sky, which was clear for the first time in weeks.

"That river is a funnel for weather," he said, "but in these parts it's kind of a wall. There's a front piling west of the river. When it does break through, tomorrow or next day, it's really going to howl."

She seemed almost pleased. Her lips relaxed in a tiny smile and she licked them with a darting motion. Her eyes were dark and beautiful, but vague, as though she were daydreaming a scene of them roughing it. As for him, he'd worked outside enough in his life to know that the way to rough it was to find a good comfortable motel.

He turned toward her, reached to touch her shoulder, but as he did the truck slewed to one side and abruptly brought him back to his driving.

Mixed with his concern for Amy were memories of background music and of a skeleton lying in a cell. When they arrived, he parked a hundred feet from the house, which he figured was a safe margin.

Amy was staring, fascinated. A hundred feet was too close to see much. The house overhung the view, but it was possible to see the façades. Windows along the porch were dull orange and red, purple, washed blue and fire yellow; the stained glass and heavily leaded frames were like subdued kaleidoscopes before an eternity of snow.

St. Paul preached earnestly to a next-door panel depicting reptiles. A goat danced, hooves pawing air beneath a blood-red Mayan sun; the face of a long-haired woman stared, one eye of green glass now only a socket of air enclosed by crumbling lead. Thunderbirds and owls mixed and tumbled before Egyptian river gods. It seemed to Tracker that he was seeing the house for the first time. His memory whispered, and the whisper was his father's voice.

"Remember, remember this."

High above the central windows was a stained glass portrayal of a brooding face. The face seemed thinking of fading sunsets, or maybe the fading of hope. The face was bearded. As John looked, it was as though the glass was making him look at his own fears, hopes, and his age. He looked quickly at Amy. She seemed fascinated, blind to him, nearly unapproachable. As though she was in a different land. Her face was tense with excitement. Her hands were nervous. She seemed ready to get from the truck and go dashing and clumping through the echoing, cathedral-sized house like a tourist tramping through five museums a day.

"It isn't that way," he said. "Look at it. *Look.*"

She did not seem to hear. She looked at him and listened seriously, but was obviously not hearing a thing.

On the protected side of the house, with the mound of freeway running in front, wind drifts were like a funnel as the wind blew down the channel between house and freeway. In spots the snow was not especially deep.

77

"I want to see." She opened the truck door.

"I want to get the truck pointed in the other direction. When we take Vera out it will save time."

Amy climbed from the truck. "I'll help you back up."

He resented it but said nothing. The door was already closed. She stood outside and waited to signal him in his mirrors as he backed up. He supposed she had seen warehousemen do that and didn't know she was being insulting. This wasn't, after all, a loading dock. He wouldn't tell her how to run a typewriter.

The ground was rutty beneath the snow—frozen mud creased where construction machinery had torn up the soil. He turned the truck, parked on a slight grade, looked up and saw Amy heading for the house and the fourth door.

Tracker jumped from the truck, ran hard, yelling after her, caught her at the edge of the porch and pulled her back. She stumbled and nearly fell in the snow, then stood quiet. He had never yelled at her before.

"All I was going to *do* was get out of the snow." Her voice sounded prim.

He didn't doubt she believed what she said, but from her pace and direction she was certainly going to open that fourth door.

He needed to get her past the illusions. He led her fifty feet back, where a windblown pile of dirt was nearly clear of snow.

"Stay here," he said, "and watch." He walked to the fourth door, stepped wide, reached out, twisted the knob and jumped back.

The door flew open, pulled by heavy springs. Nozzles swiveled instantly. A bloom of fire shot from the door at face level and burned with the red and blue light of gas above the snow on the porch. The flames went straight ahead so as not to burn the house, only someone in front of the door. When the fire died, the door automatically closed.

Tracker went to Amy. "I'll take you inside, or I'll take you home," he said gently.

"All right." All right what? Then she was moving toward the house. She was still only hearing, seeing what she wanted; one trap, it seemed, did not convince her of others. Tracker felt in his jacket pockets for flashlight, batteries and a box of heavy chalk. He steered her to the third door from the left, kicked the trapdoor, found it still on safety.

They went inside. The house seemed different. The beamed ceilings hung nearly invisible in gloom. Shadows pressed from the hall. John couldn't be sure, but he suspected this was the first time anyone other than a Tracker had been in the place. He wanted to tell her that all of this had nothing to do with him; that the diabolic constructions were creatures of other imaginations. He put his arm around Amy, who was staring at the coffin.

"Don't go near it."

"Where *can* I go?" She was acting dependent on him but her body seemed tensed for what might be independent action.

"You can go almost anywhere if I go first." He proceeded to walk ahead of her. Each time he came to a triggering device he drew heavy chalk circles. If she touched nothing within a circle, he explained, she would be safe. He also tried to explain each trap, but she didn't want to know.

"Who was that man?" Her question startled him. He looked over one shoulder. He'd forgotten one kind of fear because of the immediate fear for her safety.

"What man?"

"In the picture."

"Oh." He breathed deep. "My father. Some people said he was crazy." He leaned to trace another circle, one that enclosed a steel trap designed to break one's ankles.

"Really crazy?"

He felt angry and couldn't say why. "As a loon," he told her. "As a March Hare. Right down to the ends of his fingernails."

"Was he violent?"

"No. Maybe that's why they thought he was crazy." Strange, she'd evoked his anger with a simple question, a fair question. How was she supposed to know that the question meant more than she could imagine.

"He wasn't crazy," John said flatly. And then—"I don't know whether he was crazy or not."

"I want to see." She walked wide of a chalked circle and headed back to the hallway. He jumped to follow, saw her avoid the circle, and slowly walked after her.

Amy was now standing too close to the coffin. He looked at the painting. There were no reds in the background. He walked to Amy, moved her back. The coffin was oversized, like an ornamental piece of furniture designed to fit the proportions of the high-ceilinged hall. Rosewood gleamed dull in the half light. Gold-plated handles were massive and ornamented. As he leaned forward for the first careful look he'd ever given the coffin, he was shocked. The ornamentation was a twisting, erotic display. He rubbed at a handle and felt repulsed, but also fascinated.

"Watch." He stood at the end of the coffin, raised the lid, and the coffin tilted backward, displaying needle-sharp hooks. A muffled thump sounded from inside. He righted it, looked in and saw nothing. He searched in the faded satin, found a lever. A small trap door opened to display a compartment beneath the false bottom. He looked, slammed the lid down hard, and stood there, trying to force back an hysteric, absurd laugh that was trying to escape. He turned back to Amy. She still seemed ready to go exploring. She was not looking at him. He was glad. In a moment he would have enough control. He would be able to go looking for Vera without having to tell Amy that the fake coffin was not a fake, after all.

CHAPTER

8

Jude Tracker, son of Johan and Sarah, brother of Theophilus and grand uncle of John Tracker, died at age seventeen of scarlet fever. His was the first death in Johan's family.

Johan buried Jude and staked two dogs at the grave. The dogs howled at night. Johan wasn't sure if they howled at the moon or the Devil. He exhumed Jude and did not know what to do. He could not leave his son unprotected. The body was in such numbing condition that it could not be brought into the house. So in desperation Johan built a vault in the subcellar and placed Jude there. When the skeleton was ready, it was removed and put to rest in a cell. In this way the cemetery where John believed Theophilus to be buried was a fake. Bones lay throughout the house. The cemetery contained only a few pet dogs and cats, which bordered it like a skeletal ring of flowers.

Vera was in the same room as before. When they entered, Amy gasped, shrank back, then stood still and grabbed John's arm.

He moved in front of her and she lowered her head and pressed it against his back.

"I'll take you out of here," he said, "then I'll come back and handle this." He turned to lead her from the room.

But she stood, head bowed, rigid.

"I want to stay."

He understood. Even one room away she would feel that death lay in the space between them. If they were together, then death only sat in front of them in an old chair.

This time he was sure Vera was dead. The musty room was filled with a deeper scent, the light odor of beginning decomposition. The smell lay through the room like the rising layers of morning mist from the river. (Later, he would tell himself that a rat must have died in the walls.)

He started to move toward Vera—stopped. He turned to look at Amy as he felt time shift. He was almost glad for it. If Amy felt the shift too then it was real.

The ill-lit room dimmed, shaded back to light, and dimmed again. Distant rooms seemed to hold murmurs, but this time there was no music or child's laughter. Instead, the murmur changed to a low trilling, like winter vibrating in walls or windows. The light rapidly became normal. Amy stood there, her face reflecting wonder. Or so he saw it.

"Did you feel it?" he asked.

"Feel what?"

"Did you see the light dim?"

"I don't know. What are you talking about? I don't know." Her voice was thin, nearly hysterical. It, he, was all obviously getting to her. She looked beyond him at Vera, and seemed reproachful because he'd turned and, in turning, once more exposed her to the sight of Vera.

The house of the Trackers. No question, now it was working on Amy too. He turned back to Vera, and as he did he was sure that Amy felt time shift; he was sure she was denying the evidence of her senses, which was exactly what a person learned to do in this house.

His grandmother slumped forward. This time the body was cloaked and hooded. Robed. Like an ancient monk.

Her face was buried in shadow, and the arms seemed even thinner, projecting from the heavy cloak. He went toward her, saw one of her hands tremble. Would the old bat never die? Something urged him forward to tip body and chair into a tangled, robed heap.

But this was not John Tracker. Or rather, he feared that it was John Tracker. He was disgusted with himself. This house was a well of depravity.

Her hand was moving in front of his eyes, independent of arm and wrist. Fingers crawled, then grasped. The nails were long and looked healthy, the thin hand and almost fleshless fingers like fragile sockets into which the nails were plugged. Her hand clenched, released, trembled and again crawled. Then it became a tight fist. Her head raised slightly and her body rocked a little as her shoulders tensed. She raised her head.

He continued to watch. Her eyes were dull and glazed, but life seemed to spark from some inner tomb of spirit. Her shoulders relaxed and her head remained upright.

"Like last time," he said. He touched her arm. It was cold, flaccid beneath the cloak, and there seemed not enough flesh to sustain life.

Amy was beside him. "She's alive? Yes . . ." Amy hovered over the woman, drew the robe closer around her, looked about for more covering, then began to take off her own coat.

"Leave it," he said.

"She's freezing."

"I'll build another stinkin'-dammit fire."

"Don't curse." Amy was bustling. "It'll be all right, we'll get you to bed, we'll take care of you."

He figured she'd learn better, and she would learn it quick. Right now there was no sense in arguing.

This time his grandmother seemed to revive rapidly. Her eyes flashed, then came into focus. As the kindling began to pop and crackle, she was talking.

"Where did you get this one?" Her voice was raspy, but it was better than the other time.

"She's waking up," Amy said. "She must be nearly frozen."

"You couldn't kill her with an ax. You couldn't bury her with a bulldozer."

Vera was looking at Amy's figure, judging how good Amy was in bed. Vera seemed to have concluded that, for a punk kid, Amy was probably not too bad.

"You old scut," he said. "You flaming bitch." It was stupid. He knew it while he was saying it.

"What in the world is wrong with you? Are you going crazy?" Amy seemed to be missing everything.

"He's scairt," the old woman said. "Tracker men don't change." Her voice was smoother. She modulated it so that the tone was friendly, although the words were not.

Tracker turned away.

"It's hard to be old," Vera said to Amy. "I never thought I'd ever be this old." Her voice was getting smoother all the time. There was something antique and pleasant in the voice, like Victorian music.

"We're leaving," he said. He looked at Vera. "Walk or carry? I don't care which, but here we go." He moved toward her, half-expecting time to shift or the floor to drop from beneath his feet.

"We're goin' nowhere," Vera said. " 'Til the trouble's laid." She looked at Amy. "I feel terrible weak, just terrible." The old, parchment-like face beneath the hood was shadowed. In the dim light and the flickering glow of fire all he could see were Vera's bright eyes.

The snarl-like sound rose involuntary in his throat, like the attack signal of a cornered wolf or dog. He heard it happening and stood there, shocked. Was Amy hearing this?

"Are you all right?" She reached to touch his arm.

"Besides," his grandmother said, "it's stormin'."

Amy looked surprised.

"It isn't storming," Tracker said. "The storm is at least one, probably two days away."

"Stormin'. Stormin'."

He listened. If there were a storm, wind would echo through empty rooms, booming like drums. He heard nothing.

"I know this place," he said. "If it was storming we could hear."

"Screamin' silent-like, head fulla storm."

He gave her credit. One irrelevent statement and she had Amy fooled.

"Get some blankets," Amy said. "She's wandering in her mind. Is there any tea or coffee?" She leaned over Vera like a concerned intern viewing symptoms not to be found in any textbook.

"She's faking," Tracker said, "she's fooling you."

"She's *not*. Get busy or I'll go myself."

"Not in this house, you won't."

"I will. I *will.*"

He decided she was getting hysterical. "Please listen," he said. "Even if she's wandering in her mind, which she isn't, then the best place for her is a hospital. In the next town. Three miles down the road—"

Vera moaned, sagged in the chair, made choking noises that might be laughter or sobs.

"You see, you *see*. She's sick. Sick."

"All right, I'll go," he said, "and I'll bring what you want, but you've got to promise not to move in this room, no matter what. Don't believe a thing she says."

"Yes. All right. *Go.*"

Maybe she heard and understood, and maybe not. "Ten minutes," he said. He followed the fastest route. It was a maze, its the floors inlaid with colored symbols, leaves and crosses, chalices and flowers. It was a tightly webbed network of repeating pictures that seldom varied but which were so randomly mixed that there seemed to be no pattern. The trick was to look at as much of the floor as you could see. When you saw the largest area possible, and when you isolated the leaf symbols, then you could see how they formed a trail. They often broke off. It was not consistent, but no matter where you walked in the maze, the trail would sooner or later reappear.

He used the flashlight and followed the leaf symbols until they ran to a wall, then he pressed on the wall. A door opened into a room only two removed from the kitchens. There was nothing dangerous in those rooms if you remembered not to walk beneath the heavy chandeliers.

Water splashed in the sink. The stoves were working. This time he did not have to wonder how power was getting into the house. On Monday he had called the local utility and found that bills were being paid by a local bank. Then he called the bank and explained who he was. The name Tracker might be anathema in the surrounding towns but it still worked in banks. The bank president had limited power of attorney on a Tracker account with a balance of nearly thirty thousand dollars. The banker was handling all billings for the house and would be happy to meet with John Tracker at his convenience to further discuss that matter and any others.

Damn right, he would, Tracker thought; but the question that the banker could not answer was why the bills, while substantial, were not huge. He figured that the answer was that while the house ran on outside utilities, the power was supplemented by generators somewhere in the house.

He searched now through cabinets, found tea and sniffed at it. It smelled like plain tea, but it would serve Vera right if the stuff was poisoned.

Not much time had passed since he'd left Amy. The water boiled quickly. He figured he couldn't have been away for even ten minutes. Still, he felt it was wrong to leave Amy. Except there seemed little choice. Beyond this house, in the bustling world of buildings and trees and plans, he might have influence. In this house, with a half-hysterical woman, he was pretty helpless. If he'd refused to do as she asked she might have become really extreme. Well, what about *his* reasons for being in the house? Were they good ones? The job in Council Bluffs, that was a good job. He'd be proving some things on that job that architects and planners would be talking about for years. The job on the freeway, it didn't sound like much, but a properly landscaped freeway could be low-maintenance and still make you feel almost like you were driving through a park. Sure, there were reasons to be here. But the best, the most important reason was to understand John Tracker.

A voice was echoing from somewhere.

He grabbed the teapot and a cup, hesitated. The voice sounded distant, and almost desperate. Amy. He dropped the pot and heard it shatter behind him. It could only be Amy. No one else in this house would be calling that way. Had something happened to Vera? Maybe the old hellion had keeled over and saved them some trouble. Maybe, but he had more faith in Vera than to expect her to do anything decent.

Amy must be in trouble. He ran through the second room. The desperate voice was closer. There were distant thumps. He slugged a wall that opened a door into the maze, scrambled through, the door slammed. Once in the maze the voice was clear, bordering now on hysteria.

"I'm coming," he called out. "Stand still. Where are you?"

"Lost. I'm lost." Her voice did not hold hysteria now. The moment she heard him, she felt safe, which was a lot of responsibility to put on a man, at least in this house.

"Describe where you are."

"Between walls. Like in a long box . . ."

She was lost in the maze without a flashlight. Still, there was nothing there to hurt her, only confuse and wear her out. Maybe it would teach her a lesson if she had to wander for a while.

"Keep talking," he said.

No human anywhere, not even its builder, could walk through this maze and not become lost. Her voice seemed to be coming from both the left and right. It faded, then was strong, then faded. She could not have been in the maze for long, could not be too deep in its shifting illusion. The trail of leaf symbols was useless except to get out of the maze. It did not do a thing to help find Amy.

"Keep talking," he said again. "I can only find you by sound."

"I'm afraid . . . there's something in here with me."

It was a rat. Bound to be. He didn't want to tell her that, it would only terrify her more.

"It's okay," he said. "There's nothing in here."

"I see your light. Oh, good, thank God . . ."

He stood still. Listening. He heard footsteps, footsteps going away. It sounded like Amy was running. "It's a trick," he yelled. "Stop."

The footsteps faltered.

"Why are you running away from me?" Her echoing voice was disbelieving.

"I'm not. It's a trick. The old sonofabitch must have rigged lights that would trap someone into following deeper into the maze."

"The light's blue, it's just around the next corner."

When she went around that corner it would be just around the next corner. Damn Theophilus.

"Stand still. Sing. Whistle. Keep talking, but stand still."

"I can't. *Something* is in here with me. Every time I stand still, something moves toward me."

He hoped some rat bolder than the rest would not advance under cover of darkness and nip her. She was, he thought, handling the situation pretty well. Then, abruptly, it occurred to him that it was not a rat and not her imagination.

"What does it sound like?"

"Like sighing, like someone is sad—"

"It's a trick. You've activated recording equipment. There are concealed speakers in the wall. No matter where you go you'll hear it. Just stand there, don't move."

The maze was like an echo chamber. He walked in the direction of her voice, but every time he heard her voice it seemed to be coming from an opposite direction. A memory was trying to break through, some past knowledge that should help him find her. He stopped. If he could figure out what he knew, it might not take hours to reach her. If he couldn't, he would have to go on walking the maze. Finding her would be pure chance. He would be as confused as she, though he could get out whenever he wanted. So spend a little time reflecting, and save a lot of time.

Once, when he was little, and when this maze was already built, there had been an awful fracas. It seemed he could still hear Vera's laughter, could hear her scorn. His father had fussed and worried, and for a while Theophilus had been like a madman.

The old man was sitting in the kitchen with his shirtsleeves rolled up. There was plaster in his gray hair. The muscles and cords in his forearms made his fists look like hammers. Vera was standing in an entry, laughing. Justice, curly haired and slightly beefy, sat across from his father.

"It's plain fact," Justice said. "It's new theory, but it's also fact, and the fact is you're proving the theory."

"Theory." Theophilus was digging into the tabletop with a pocket knife. Slivers and shavings erupted. "You

90

can take your theories and stick 'em where the sun don't shine."

"You use theory every day," Justice said. "You just call it practical."

The knife scraped, scooped, and on the tabletop the shape of a bird began to form. It rose from the wood in that magic way that always fascinated John when he was a child.

"Your whole life's wasted," Vera said. "Your whole raggedy no good job don't run furder than your foreskin to your tailbone."

The knife left Theophilus' hand, whirled, struck into the frame of the door beside Vera's face. She laughed, plucked it loose, tossed it back to him.

"Grow an extra hand . . ."

And that was it. John remembered that the whole scene had come about because Justice was demonstrating that Theophilus always built to the right. Justice had innocently begun talking about psychology, and it ended in the implication that anyone could solve anything in the house if he thought to the right.

Tracker turned the flashlight on, calling out to Amy that he would be there soon. No answer. He called out again. No answer.

He quickly followed the leaf pattern and got out of the maze, rapidly moved through a half dozen rooms until he returned to the room where Vera was supposed to be sitting. The firelight flickered and danced on a shadowed, empty chair.

Vera had tricked Amy, and he had allowed it to happen. He could not really blame Amy. Leaving her with Vera was like leaving a rabbit in the tender care of a bobcat. Now Vera was loose in these endless corridors and rooms. It might even be Vera trying to lead Amy deeper into the maze.

He was back at the starting point. He entered. Each time

there was a choice he moved right, his moves carrying him deeper and deeper into the maze. It was almost as if he could feel the depth of it crushing down on him. He could see, using the light, how options for turning always led slightly to the right. It came from the subconscious of the builder. He figured that Theophilus, once alerted, never made such a mistake again. Well, he was glad Theophilus had not been alerted when this thing was first built.

Tracker walks . . . he tensed at the thought, moved rapidly, was nearly running as he made his decisions. He wondered how much space the maze covered and figured it must take up a quarter or more of the first floor.

He flicked off the light. Waited. Listened. Vera must be in here somewhere, otherwise he would also be seeing blue light, hearing sighs. He wondered how anyone that feeble could move so quickly, then told himself that she knew this house like he knew a ledger sheet. She would not need to be quick.

He found Amy curled with her knees tucked to her chin, shoulders wedged against one wall and feet pressing against the other. She was moaning as he approached, seemed to draw herself together even more tightly.

He rushed to her, knelt. "It's me, it's all right, you are safe." He touched her. She tensed, tried to straighten, tried to scream. He looked at her face in the reflected light from the flashlight that he'd placed on the floor. He could tell that she thought she was screaming.

"It's all a trick," he said. "You are safe." He repeated it over and over, and as he did she gradually seemed to comprehend. Finally the message seemed to overtake her, and as suddenly as a scream, she relaxed. She recognized him. She huddled into his arms and lay there, breathing short breaths.

"I'll get you out of here, I'm so sorry . . ."

She stiffened, seemed to rebel, then relaxed.

"Can you walk?"

He helped her to her feet. She leaned on him. He directed the flashlight to the floor and followed the leaf symbols, and in less than two minutes they were free of the maze and headed for the kitchens. As they walked he grabbed a blanket from a bedroom and draped it over her shoulders.

"Tell me what happened."

She shook her head dumbly. Her mouth tried to make sound, was soundless. She was clearly in some form of shock, and he tried to remember how to treat for shock. He talked gently to her. The house was silent, but Vera was out there somewhere. Walking.

CHAPTER

9

Not all violence in Tracker history came through deceit. If Theophilus was a master of tricks, and if Vera, walking (animated by Theophilus, by the evil genius of him, of her forbears), was a master of spiritual violence, others were not as subtle. As time shifted in the house of the Trackers, every crime seemed to predict a future crime.

Matthew Snider was John Tracker's great great grandfather on his mother's mother's father's side. When he was alive he had no fun except when some neighbor became crippled or died. His envy was overwhelming. His fields amounted to three hundred and twenty acres. His family amounted to five healthy children and a wife. His stables were full, his barns brimmed with life, yet Matthew Snider was known to curse himself as a victim of God's wrath when a neighbor's cow calved twins. When the church was built he took his tools and went home because someone else was working on the staging for the altar.

His wife Gertrude had been known as a gentle and quiet girl. Life with Matthew changed her. She surrounded herself with children and food. She became fat and dictatorial.

Matthew Snider was murdered shortly after the Civil War by his wife, the former Gertrude Drucker. She put rat poison in his supper. This caused him to "swell up and bust," according to the coroner's report. A jury of two men traveled eighteen miles in a one-horse rig over bumpy, trail-like roads; not to condemn Gertrude but because they wanted to be sure that Matthew Snider was really dead.

Of the murder nothing was said. Conditions were different in those days. Gertrude was a young woman with five children and good land. There was no place to send the children if she was charged with murder. Matthew Snider was no loss. The coroner's jury ruled that he committed suicide. Gertrude Snider lived until age forty-six, when she died of a stroke.

Amy slumped on a kitchen bench. She was not, after all, one of those strong German women of the kind that had issued generations into this house.

She made small sounds but could not talk. Before they got to the kitchens she twice delayed them by stopping and trying to look backward, and each time she did he made the mistake of releasing her, and each time she nearly fell. When they got to the kitchens he helped her onto an upholstered bench that ran along one wall. A regular table could be raised in front of the bench from its storage place in the floor. A desk-like table could be lowered from the wall for work on papers and ledgers.

"Amy, can you talk? Tell me what happened."

Her face was drawn tight, eyes too bright. She was very pale. Her lips tried to move. Sounds came from her throat but her lips only tightened. Whatever the trick was, it had thrown her into too deep a shock to be answering questions.

"Some of the tricks are so real," he said quietly to her, "you can't believe they are tricks. It's what makes them so awful."

Her breathing was light now. He knew something about her strong will, and now he was glad for it. He rubbed her arms, feeling their softness, surprised a little because the texture of her flesh did not seem quite as firm as before.

Shock would be followed by fatigue.

He worked with her, mostly rubbing her arms and legs

as much for the soothing effect as to help restore circulation. He rubbed her forehead, her temples. It occurred to him, as it had earlier, why Amy had at first accepted the house so easily. She had been seeing it as a set for a play. She had simply walked through it, thinking it no more than staged make-believe. He nearly smiled, and at the same time felt guilty for bringing her here. Well, he was willing to bet that her acceptance of this place would not come as easily from now on. He told himself that as soon as she could walk by herself, he was taking her out of here.

She seemed to go through several stages of recognition. At first she was helplessly dependent. Then her eyes showed that she was afraid of him. That passed rapidly, her body relaxed, her eyes were submissive. And when the submission passed her eyes became trusting. He estimated that he worked with her for the better part of an hour.

"Touched me." Her voice was small and childlike. He could hardly hear her.

"What?"

"Touched me."

"Who?"

She shuddered, half raised up, lay back. Tears stood in her eyes but she controlled them.

"Did you really see? Who did you see?"

"Didn't see. Felt."

"Touched you where?" He was afraid of the answer, because he knew Theophilus.

The tears came, and she wept like a small child caught doing something she knew was wrong.

"It was Vera," he said. "It was bound to be Vera, if you knew her you would understand—"

"It was strong."

"Then it was a trick," he told her. "That old bastard, my grandfather, could rig anything. You were touched by some kind of device he rigged up."

It was true. He didn't know how to convince Amy, but he knew it was true. There were no theatrics Theophilus couldn't rig. If you wanted a mist that drifted and talked, Theophilus could rig it. He could rig slow poison accumulating over years through a water system. He could rig the memory of a skeleton in a cell. Could he rig the apparition of death—something that looked like death, but which waked and walked? Impossible. Not even Theophilus could have rigged and manipulated some replica of Vera. Just impossible . . . but, if he had, it meant that Theophilus had not only lived after her . . . he was still alive.

The house of the Trackers. Now it was taking him back to the irrational beliefs of the Middle Ages. Then he seemed to hear his father's explaining voice . . . "remember, remember this. . . ."

Impossible.

"Sleep," he told Amy. "At least try to rest. I'll be here every minute. Then if you want I'll go back with you and show you what happened. You won't need to be afraid." He was talking to himself too.

She actually did sleep. He watched her narrow form beneath the blanket and told himself not to be impatient. Amy clutched the blanket to her face, her hair lay rich and thick as it spilled from beneath the blanket. A gray hair here and there showed almost incandescent in the thick hair. He was glad she didn't dye her hair. Honesty worked for her, ordinarily you didn't notice a single gray hair.

He wanted to get the job *done,* told himself he could not be impatient but must get Vera out and set the place up for demolition. If he didn't get the contract written for demolition, the whole affair would take time next spring; and hell or house or the hereafter, he intended to be in Council Bluffs in the spring.

Amy moaned now in her sleep, clutched the blanket

tighter, shuddered, then relaxed and seemed to go deeper into sleep.

So terribly innocent, Amy. Either that, or she trusted him more than he trusted himself. He began slowly to pace up and down the main kitchen, telling himself again he should not have left her for a minute. Well, he would not leave her now. Instead, he sat looking at all of the house that he could see.

These kitchens, which were the only safe places in the house, stretched in a long line. The main one was tiled with a color that just missed being purple. It was ugly but efficient—the countertops and cabinets old-fashioned, painted white and red and brown. Sinks were deep like small tubs. An enormous commercial range dominated one corner of the main kitchen, all nickel and brass and blackened steel. Flanking the main kitchen were two smaller ones, and behind them were pantries.

He'd had intimations of it before, but now he knew that he had two sides to his mind, knew that the business, decision-making side seemed frail in this house, that the other side harbored an ancient fear, and cruelty, and that it kept trying to get free in this house, was trying to get free from him right now. Well, even at his worst he would not leave Amy. Suppose she woke up and found herself alone in this place.

On the side of the kitchen opposite the pantries the house gave onto an ornamented dining hall with leaded glass windows that looked onto a first floor terrace, a cold and sunless terrace, the sky a small patch in the tunnel made by the house. Not even shade-loving, resilient plants like azalea or rhododendron had ever done well there. Even in the hottest summer that terrace was cool, sometimes cold.

Across the terrace the house rose sheer like a cliff, un-windowed and faceless. Somewhere beyond that blank façade rose up one of the towers. Stairways wound through darkness into parts of the house where he had never been. He stood now, looking at the kitchens, and he believed he could remember enough to get around the first two floors. Perhaps he could manage the cellar. The subcellar, the third and fourth floors, and the towers were mysteries, except for a couple of terraces on the third.

Beyond that blank façade was new construction, which could be anything. The only thing he could be sure of was that it would be some sort of a trap.

He turned to look at Amy, and thought he saw movement as something seemed to disappear through a doorway of the kitchen. He raced to the doorway. Nothing. From where he stood he could see through a line of doorways, a sort of hall of doors. He told himself that he was edgy and imagining things. If Vera was out there she could hardly disappear so quickly. Surely he was imagining things.

When it came, the time shift was so slight he was not sure it was a shift. For a moment the kitchen seemed warmer. His nose wrinkled. He smelled something light and flavored, like flowers or perfume. The light did not alter. There was no sound. Then, four rooms away, a hooded figure passed one of the doorways. It drifted easily and slow. He could catch her if he moved quick. He ran into the next room. Stopped. He was in the house of the Trackers. He was nearly decoyed. Wasn't he?

Decoy or real, he could not leave Amy. He told himself he was relearning fast, and felt he was doing pretty well for having been away so long.

A memory nudged at him and he let it come. He'd visited his father here one summer, when he was fifteen. He'd had a summer job on the other side of the river. He recalled the clear, early mornings as he walked the long road down to the river where the workboat waited. Once across, the crew planted seedling trees in a burned area on the Kentucky side. It was easy to remember if you tried.

What was not easy was training yourself to forget, and he had done that for years.

When he was fifteen his mother was busy going through one of her interminable divorces. She always took them seriously. She was busy and slightly hysterical. He remembered her only vaguely in those days. He could remember significant incidents about his father, Justice, but he had lived with his mother from the time he was ten until he went to college. The day-to-day experience seemed to cloud what he remembered of her.

Justice was hopeful in that summer when John was fifteen. It was almost like he still believed that, once more divorced, John's mother would return to the house. They would be a family again. And at fifteen, John, his son, had been wise enough, had seen enough, to know that his father was being foolish. If asked, John would have added that Justice was also nuts to want such a thing. Anyone married to Sarah Tracker-plus-other-names would have to love living in a carnival, especially on the carousel. She was always trying something new, and while she usually married the men, she never married the projects.

Vera was nearly civil to him that summer, and John could still remember his suspicions. When Vera was civil it meant she was planning something. She'd said she wanted him to stay. He remembered now. Right here in these kitchens, with Theophilus sitting over there at that table, and with his father sitting beside Theophilus, and with Vera standing there by the stove. Justice and Theophilus had a ledger open in front of them.

"You aint goin'," Vera said. "There's a high school in town, and a college across the river."

"I never needed no damn high school," Theophilus said. "Go ahead and get your brains stewed."

"Finish high school, go to college, any college you want." His father was abstracted, was fooling around with totals in the ledger, was responding to Vera and Theophilus in a way that told all of them that he was only partly listening. When Justice was absorbed in something he made small, snuffling, worry sounds; but as far as the ledger was concerned there was no cause for worry. It was said of Theophilus that he had tied up half of the soybean crop in Indiana in 1942. Then he did it again in '43. He had not only rigged it once, he had rigged it twice.

"Your place is here," Vera said. "They's enough here to keep anybody named Tracker busy."

"I'll learn to drive a bulldozer," he had answered her. "Then I'm going to get the world's biggest damn bulldozer and I'm going to start at one corner of the place—"

"You got a smart mouth."

"Come by honest."

"Sure you do," Vera told him. "What you don't ask, is what else you come by."

"Tinkering," he'd said. "Well, I'm not about to waste my life building a junk pile."

"A smartass with a smart mouth." Theophilus pulled a knife from his pocket and began cutting intricate designs on a table leg.

"Study history," his father said.

Vera looked like she was trying to be honest, which could not have been easy. "It aint tinkering. None of us would fool with all this here if it was only tinkering."

"We're in a race with power," Justice said. "Stay out of it."

Vera turned to Justice, and she seemed tense, on edge. "You think you're a smart one, but it's just the same old Tracker dumb."

"A'course, there's all them sorority girls," Theophilus said, changing the subject. "You could study sorority girls. I always regret I never had nothing to do with anything but common women."

"You'll come back," Vera said. "You can kick and fight agin it, but you'll come back."

" 'Cause all of them people out there are stark staring shithead nuts," Theophilus told him. "Go ahead and learn it. We all got to."

"Study history," his father muttered from the depths of the ledger.

Well, he *had* come back; because here he was, standing in the old kitchen and watching the sleeping form of a woman named Amy. A woman he'd helped scare out of her wits. If anyone had asked him if he'd come back willingly, he could not have answered. He did not *want* to be here, but he knew now that it was not a matter of his want. This house held part of him captive, as surely as if he were locked behind bars.

The tension and the pacing were tiring him. He brought a chair from one of the smaller kitchens, sat down, rubbed his eyes, looked at his watch. For a moment the watch seemed like an alien trinket strapped to his wrist. It seemed without purpose. This particular watch came from an insurance inventory, he recalled, that had been raided by the former owner, by truck drivers and claims adjusters until most of the value was drained off. The insurance company really took a bath on that one.

When he was twenty, the last time he'd come to this house when his father was alive, it was because Justice wanted to see him and maybe advise him. Of what? Concentrate. That new construction, twenty years ago his father talked of that new construction, and John now found himself remembering a phrase like "life's work," and words like "sanctuary" and "preservation." He'd definitely have to check on that before this place was destroyed. His father advised him to do something, take some kind of action, but he couldn't remember what.

He yawned. His knees ached slightly. Two days before he'd done some pretty fancy scrambling on that snowy grade. A man shouldn't let himself get even the least bit out of shape. Then his blinking eyes opened, startled. He checked his watch again. The watch—a mind of its own—held to the opinion that the time was 6:30 P.M. He shook it, looked at its lighted dial. The thing was moving, seeming to speed. Fear clouted him like a hammer. He'd been desperate over Amy, angry with Vera, and afraid for Amy. On this second visit to the house, though, he'd felt neither his own unreason or very much shock. Even the skeleton that had rattled like dice and appeared in the false bottom of the phony coffin had caused no fear like what he now felt. Fear that time was misshapen. He shook the watch again. They could have been here, at most, three hours. Surely it could be no later than early afternoon.

The halls and rooms and doorways did not look different. Inside this house it was impossible to say whether it was day or night unless you found a window. Always there was the perpetual gloom of this house, where lights sometimes flicked off as you entered a room bringing you into total darkness at midday.

He looked at Amy, still huddled into the blanket, and battled a panicky urge to run and find a window.

This was a trick, and to hell with it. That was becoming his answer for everything in this house. It was one thing to know about tricks and traps, it was quite another thing when time not only shifted but went haywire. The silent house felt like a slowly descending weight, exerting pressure, like the piling on of stones, like a force that entered his chest and legs and arms to dull and slow them. He remembered dreams about trying to run underwater. It felt like that.

All right, try to reason it out. Perhaps he had slept. No doubt he had slept, but surely not for four or five hours. He felt displaced, as though he had been carried to the edge of an abyss, as though he were standing at the edge of the Grand Canyon with the wind at his back gusting, popping, echoing. He felt the way Rip Van Winkle must have felt as thunder bowled between the mountains on his return from sleep. But that was not the Hudson River out there, dark and roiling beneath the cliff. That was the Ohio, the wall against weather; the liquid symbol of movement that, since he was a child, always let him know that he could leave. That river, symbol of trade to some, of power to others, always meant to John Tracker that there were options if things got too terrible.

He raised his head and listened. This deep in the house the only weather sounds you ever heard came from wind. In this great well of a house, built over a well, even the sound of thunder did not penetrate. In that huge dining hall that looked onto a terrace, that looked up as if from a well at the towering sides of the house, sound did not penetrate. Rains came to the terrace, and ice, but the wind rode high up there and was like a cap on a well.

Tracker listened and felt, more than heard, the far off pressure of wind.

A trick. His mind now automatically responded that way. The storm was not due for a day, or perhaps two. They had plenty of time. He looked at Amy. If he woke her up while he was afraid he would telegraph his fear to her, and that would slow them even more.

At least he had to discover if darkness had come, if the distant winds were real. But he couldn't leave her. He began to back slowly through the kitchens, Amy in sight, and headed for a doorway that would allow him to look into the dining hall. He was ready at the first sign of any trouble to rush back to her. He was taking a chance and knew it. These kitchens were safe, but nothing in the house of the Trackers was ever one hundred percent safe. That would have ruined its reputation, denied Tracker history.

Step at a time, half-step at a time he eased backward until he stood beside the doorway. Amy was still asleep. He turned from her and looked into the dining hall, waiting for his eyes to adjust. The great floor area was as black

104

as ocean depths, there was no light on the terrace beyond those windows.

Then like a burst of phosphorescence on the crest of a wave, a glimmer of blue light began to radiate and build from a dark corner of the terrace. He stood watching it increase, and, in despair, could now see through those lead-enclosed windows just how heavily it was snowing.

CHAPTER 10

Christian Traker was John Tracker's great great grandfather on his father's father's father's side, and he lived in Darmstadt, Germany.

Christian was a fat man who made his living as a butcher. His health, of which he was known to brag, he credited to the custom of drinking blood then current in his trade, and which, of course, violated Genesis' rule. Christian, after hammering the beast, would string it to drain, open the artery at the throat and catch the steaming blood in a cup. On cold mornings, or on mornings after nights when he had drunk too much schnapps, he was known to brag that he could drink an ox dry. Like most men of his time he had a mustache and beard, which often sported dried and caked blood.

Christian Traker died of a heart attack at age forty-five.

John and Amy sat together in the kitchen while she blinked herself wider and wider awake. Actually she seemed in rather good spirits, considering the situation. It was almost as though she remembered the maze as something that had happened years before.

Tracker rubbed at his elbow. It was sore, he must have bumped it as he scrambled through the maze. He doubted that they could leave during that storming night. He also

106

doubted if he would keep much of his strength if he didn't eat something soon. It felt strange to be hungry when you'd never had any practice. It felt doubly so when you were accustomed to eating in the best restaurants. Of course the kitchens were well-stocked with food, and in back of this kitchen those pantries were well-filled. The food might even be good, but it might also be salted with poison.

"Is there any coffee?" She was smiling, and looked wonderful to him, considering the dishevelment of her hair and clothing. In fact, that made her look good in a special, personal way that he liked.

"We don't dare drink it, we don't know what's in it."

"That's silly. If Vera was going to drink it—"

"We don't know what Vera was going to do."

"She *was* pretty mean, but so were you. You were insulting."

"I was only describing her—"

"You cursed, I hate it when a man curses." Her eyes told him she meant what she said, but her voice was soft. She was pleased by the memory that came to her. "I brought lunch," she said. "Two sandwiches and two apples. In the truck."

"Let's go."

Beyond the kitchens the house seemed colder than before, and his flashlight seemed a poor tool in the dark rooms that lay like crypts. The boom of wind came through clearly as they moved toward the outside of the house. Although they came from deep in the house, it was familiar territory and it did not take Tracker long to lead them to the front hall, where the coffin stood beneath the portrait of Justice. He opened the door against a crush of wind. The trap was still on safety. The wind funneled at them. The mound of freeway lay like a white mountain in the darkness. Snow blew along the grade, and from the river far below the wind rose over the bluffs and moaned through the channel between the freeway and the house.

Tracker recoiled from it, then gathered himself to make a dash to the truck. There was no chance in the world, even with that truck, of driving through this. The truck looked isolated, but also real and sensible and reassuring. Then he took a second look. He'd deliberately parked the truck on a slight grade, and was sure he had set the brake, sure the truck was left in gear. The equipment could not possibly have a tare weight of under three tons, yet the truck was slewed sideways on the grade, the front end slightly lowered, like it sat in a pothole. The wind had seemingly twisted it as easily as a child might turn a toy car.

"Stay on the porch, I'll be right back."

"I'm coming with you."

So he took her hand and they plunged into the wind. Blown snow stung their cheeks, their eyes watered. When they reached the truck they found the doors were frozen shut. Tracker muttered under his breath. You never parked a rig in winter without making sure you could get back inside; he shouldn't have closed the doors tight. Some moisture always collected in the cab of a landscape truck; condensation had him beaten. He hoped he at least hadn't set the brake. If an emergency brake froze, you were really in a fix; unless you liked to drive in reverse.

And then he remembered. He'd jumped from this truck to save Amy. Maybe it wasn't in gear, maybe he didn't have time to set the brake. The keys were still in the ignition. He wiped snow from the side window, then from the windshield, and shined his flashlight into the cab. The few tools he'd had with him were in the cab. He pounded on the door, then backed up and kicked it as hard as he could. It wasn't much of a kick because it wasn't solid, his snowy shoe skidding across the surface of the door. His knee felt like it was wrenched. He just was not going to jar that door loose with a kick.

There was still a crowbar back in the house, laying somewhere in that room where he saw the projection of Theophilus. When he'd run from the apparition he'd been in no mood for carrying crowbars. He could use it now to wedge the door open or break the window. His mind automatically flipped figures and told him it would be cheaper to break a window. He told himself that he really was crazy. Here they were, half-starved, in the middle of a storm, and he was thinking about *economics.* "Let's get the hell out of this," he yelled, but the wind swallowed his voice. He motioned to her, took her arm and they trudged through the blowing snow back to the house.

After the wind, the house seemed a warm shelter. Amy stood shivering, but not the way she would if she were tensing against weather. Tracker felt something between disgruntlement and anger. If he'd not had to jump from that cab in the first place he would have remembered the door. If, on the other hand, he'd been half as smart as he thought he was, he would have left the door on half-latch.

He looked at the portrait of Justice, at the empty hall, at the unempty coffin. His belly rumbled. His knees and elbows twinged. Wind was banging the house like a fried-out drummer kicking over a set of drums. His grandmother was walking and planning devilment. Behind him snow was chin-high to a tall giraffe. Tracker felt a choice between total despair and laughter, so he chose the laughter. It did not fill the belly, it did not tell him the right time, but at least it was better than letting this crazy, rum-dum carnival show overtake him and make him so afraid he couldn't act.

Amy looked at him nervously, and then some of their situation dawned on her and she began laughing with him. Two children standing in front of a Frankenstein movie and giggling because they knew they were about to be scared witless.

"We can do this just as easy where it's warm," Amy said.

She did not know about the crowbar. He decided to take the long way around to the kitchens and pick it up. Food or not, he wanted to dig in the snow and check out that truck which now sat at an awfully peculiar angle. He might just as well get the food she'd brought when he checked the truck.

"This way." He explained what they were doing as they walked. "You can watch the old man standing in sulphur if you want, but it isn't really worth it." He tried to make his voice light, but the tones were wrong.

"You're afraid."

"It's a little shocking, that's all. I don't mean to frighten you."

She did not look reassured.

He thought that by now she might understand some of the dark in his past. He couldn't tell her that for nearly twenty years he'd tried not to dream. He couldn't tell her that at one time a psychiatrist was the only thread that anchored him to an otherwise crazy world. All he could do was walk silently beside her, feeling clumsy. This woman trusted him, had lain naked beside him, had whispered to him and touched him and smiled at him. As the world operated, this woman was his lover, and the problem was that he did not know how to love. He only knew how to try. That would make anyone lonesome.

"It's just this," he said in a low voice. "This place was once very real to me. It isn't real anymore, but it seems a part of me doesn't understand that."

"Me too," she said. "I mean, I think I know what you mean."

"How could you?"

"You hardly ever drink," she said. "In three years I doubt if I've seen you take a dozen drinks."

"The only way to do business is over nothing stronger than a cup of coffee—"

"That's not what I mean." Her voice was intimate in a

110

new way. Confessional. It was a voice that cared little for nice clothes or bright talk or to be seen in stylish places. "My father is a good man," she said. "A *good* man."

"I understand," he said, and he did. Her voice was filled with years of sadness. Sometimes she would cover a confused situation with a casual, or would-be sophisticated voice. There was nothing of that in this confessional voice.

"They say a part of us never grows up," he said. "We stay frightened little kids." He'd never talked this way to anyone.

"I think that's true," she said. "No, I know it's true."

When they got to the room he played the flashlight beam across the floor. The crowbar was lying in the center of the room. The light played on a tapestry of camels and palm trees, across dusty furniture.

"Stand here," he told Amy. "Unless you want to see."

"I don't." She was hugging herself because of the cold.

"I'll be just a moment." He stepped through the doorway, knowing that he was about to see the apparition. Nothing happened, which gave him a chill that didn't come from the cold room. Apparently he'd missed the tripping device. He stepped into the hall, reentered the room.

Still nothing. An idea came back. It wasn't exactly shocking, but it began to work on him. He knew Theophilus, he knew that old man like saints know their Bibles, and he was beginning to feel that he'd set himself up by not listening carefully to Vera. He tapped the crowbar all around the entry, kicked the floor inside the room. Nothing happened.

"It must have been a one-time show," he said to Amy. "Some of the traps are good for only one shot." He remembered the burnt flashbulbs and sheared-off sword of a former trap. He also did not know if he believed a word of what he said. He wanted time to digest this new idea.

"Let's get back where it's warm," he said, and took her arm and walked toward the kitchens. He tried to add up what he knew as he walked beside Amy. The apparition was not an apparition at all. It was a crazy old man who could use lights and mirrors and smoke to produce illusion. It was a man who must be in his eighties, at least; but who could still rig a set-up if he was given a little advance notice. John figured he'd maybe even seen Theophilus himself, and not a projection. Theophilus was still alive.

If Vera was still here, why not believe that Theophilus might also be here. He thought about it with a different slant and his mind sparked with a sudden, painful hope. If those two were still walking this tomb of a house, then there was no reason to believe his father was dead.

The empty house suddenly seemed peopled. It felt like years had not passed. Vera and Theophilus and Justice were all here somewhere. Tracker felt nearly optimistic.

When he was twenty he'd rejected his father, had rejected everything he knew about this place. Now at forty he could understand how he could grow in experience, knowledge, and wish it had not happened.

As soon as he found Vera he would get the final truth of it. "I've got something worked out," he told Amy. "When we get to the kitchens I'll tell you." They were passing through a corridor where the dim, night-sleeping lights were fairly close together. Shadows heightened the drama of Amy's features; her high forehead and cheeks were even more distinct.

She stopped. "I'm feeling sort of tired. Even though I got some sleep." She sounded apologetic.

"We'll be in the kitchens soon."

"That isn't why I stopped." She smiled. It was a smile that came slow and built slow and ended slow. Her eyes were fatigued but they also seemed lighted with an interior joy. Her soft hair framed her face and covered her shoulders. "Now this is really dumb," she said. "I don't

112

mean that what I'm going to say is dumb, but it's a dumb time and place to say it."

"What? Is something wrong?"

"I haven't said it before . . . I mean, I've said it a couple of times when we were in bed but it somehow means something different with your clothes on."

He understood, dared to understand.

"I love you," she said. "You are a good man and I love you. I don't know why I'm saying it here and now—" She broke off, but it was not from confusion. It was shyness, and he even understood that too.

He fumbled the flashlight, dropped the crowbar, and then held her close. He swore to himself that he would love her, he would *learn* how. He would learn about trust, and she would be glad, not sorry. "I want to say the same," he told her. "It's just that I want to say it as well as you have and have it mean as much."

"It does."

"But I want to say it well—"

"Are you still afraid?"

"No," he answered truthfully. He was not afraid. How could he be? She had just said the truest thing she felt, and he understood, even if she did not, that the house of the Trackers was not omnipotent. It was dangerous, but it was vulnerable. It became vulnerable and even stupid in the face of truth.

"Let me take you to the kitchens and we'll get warm."

"I wish we could leave."

"In the morning," he told her. "Even if it's still storming, we'll do our best to make it then."

"But I won't ever leave you. Not after this." Her voice was so soft that he could scarcely hear it even in the silence of the house.

"I'll *care* for you." He said it almost fiercely. "If anything tries to touch you, it has to come through me first."

"It will," said Vera Tracker.

Amy screamed. Tracker spun around. There was no one in sight. The long, dimly illuminated hall was as empty as an abandoned tunnel.

"That tears it," Tracker said. "I'm coming to get you and hog-tie you." He started to move forward, looked at Amy. Her face was a mask of horror. "I'll get you," he said to the empty hall. He led Amy back toward the kitchens, and watched her try to gain control as they walked.

It was clear that Amy was still not used to the way things were done in the house of the Trackers.

Was he?

CHAPTER

11

The endless halls where Vera walked had long since grown beyond the original designs of Johan Traker. Even Johan's fear of the Devil could not account for that endless building of traps. Fear cannot be sustained with so much force for so long. If Johan feared the Devil, it was likely that either Vera or Theophilus or both of them welcomed the Devil in any form.

Still, the house was originally Johan's idea. It was fear for his soul that caused him to begin to build. History does not record exactly how Johan's fear began. It does record that he began building the house about a year after his mother's death.

Hildegard Schuder was Johan's mother. She was John Tracker's great great grandmother on his father's father's side. She left Berne at age seventeen for Darmstadt in unusual haste, the pressing reason being that Hildegard was ugly. She married Christian Traker, because there was no one else to marry. The casual vacation that Christian had taken returned him to Germany with a wife he never tried to understand.

Hildegard was a small woman of the kind who becomes tougher with hammering. She was not educated beyond religion, and that was an education of practice and not theory. She raised her family in the same manner. She bore seven children. Johan Traker was the first. Hildegard lived to bury three of those children and see Johan leave for America. She died at age thirty-nine when her husband

115

was two years dead. The cause of her death was internal hemor-rhage brought on by an abortion.

In Tracker family legend, mothers were not allowed to fail. It may be that those endless halls where Vera walked had their begin-nings in that one incident that, while seeming only pathetic, nonetheless changed Johan's youthful confidence to fear.

John figured Vera was not going to leave them alone, and realized he did not know how to make Amy understand that Vera would enjoy being drawn and quartered if it made her the center of attention.

When they arrived in the kitchens, John flipped a switch. A section of the floor rolled back, a table rose from the floor and the floor closed back around the table's pedestal. He told Amy to sit on the bench behind the table. She had a wall at her back, which she huddled against.

"She'll come looking for us pretty soon," he said. "Meanwhile, we've got to eat. There's bound to be a way to figure this out." He opened cabinets, pulled out canned vegetables and tinned meat.

Somewhere in his memory were instructions about this. He tumbled a can over and over in his hands. To solve anything in the house of the Trackers you had to think like a Tracker.

He looked through a doorway, expecting to see Vera drifting somewhere on the edge of vision. He could feel her out there, circling the action. Of course she had a motive to hide from them—to make them afraid, to run them off. Maybe she would not show.

Trackers inevitably created tricks, traps to snare the unwary. Theophilus had learned his fear from Johan, and then had built his own purposes for setting traps. What-ever a packing company could seal, Theophilus could open and reseal. Each can lid carried a code stamped by

116

the packer. If you handled enough distressed merchandise, the way John did, you knew something about those codes.

He looked at a series of cans, then at another series. After he'd examined two dozen cans he thought of what the bad ones might contain; poison that would turn to gas when air hit it, or maybe rolls of twenty dollar bills. More likely, the latter. This kitchen was a sort of practical, functional center for the house. When the gray dog first got into the chickens Theophilus had kicked open that concealed locker over there in the wall. Guns were like money. Both could be kept for an emergency. The kitchen seemed almost homelike. He remembered . . . Theophilus had invented his own code. If Theophilus opened a can, replaced the contents and then resealed the can, the code on the can would contain the letter A, and the bar of the A would be broken. Any can with a broken barred A was dangerous. It was easy, after all. He found untampered cans, useable coffee, corned beef and vegetables.

"I'll do this," he told Amy. "You've had enough scares to wear anyone out."

"It's nice to be warm." She no longer huddled against the wall.

"Coffee in a minute."

He checked his watch, which now claimed that the time was 8:30 P.M.

"We're in for a long night. When Vera shows up, don't be afraid."

"I will be," Amy said. "But I want you to know she didn't fool me into going into that maze. I just went through the doorway to be away from her."

"And you won't make that mistake again." He grinned. "She's crude, like that show of hers just now in the hallway."

"It's more than that," Amy said. "Her eyes looked funny."

"Mean?"

"Worse than that."

The coffee began to perk, the food was warming on the stove. He marveled at how normal the kitchen seemed.

"You said you'd figured something out." Amy's voice was brighter. She seemed to be trying to push away thoughts about Vera. The comparative security of the kitchens and the promise of food worked a sort of civilizing magic on her. With no immediate threat, some of Amy's early interest in the house was returning.

As they ate he explained why he believed Theophilus was still alive. He didn't express any similar hopes about his father. Almost superstitiously he did not talk about Justice.

"Why does Vera act that way? And why do you act badly when you're around her?"

They were sitting side by side at the table. Tracker was taking a good deal of pleasure in the food and lack of tension. "I live in the world and Vera doesn't. We're automatically adversaries. Long ago this place separated from the rest of the world. Theophilus and Vera despised that world out there, but they sure knew how to use it."

"Money?"

"Sure, money. Also tools and technology and materials. Millions have gone into this place."

"I hadn't thought about that."

"I don't know everything that's here. I do know there's a transportation system, elevators and conveyors. The old man could move heavy equipment around almost on a whim."

"It really did cost a lot, didn't it?"

"And they made a lot. Johan was a hustler. Theophilus exploited a depression, two major wars and two or three minor ones. My father was honest, and as spare in his dealings as a Yankee peddler."

"You trained in a pretty tough school." She actually grinned. Clearly she was feeling better.

"It answers your question about Vera. They all, except Justice, looked at people and material like so much fodder."

"You've got a legal problem." She pursed her lips, looked around the huge kitchen, then toward the smaller kitchen that she could see. She was estimating the place with a new set of facts.

"If Theophilus is alive the legal problem is nearly the same, only doubled-up."

"It makes me almost mad," she said. "At least it makes me feel bad."

"Why?"

"If they withdrew, and their lives stayed here, and then the outside world came along and built a road, I can see how they'd be pretty mean."

Except, Tracker thought, the house and the forces that built it should never have existed in the first place.

"I suppose you could say they were in a war and they lost."

"A war with what? The Devil?"

"I used to think it was that simple. I don't anymore."

"As long as we're here," she said, "we should take a look around."

"I think it's more of the same. Traps and gimmicks."

"I wonder. I can't believe that something this big and ambitious is haphazard," she said.

"An overall plan?"

"Something like that."

On his return, the first time when he was frightened by the specter of Theophilus, John remembered thinking the same thought. He remembered thinking that the place was sane and orderly, if one granted that the premise on which it was built was insane.

"Let's explore it."

"All right," he said. "We have to figure how to spend the night. One of us will sleep while the other watches—"

"It's really that bad, isn't it?" She was excited again.

"Vera's that bad," he said, "and if Theophilus is alive he can't be more than ninety."

She looked to see if he was joking, and saw that he was not.

"Age doesn't mean much if you can move, and if you have the right tools."

"Especially a machine that changes the way things look," she said.

She had to be talking about time shifts. So she had experienced them, after all.

"It isn't a machine," he told her. "In this house time goes haywire. It just always has."

"Of course," she said. "That's what it is."

She seemed pleased, even relieved.

"What happens? How does it feel?" He was pretending to be casual.

"Like being on stage," she said. "Like being in the second act of a play that's going well. The props are right. The players are with you. Then you deliver a line, look around and find that you are in a different act in a different play with different players."

"You seem to be taking this awfully easy."

"Happens all the time," she said. "In this place you just notice it more."

He did not understand.

"You weren't raised a Catholic," she said. "You've never even been an actor. It's like going to church," she said. "People say it's like stepping into another world. On stage you do step into another world . . . except it really isn't. It's like a frame in time that's separate from the rest of time. That's all. Easy." She actually smiled.

"Hell isn't hot," he told her. "Hell is cold, like that storm out there. Hell imitates fire, imitates heat, but fire is the enemy of evil—" He stopped, surprised at his inappropriate answer.

"She's coming," Amy said. "Is that what's the matter? Is Vera out there?"

"This is the Middle Ages around here." He had fumbled, and felt he was recovering badly.

"And Vera is coming?"

"I suppose she is," he said dully. "And here we go again." The trick was to draw your strength together, prepare yourself, and turn your face blandly toward the unspeakable.

"You're looking better," he now said to Vera, in flat bored tones.

"You aren't."

She was walking awfully slow, but there was no hesitation or uncertainty. A few hours ago she'd looked like something recently excavated. Now her face showed a faint flush of color. Her hands did not crawl or tremble.

"You look tard," she said. "You look all crackeldy and 'bout to blow up."

His elbow, which had ceased aching, twinged. His knee felt fine, but behind his knee was a dull torment, as though his leg had been held too rigidly in a cast or brace.

The sag seemed to be leaving Vera's face. Wattles of loosely hanging flesh seemed tighter. Her face was old, old. She wore a red scarf over her baldness. Her eyes were brilliant and diverted his attention from her face. Her eyes seemed to demand that he concentrate on them.

And time was shifting. Was—is—will be; he didn't know. Vera's eyes were bright spots floating in her wrecked face. Mesmerizing spots that drew you painfully from inside yourself.

Amy clutched his arm so tightly that he had a momentary impression that she was drowning, or falling, or felt her sanity was being robbed.

121

It was what he needed. *Protect Amy.* He stared at Vera's eyes, challenging them. As he stared, her eyes became bland. She faltered, appeared ready to fall. Her mouth moved silently. She was calling him something.

"Same to you," he said.

Amy had helped him. Now it seemed that he was helping Vera. Before, on his return, Vera gained strength from making him hate her. Now it happened again. She stood more easily.

Amy pressed her leg against his, and his reaction shocked him and made him feel silly. He knew she was taking comfort from the contact, but it gave him feelings he believed were hardly appropriate in this situation. It was warm and personal. Sexual.

Vera was estimating Amy again, then estimated him.

"I don't see why you bother," she said to Amy.

It was crazy. They were feeding strength back and forth to each other, and Amy was sitting there missing what was happening.

"Leave her alone," Tracker said. He turned to Amy. "She hits where you're least able to stand it."

"You aint too far over the hill," Vera said. "With those legs you could get a real man. Lead with them legs and nobody's gonna notice that chest."

"Once more," John told her, "and you get tossed in the snow."

"Not you, ner any other man."

"Stop it," Amy said. "Just stop it, both of you."

"You're right," Tracker told her. "I don't know how she does it, but she always pulls me down to her level—"

"I said stop it."

"He's just scairt." Vera's voice was not spiteful, the musical voice was back. With Amy in control, Vera was looking feeble again.

"You want something," he said. "I'll be civil, but spare me any games."

"I better sit for a spell." She was drooping, almost pitiable.

"Get a chair, John. We don't have to behave like animals."

He kept his eye on Vera while he went for a chair. Amy might think the old bat was helpless, and maybe she was, though he did not believe it. He returned with the chair, and Vera sat down suddenly, like all her strength was gone.

"Are you all right?" Amy started to get to her feet but John motioned her away.

"A sight better off than him."

"See," Tracker said, "see, she doesn't let up." He turned to Vera. "The old man's still pooting around here someplace. Where?"

"Which old man?"

"You know. Don't kid me. He's here and he's up to devilment."

"You come back. What I want to know, why did you come back? I aint a goin', but why did you come back?"

It would be better to lie, to tell her that he came to rob her, or find out about his father, or any other lie that was convenient. He didn't know how she would take the truth. She was cruel, she was like everything painful he knew, but he did not want to be responsible for killing her.

"I'm sorry," Amy put in for him. "Truly, truly sorry. Because of the new road the house is condemned." She started to say more, saw what was happening, stopped.

Vera fell to the floor, rolled over, moaned and passed out.

"Wet towels," John said, and knelt beside Vera. Amy ran for the sinks, fumbled in cabinet drawers, found a towel and ran water on it, breathing in sobs.

"You aren't responsible," Tracker said over his shoulder. "She would have known sooner or later. You said it nicely. I probably wouldn't have."

"I didn't know, I didn't know—"

"There's no possible way to know anything about this woman. There never has been." He had Vera's head raised. Her mouth was twitching and gasping. Her teeth were small, they looked like the teeth of a young woman, or even of a child. The rest of her might be stained and wrinkled, but her teeth were horrifying because they were perfect. Like her nails, he thought, things that could cut—

His grandmother was suffering a seizure. She kicked her legs and flailed her arms. As he knelt beside her and almost lost his balance her eyes opened, staring, staring. Her feet began to drum on the floor. Her dress moved above gnarled and bony knees, and Tracker, absurdly, struggled to pull her dress to cover her legs. Amy stood there, helpless with her warm towels. And then Vera hit him a sharp blow that missed the groin but caught him in the lower stomach. And then, as suddenly as it had started, the seizure left. His grandmother's eyes focused. "You was always a hellion."

She was not even gasping, it had to be an act. She looked stronger, when she should have been depleted.

"Get her to bed." Amy seemed to overlook everything, the blow, the hard words.

"On your feet," he said. He gave her his hand, reached behind her to help, and was surprised when she cooperated.

"We'll take care of you," Amy said.

"Fits happen," Vera told her. "Then they go."

"Help her, John."

"Stay close to us," he told Amy. He took his grandmother's arm, which seemed as thin as wire. He led her from the kitchen. She tried to resist. He pressured her arm with firm fingers and kept her walking, then suddenly found himself walking scared.

"I'll get you," she whispered. "Ass 'n appetite."

"You'll not. I had nothing to do with this."

She was walking good. Now she tried a different tactic, looked at him almost as though he were a friend. There was a smile on her face, he could swear it. The smile of a whorish girl, but a girl nonetheless. Then her face tensed, her eyes opened wider. In the center of them, deep from something or somewhere else in time, luminous red forms moved. Her eyes were not red, but there was red in her eyes. Her tense face tightened more. It bore hatred mixed with something John Tracker had named at various times but had never really seen on a human face. He thought he knew the look of greed, lust, envy; but he realized without question that he was now looking at the force that embodied them all. He was looking at absolute evil.

Tracker faltered, and as he did his grandmother's face changed. Now it was old and bland, although her movements were still strong, and he decided that his grandmother was the greatest actress he had ever seen.

"What's got hold of you," he asked. "You change from one thing to another every minute."

Later he would remember that she tried to speak, her jaw tried to move. Once more she tensed. "I give you one answer," she said. "I aint changed, and neither have you. You're just growin' toward what you already was."

They arrived outside a closed door. "This here's my room."

"I know, it always was."

"Go away."

"We'll get you comfortable." Amy was trailing behind, missing some of the conversation, but now she sounded like a nurse.

Tracker gave Vera credit. When she wanted something, she had the moves it took to get it.

"I've lived here all my life," she told Amy in a pathetic but curiously dignified way. "You want to tear down my house. At least let me have my room."

"I'm sorry." Amy was also near tears. "We really had nothing to do with this."

"You are a good child," Vera said. "You are a good girl. Please go away."

"I'll come for you after the storm," Tracker told her.

She looked at him, her ancient face cross-hatched with wrinkles, with hate that she was hiding from Amy; and with sagging flesh around a face that still looked so much like a death's head. She whispered so softly he could barely hear, and he was sure Amy could not hear.

"Which storm," she said. "The real storm only just started."

CHAPTER

12

If John Tracker was uncertain about his grandmother Vera's power, and its source in witchcraft, some of his confusion came from his own past. Although he had not known his mother, Sarah, from early childhood until age ten, he had spent his teenage years living with her and so came to know a woman who was sometimes an example of confusion. Sarah had been a woman with many and various directions.

She was the daughter of Samuel Lily, a lay preacher who worked in the shipyards. Like his daughter after him, Samuel was a questioner. Eventually he rejected religion because of the emptiness of dogma, and in his continuing search for understanding he read all manner of radical tracts. His friends tolerated Samuel's radical speculations because they liked him. Samuel was a gentle and sometimes befuddled man. He was killed during World War II when oxygen tanks blew up in a welding shed. Considering his befuddlement, and his innocence and openness to all ideas, it is likely that there was no really viable spot for him on the face of the earth.

The word "sanctuary" echoed in John Tracker's mind as he and Amy returned to the kitchens. Vera frightened him. The clear-headed, business side of his mind, ironically, did not know what to think or do, though it was juggling possibilities.

A psychiatrist, he speculated, might say that he had repressed fears for so long that his mind was now giving sensory form to those fears. A believer in genetic memory might accuse him of questioning what was inevitably there, and so missing the obvious answers. One thing was certain; no matter how he tried to apply worldly logic, Vera was stronger than Vera ought to have been.

In any case, the side of his mind which he'd never trusted was like a dog with its hackles raised. Bad as it was, it had sense enough to tell him to leave this house, even if he and Amy might be lost in the storm. Fight or run, but at least move.

He felt an urge to return to Vera's room and kill her. The thought repelled him. He might be a lot of things, but he was not a murderer.

He was afraid, though, of a man in at least his eighties or early nineties. In this house, if Vera lived, Theophilus was king. Theophilus had choreographed this house, orchestrated it. He could play this house with all the dexterity of a concert pianist. Men's minds deteriorated as they grew old, which meant that Theophilus might be even more dangerous now than before.

Sanctuary.

It was his father's word. His father used it when referring to the new construction, still in the planning stage when John Tracker was twenty. John saw no better alternative now than to reach that new construction. With a safe wall at his back he could figure out why Vera was so changeable and so strong. It was almost as though she were two people, as though she tried to talk to him but someone else got in her way and did all the talking instead. Sometimes, he realized, she seemed almost mechanical. Tracker did not know what he thought, or believed. He only knew that he and Amy must get to a safe place.

They reached the kitchens, where she went to the stove

to heat the remaining coffee. She didn't seem exactly frightened, but her face was drawn.

"What did you see? What do you think?" He watched her closely. She was moving well but with fatigue.

"I think Vera is crazy," she said. "Living here all alone, or with Theophilus, she'd have to be."

"Anything else?"

"I'm afraid of her, but mostly I'm afraid for her." Hovering above the warming coffee, Amy brushed at her long hair with one hand, reached back and rubbed her neck.

"Afraid for her?"

"John, when I was a little girl, back in the days of angels and demons—" She broke off and turned to face him. "I made a mistake someplace." A hint of the confessional voice returned. "Sometime or other, I learned to laugh at things I couldn't explain."

"That might not be such a mistake," he said.

"Not according to catechism. You trust your good angels."

"I don't believe in angels." He did not like the way the conversation was going, it seemed too close to Justice's forgotten words.

"I believe in angels. Anyway, I do now."

"These kitchens are central," he told her. "I've changed my mind about staying in them tonight."

"All right." Her fatigue was clear in her quiet voice. It bothered him that she seemed so tired. She had slept, after all, and he wondered how long he had slept.

"It's warm here," she said. "It's nice to be warm."

"I think it will be nicer where we're going."

After two hours he was not so sure his decision was a good one. Defenses stood in front of the new construction, as if Theophilus had thrown every resource of his mechanical genius into making Justice's vault inaccessible. Still, if you were careful it was possible to make slow progress in the house. He pushed heavy pieces of furniture ahead of him, which took care of the cruder mechanical traps. What bothered him were chemical activators or traps hooked to a timer. A man could trip one of those, proceed with his business and be killed five minutes later. To defend against them he waited for ten minutes after each major entry. Only then would he explore the room.

The traps were a large, curving spectrum of mixed violence. Rooms halved as sections of wall twisted; concealed lamps bloomed to burn eyes; compressed air exploded to fill rooms with salt and sand and roofing nails—grapeshot, a scarifying material not much different than what was once fired from muzzle-loading cannons.

He tripped a pressure switch and jumped back as the door shut and snap-locked. There followed sounds like the whoosh of a train blowing, then silence. In ten minutes the door slid open. He and Amy were hit with a cold blast, a rushing and sucking of air. The cold dispersed. The room had been pumped full of carbon dioxide.

When the room was safe, John reentered, checked routinely. The door jamb of ornate framing stood slightly away from the wall. He ran his fingers behind it, found a switch, pressed and got out of the room.

A wall panel raised to reveal a plain wooden door with a passage knob. No lock. It seemed like an invitation to easy destruction, but by now Tracker was picking up a pattern in Theophilus' design. This door violated the pattern, it was too simple.

He crossed the room, shoved the door open with his crowbar. Nothing happened. Then, through the open doorway, lights flared to reveal a set of concrete steps leading downward. Fifteen feet away, and about two feet above eye level, rose a concrete wall. He watched, waited and understood that he was seeing a building that was partially underground, like a bomb shelter or an Egyptian tomb.

Or like a treasury, he thought. This was the kind of

place that might be built to contain a fortune. Perhaps he had not found Justice's sanctuary at all.

He was worried about Amy. She was so quiet, just following. Her fatigue was obviously great. He didn't know which of many fears might be assaulting her, but he knew that guilt was attacking him. He should never, regardless of her pressure and his needs, have allowed himself to be talked into bringing her along.

"How do you feel?" He touched her shoulder.

"Could be worse." Her voice was flat. It was unlike her. She didn't say trite things like that to dismiss serious situations. Almost, it seemed, she was acting, and he was being allowed to see only a projection of what she wanted him to see.

"It's almost over, I think I've found what I'm looking for."

"Let's go, then. Right away, right now."

"Follow me, but stay at least ten feet back."

It turned out that he was entering a building within a building, the outer shell distant enough from the inner shell to cause an insulating crawl space. Tracker descended the stairs and pressed hard against a door that moved slowly inward. The door, made of steel, asbestos and concrete, was a beautiful piece of engineering. One man could move it, and yet, Tracker thought, the thing could not possibly weigh less than a ton. A fire door. No locks.

Beyond that door stood a second door, also huge, but with a combination lock. At first glance it looked like the door to a bank vault. Tracker faltered, he hadn't thought of this. Even high explosives placed in the space between those two doors might not move that massive piece of steel.

Then he looked closer, and remembered one of the first traps he'd encountered on his return to the house—a silver sword had been sliced, clean, as though with a cutting torch. Now this door, seemingly impregnable, stood slightly open. The bolts were cut clean, as though they had been lasered.

If this was what his father, Justice, had believed was a safe place, then Justice had been wrong. Very wrong.

Amy stood just outside the entry to the first door. He turned back to her. "I'll check, and be right back to get you." He pushed on the vault door and was unsurprised to find it as thick and heavy as the first one. As the door opened, lights came on. He stepped into a comfortable room, the reinforced concrete walls of which were covered with paneling. Soft rugs. Ceiling-high bookcases on one wall were stacked with what appeared to be ledgers as well as the worn browns and reds of aging books. A work area contained an immense desk, files, papers, scissors, gluepot, work table and drafting table. At the other end of the room was a living area.

It contained no remains. Large bed, dresser, a night table. A radio and an old-fashioned phonograph. There was no lavatory and no toilet Pipes would violate the fireproof integrity of the place, and he estimated that the room would rate out to any number of hours and degrees that a fire insurance company could imagine.

He stomped on the floor. There was no echo and the thick carpet did not give, but the stomp caused a flash of pain in his knee, which told him that the floors, like the walls and door, were asbestos lined with thick concrete.

There was a sense of strength that rose as he looked at his father's domain. It was not, however, the strength of the known, and as Tracker looked about him he felt acutely his own ignorance. Rather, it was the strength of the discoverable. In this room, with its occupant long gone and probably (possibly?) dead, John Tracker felt that he was now coming to terms with the house. He only had to discover what those terms were.

There were sounds behind him—Amy pushing the massive fire door of the outer building. He turned, and she stumbled through the doorway of the vault. Her face was drawn, blanched as she emerged from shadow. She was moaning. Her eyes closed, then opened in a frozen stare. She sighed, like a last breath. She pitched forward, and he barely caught her. Her body relaxed. She was dead weight.

Grief and fear and guilt swarmed at him as he carried her to the bed and eased her onto it. He turned to meet the attack, saw nothing, and headed toward the door.

He passed through the first doorway with an anger that seemed capable of breaking concrete. His mind was direct and clean, a killing mind. It was a mind that had been under pressure for so long that there was no patience left. Theophilus *had* to be out there, and he hoped that Theophilus was capable, even armed. The pleasure of killing him would be that much greater.

He leaned on the fire door, felt it swing slowly, and impatiently leaned into the swing. He would come off that door with hands tearing into anything that moved.

He got clearance and slid through, hands flexing; and he halted, midstride, as though pole-axed. Someone, something, screamed. He had no experience with such sounds. The rising, prolonged cries rested like a base under the entire structure of the house, rose from the subcellar to wash through empty passageways and the corridors; hung in the updrafts of wind-scoured chimneys; bounced from ice-rimmed windows. As though from a subterranean monster squalling through the depths of the soul of man. Something, someone out there was dying with a scream that was ancient, that seemed to bespeak every agony ever wrought by history. It swelled, burst, and died choking.

John fumbled, tried to move. The wake of silence left by the choking began to intensify. All else seemed remote. He returned, staggering, pushing the heavy weight of the door, to go to Amy and sit beside her. He knelt to rub her hands, her face, her arms. He cradled her head, moved it back and forth—direct, simple movements to help restore circulation to a person in shock.

The silence enclosed them like a vacuum.

Amy's breathing was better, but for a long while his was not. They seemed to come out of the shock together. As his receded, his fear reorganized thoughts, his feelings combined into a profound despair. Amy had just been subjected to too much. They might survive this, but survival might be a very cold victory. Too much had happened. He'd never really been loved before, and he remembered the tenderness in her voice, saying that she loved him, and felt this last awful thing was too much, too much for them. And so his sense of loss, of grief.

Her breathing was regular now, becoming stronger. At least he could discard his fear for her immediate safety, and wonder about the incredible screams. His first impulse, as for so much that was inexplicable in this house, was to call them a trick. Theophilus could build anything, could imitate anything; and telling himself that, he had to believe that the screams were *not* a trick. You couldn't imitate something that had never been heard before.

Amy continued to improve, and passed from unconsciousness into sleep. His watch read a little after 11 P.M., and he became aware again of the enclosing silence. He reached to the bedside table and turned on the radio. A low hum as it warmed up, then an announcer speaking with detachment of traffic accidents caused by the storm. He changed the dial. Hard, pulsing music. He lowered the volume.

"I'll be all right." Amy tried to sit up.

"In a little while. You've had quite a shock. Just lie there and take it easy." He touched her cheek, her lips. His voice sounded stronger than he felt. "You'll be all right soon," he told her. "We'll stay here until morning, and then leave if it's no more than a normal storm." He hoped he could drive away in daylight. They might even be able to walk to the nearest town if they could get over the grade and onto the county road.

He recalled the strength he'd felt when he'd entered this room—the strength of feeling that the unknown was discoverable. It was still here. "I'll be in this same room," he told her. "At the desk."

He went to the work area. The large, functional space was intelligently organized. Tracker opened one of the files and whistled into the muffled silence and the dull beat of the radio. It seemed Justice went first class. Here were heavy fireproof files in a fireproof vault encased by a fireproof building. More of the ledger-type books were in the files, and in the bottom drawers he found blueprints.

It was the best of luck. It seemed that the entire house was charted. Traps were designated and trips shown. He turned to make a careful examination of the rest of the room. As he turned the radio seemed louder, the silence lifted. He wasn't sure they'd been in one of these seeming time shifts, but he felt it was something he could no longer afford to worry about. If time really shifted, then there was nothing he could do about it. Worry and preoccupation only made him weak.

As the silence lifted the room felt larger, safer. It was much bigger than it seemed at first. An eight-foot table beside a six-foot desk halved the room. The low ceiling was dark and richly paneled. Tracker sat at the desk on which lay a normal clutter of work, but it was work long forgotten. One of the ledgers lay open on the desk. He looked at Amy who seemed all right. He wondered what she was thinking.

The ledger, he now realized, was not a ledger at all; it was a journal . . . "Not a question of price, at all," he read, "for goodness, I understand, is free."

He flipped pages. It seemed to him that he could almost

135

hear his father's explaining voice. This volume was nearly filled. He read the last entry: "Will die, am dying, weaker than yesterday. The reason is in the mind of the old man —curious to be dying, father father burn it, burn . . . to get from under the heavy hand . . . Victory."

CHAPTER

13

In a world of few absolutes, Justice Tracker's journal ended with one. From the journal his death was certain. His ending, though, implied struggle, and thereby some uncertainty about the precise time and manner of his death. It was the usual condition of Trackers. Few in Tracker history exerted continuing directed force of a single kind. Except for one or two. . . .

Amy Snider was John Tracker's grandmother on his mother's side. Her life is almost completely documented because of an irony.

Some years ago a cynical man attended a funeral in Boston. He watched the expensive hearse and flower cars, the rosewood and ebony coffin, the machine-cut grave and the waterproof vault. Then he strolled across the cemetery to his car.

A large stone among many small ones marked Amy Snider's last resting place. The stone said that Amy had been good and kind and just and loving, and never told a lie in her life. She had been charitable, merciful, noble, beautiful and wise. She was the giver of grace, hope, honesty and good work.

The cynic decided to prove the hypocrisy of humanity by disproving the claims in this specific case. He interviewed every person who ever knew Amy Snider.

And he found that Amy Snider was good and kind and just and loving, and had never told a lie in her life. She had been charitable, merciful, noble, beautiful and wise. She had been the giver of grace,

137

hope, honesty and hard work. Everyone who ever knew her remembered her not with weeping but with joy.

Everything was always changing, Amy Griffith thought, and that was the reason life was so uncertain, that was why, no matter what you tried to do, you always seemed to end up doing something else. Such thoughts went through Amy's mind like the first curls of smoke rising from dry leaves that kindle a forest fire. She lay on the bed while John sat, quiet and intense, at the desk. The radio was too loud. She turned it down to barely more than a hum.

She felt almost safe for the first time since entering this house. It was good to feel safe when you were so tired and weak. It was good, and lucky, to feel loved. Her thoughts jumped from present to past, from past to trying to plan the future. You could still have a baby when you were thirty, if you were married. Her mind rebelled against it, though. You could never be an actress and a mother both; except wasn't it too late to be an actress anyway?

She wondered if the real reason her mind rebelled was because she lost the first baby. The man had been bad, she'd only gone with him because of the loneliness after Jim Randall left . . . and he *had* left, he had. She didn't send him away. Not really. Well, he should have stayed, because then the other man wouldn't have happened, she wouldn't have gone through the hell of losing a baby, she wouldn't be in this crazy house. She told herself she should be grateful. John Tracker was a good man, especially when you compared him to all of the crazies who were walking around out there, in here . . . She felt near to sleep, almost dozing, and from old and nearly forgotten recesses of her mind she whispered a Hail Mary. It was comforting, the drama of the words long since lost under repetition and habit.

138

The air tasted fresher. John's movement as he shifted in his chair sounded sharper. The vault had seemed almost like it was stuffed with cotton, and now the cotton was removed. Maybe she was dreaming. Had she ever really done wrong? Here she was, thirty, and had slept with three men and was not married to any of them. It wasn't much, these days. Other women would laugh. She was not other women. She was herself, and herself was honest when she dreamed allowable dreams. Her first love was Jim Randall, but he might no longer be an allowable dream.

She was casting and recasting a future, fitting out a new role. The trouble was that she remembered the past, and especially she remembered the lonely time with the bum. . . .

"I missed, I'm scared, it's been six weeks."

"No kiddin'. I mean, no kiddin'."

"Listen to what I'm telling you."

"You already told me, baby. I'm sorry. You got a tough break." . . .

Not like last time, no more mistakes. No more millions of stupid words in company with executives and executive typewriters. John Tracker was not a mistake. John Tracker loved her, at least she was almost sure he did . . . and forgive me father for I have sinned . . . father, father, oh father, dear father—

She did not want the memory. Her mouth tightened. She rolled on her side, huddled, and knew she must be sleeping because she couldn't seem to wake. Other memories . . .

Her father, Jefferson Griffith, showing up with a girlfriend. "This here's my kid. Agnes, meet Amy. Amy, this is Agnes."

"What a pretty little girl."

A lie, a lie, I'm ugly with a big nose and they're drunk, he's drunk again, he said he wouldn't get drunk again. . . .

139

She dreamed and remembered other voices and tossed in her sleep. Her father had caused the voices, voices of strangers or neighbors who felt sorry for her . . .

"Kid, call a taxi."

"Kid, does Jefferson Griffith live here?"

"Kid, he crapped out on the front steps. Again."

"Oh, father, dear father, our Father which art in . . . oh, father, you're hurt.

"A scratch."

"You're bleeding."

"Just like a Mick. Caught with a roundhouse. How can you get caught with a roundhouse?"

But Jim Randall had loved her. For a moment he was an allowable dream. She stiffened, tried to rise from sleep, and then relaxed. It was John who loved her. The sleep deepened. Her face became calm. She lay wearing a long-sleeved cotton shirt, a pattern of pastel stripes, tucked into a wool skirt which lay across the relaxed curve of her wool-stockinged legs. Her hair was loose on the pillow, full and long, accenting the now warm and fuller lips.

When Tracker turned ten minutes later he couldn't be blamed for watching her, loving her. He found that he was even loving the act of watching.

Amy breathed a little irregularly, moved one foot which changed the pattern of light and shadow on her legs. He wanted to wake her. Instead, he turned back to the desk, then hesitated, turned back and looked once more at her. At least she was safe. He must get to work.

He forced himself to accept Justice's death, his hopes in that direction passing almost without a flicker. At the same time he was excited by the notion that the blueprints could solve more than the problem of moving through the house. They could solve the grand scheme of the house. Looking at Amy, he felt his humanity, felt a sexual rush. His head seemed like a punching bag for vying emotions.

He tried to shove Justice's journal away. How Justice

died, and why, was surely recorded in that journal. As long as he did not read the journal there was still a chance that Justice might be alive . . . irrational to behave that way, yet he was taking satisfaction in thinking irrationally while rationally knowing he was doing it.

Besides, the blueprints were probably more important. If you were in a battle, as he now knew that he was, then it was of first importance to know the terrain. There was a madman out there in that house, walking, scheming. There was no question in John Tracker's mind that Theophilus was still alive.

He sat with a still folded blueprint in his hand, picked up a pencil from the desk, laid down the blueprint, and randomly marked on a legal pad.

A face was forming on the pad. It started slow, began to peer through angular marks, circles, designs. The face became more solid. He felt he recognized his feeling of sadness as old and heavy, out of the gloom and forgotten loss that forced itself onto paper. He watched his hand make the final delineating strokes. And then he recognized the face, the face of the sorrowful man of the stained glass window who seemed to comprehend aeons in the very presence of death. He grasped the pencil, heard it snap. He pushed the pad away, stood, looked back at the sketch. The picture was of somebody, and then it burst on him as something he'd suppressed all of his adult life began to surface. It was coming in a flood. It was the beard and the leanness of the face that had fooled him. He had just drawn a picture of his father.

There was no madness on *that* face. Only understanding, and a sadness that seemed to ride like a vapor, a knowledge that understanding had come too late. But perhaps not for John, the son. Suddenly he felt corded and strong. It was a new kind of consciousness. Not smart, not clever. It would never bring ten cents on any market, but for a few moments his mind was flooded with the total

awareness of a revelation. He did love his father. He *did.*
And with that knowledge came strength of his own, yet
undiscovered.

It was also exhausting to have one's mind work so well.
For an instant he felt that he was going to understand
every mystery that had ever hovered in his life. And he
knew he would not. He did not know enough.

Where to begin? He looked at Amy. He touched himself, his legs, dulled for so long he was forgetting they
ached. He told himself that he was forty years old and
ignorant as hell.

But, that was just an expression people used. How ignorant was hell? What had Justice written in that journal,
that goodness was free? Did that mean that goodness
knew no bonds, or did it just mean that goodness was
without cost? He resisted the temptation to pick up the
journal. Better to figure out the ground you had to fight
over. It was really that simple. Vera and Theophilus were
in a war and had lost. Now he was in a war with Vera and
Theophilus. Even if the old man had no vigor, Vera
seemed in pretty good shape. She could make manifest
whatever Theophilus schemed.

The blueprints were like reading seventeenth century
maps. Gaps lay in them like those white spaces on old
charts that were once marked "unexplored." Either Justice had not known, or felt compelled not to tell. Likely the
former, because the blueprints seemed scrupulously honest in everything they did report. Justice had been a fine
draftsman. Traps were lettered with explanations attached to each blueprint. John whistled under his breath.
There were a couple of things that appeared impossible
to beat. Again, examining the blueprints, he felt that the
house made terrible sense.

The past ran in his mind. Old conversations, old read-
ings, heroes that walked through the tales and instructions of his father. John tried to remember all of it; could

142

not, but names came to him for a moment. It was almost as though the names were spoken by Justice . . . Herbert of Cherbury, Fox, Brattle. He couldn't remember a thing about any of them. As other names began to unreel he felt neither good nor bad about them . . . Calvin, Mather, Travers. He knew he was naming men who had walked through the light and shadow of times past with prayer, teaching or threat on their lips. He did not know if any of them were good or bad or only obtusely sincere.

On the third floor the blueprints showed fewer and larger rooms. There were no blueprints for fourth floor. The house got more old-fashioned the lower one went, the subcellar a series of grottos and passageways and open unwalled places, doubtless earth-smelling and damp from a century of subterranean and sunless air. He looked at the blueprints, traced the passages; read the simple but effective traps . . . deadfalls, pits, self-sealing cells that operated at the tip of a counterweight. One was fairly sophisticated, a room that sealed and then flooded, the water coming from a huge well in the center of the subcellar.

Tracker shuddered. He knew that this was the site of the other well—the well against which he'd been warned as a child . . .

"Don't go near that other'n."

Theophilus' voice flooded the silent room, but it was his own imagination, John was sure. Still, it seemed that Theophilus was right behind the door. John got up, walked to the door and looked. Nothing.

The blueprint's explanation said that the well was poisoned. Of course, that would have been a long time ago, but John told himself that the well was undoubtedly still poisoned.

He could ignore facts no longer. Someone was maintaining this house. Electricity was being generated. He turned back to the blueprints. There had to be a machinery room. He found the description of it in the subcellar, a fairly sophisticated rig run from diesel engines, which meant maintenance, though not necessarily very complicated maintenance.

This fact of maintenance was one more argument in proof that the old man was still alive. There was no other explanation. The cellar had several interesting features he'd either never known or forgotten. One section of concrete floor and rising concrete pillars had apparently been installed long after the house had been built, straddling the subcellar to stand Herculean beneath the massive construction. Double walls ran like fences, and even with the rock-hewn foundations there was an enormous weight problem.

The decomposition room was also in the cellar.

Shocked, Tracker thought of skeletons as he examined the blueprint. It was a small concrete room. Johan had done a germanically exact job. The door must be a perfect seal, he thought, one that dogged down like a ship's hatch. Temperature could be raised to one hundred twenty degrees. Fans cycled air from an intake, ran it over electric coils for the heat, exhausted it through the well in the subcellar. The pipe entered the well in the subcellar and then traveled downward to break free of the well and travel further downward. It looked to Tracker like the thing exhausted burbling into the river.

Attached to the first description was a second, showing that the decomposition room was wet, water intruding as a mist from fine spray heads. Johan had contrived a hot wind in tropical conditions that would strip a body fast. Tracker read the description, which gave locations where the dead were interred. The long-remembered skeleton in the cell was Jude Tracker. Johan was in the fake coffin, Johan's bones that had tumbled like dice. Johan's wife Sara's bones lay in a concealed compartment in one of the rooms near where John had seen Theophilus. No places were listed for Vera and Theophilus, naturally, and if his father was the draftsman here and his father was dead, then there was no surprise that Justice Tracker had no entry either.

John looked at other features, then picked up a blueprint of terrible efficient devices like those perfected during the Inquisition. He was scanning now, missing most of what he saw. His mind rebelled against taking in anymore.

He picked up the picture he'd drawn and studied the face, then turned to the long row of journals, chose one at random, hesitated and read:

"What is to be said of a man who goes to a fine hotel and pays a higher rate for both himself and his wife (the man being then unmarried) and goes to the room to spend the afternoon taking baths, masturbating, listening to a baseball game on the radio, and getting drunk?

"Once, when he was little, I slept all night beside my son because I knew that at least he loved me.

"It is awfully difficult to be lonely."

Tracker closed the journal and turned to look at Amy, who was asleep. He felt tears pressing forward, tears he had denied too long. He was grateful that Amy was asleep and would not see.

CHAPTER

14

The American branch of the Tracker family grew in a nation where first settlement was made by zealots who represented the highest development of the medieval mind. That mind had been dead in the books since the fifteenth century; but because a thing is dead in the books does not mean that it is not out there in the world—walking. It walked strongly through most of the seventeenth century, then fought from its knees through the eighteenth. Other theologies arrived, together with modern political ideas. But theology in America declined as the Civil War approached, and when the Civil War ended, dogmatic religion, unrelieved by theology, emerged. . . .

James Miller was John Tracker's great great grandfather on his mother's mother's side, a preacher who broke jail to answer his call. His success came because he was intolerably handsome, with flowing blond hair, a pointed beard, and a figure like a masculine arrow of promise. The jailer's wife released him.

To say that Miller was vain would be to misunderstand the word. Miller was vain when he was asleep. When awake, the vanity took a sort of Spanish flamenco presence. Over the years an unusual number of blond-haired and blue-eyed children were born to his congregation.

To say that Miller was lazy would be like describing a dead turtle as indolent. At the same time he was a flaming good preacher of the hell-raising sort. On stage, though, he became mesmerizing. From

146

the diaries of two of his admirers—behind the lumpy misspelled prose of one, the smooth-flowing and articulate self-lies of the other —rises a picture of a man who was a vision of ambivalence. He was sometimes kind, but the kindness always turning to detestation or vengeance or both.

At age thirty-three he was killed by a man named Bill McCord, who was drunk enough to be suspicious and sober enough to act. McCord followed Miller through dark streets until he was near McCord's house, and wife. He stabbed Miller. The jury looked upon adultery in a traditional light and released McCord. Mrs. McCord did not testify.

James Miller left two good suits, three hundred dollars in gold and a near-idiot Indian girl named Mary who was found crouching and pregnant in his apartments. Mary was at least fourteen, did not know her last name; but her issue, Ruth, acquired Miller's name and became a member of the parish. Mary went to an insane asylum where she died early in the twentieth century. She never realized that she had briefly lived beside a nightmare more terrifying than madness. After all, it was born of a man of God.

The dream came and went and came again. It cycled through the muttering of John Tracker, pulsing, throbbing, as centuries of nightmare culminated, centuries of which John believed he knew nothing; of blood-smeared swords and cries of "Santiago"; centuries of the carnal muttering of dogmatists, the blood revenge levied beneath the shadow of steeples. He dreamed of twisting fires engulfing staked figures, of Indians roasted alive by sacred flames, of the iron tongs of the Inquisition and of Jews grimacing skeletally from lime pits as machine guns chattered. The sound of the guns drew a historical line: through history most men would live beneath that line, a few would live on it, and a very few would live above it . . .

Stiffness in his arms woke him. The emotional depletion

of hours in this house, plus the revelation about his father, had overcome his determination to stay awake. He raised his head from his arms, felt the journal at his hand. He turned quickly to look at Amy, noted her even breathing and was relieved. He checked his watch. Nearly five A.M. Time to leave soon. He leafed through a journal, stopped, was captured by a phrase:

"Evil will attack the woman first." In Justice's opinion, there would be two reasons why Amy had been attacked in the maze and later by the screams. The Devil, being revolutionary, sought fecundity; sex was the Devil's revolutionary act. Institutions, being counterrevolutionary, sought heaven. Justice seemed to take wry amusement from the thought that the Devil was technically on the side of life, while institutions were on the side of death, or life after death. John felt neither wry nor amused by it. "As important," Justice wrote, "evil attacks those who are most vulnerable. Women and children are most vulnerable. In denying their humanity society has made them so. It has taken their humanity and given back only vanity. The Devil takes to vanity like a vulture to carrion."

Tracker put down the journal. He shouldn't have slept, too risky, but nothing had happened. He stood slowly, nearly lost his balance. His knees were weak, his shoulders ached from the awkward sleeping position, he was hungry. He moved his body to loosen it and felt like he was tottering. He thought dully of all that had happened since they'd come to this place less than a day ago. The strange behavior of Vera, the dying screams, Amy saying that she loved him . . . that made him feel better. He crossed the room and sat down beside her. She might even be sufficiently rested and in control for them to leave. Then later on he could come back to finish his business. It was a sensible feeling that came from the long rows of journals and books, from the orderly and businesslike arrangement of the room, and it nearly proved to him that the

148

house was as ridiculous as he thought. Except he did not know what to think of the dying screams.

He touched Amy and she woke up, but she seemed no more rested than he was as she blinked, lay still, tried to become oriented and then closed her eyes.

"It will be dawn soon," he told her.

She shuddered and refused to open her eyes.

"Have you been dreaming?"

Her mouth tightened.

"We have to leave now," he said. "There will be time to come back later."

"I have to stay, at least for a little while." She reached for his hand and brought it to her face.

Her hand felt thin. "Something out there is capable of killing," he told her. "I think we really must leave."

"We can't."

"Why not—?"

"Something bad is happening to me, I don't know what it is. I'm afraid if we try to leave it will get worse—"

"What do you mean? What's happening?"

"I don't *know,*" she said. "Maybe I'm wrong."

"We should eat something," he said, stalling, trying to divert her. "Come with me to the kitchens."

"Yes." Her voice sounded more filled with despair than fear, although the fear was there too. She seemed trying to see his face. She sat up, nearly lost her balance—as he had—and then stood.

He took her arm, which seemed thinner, the bone rising under his fingers at her elbow. Her skin seemed terribly fragile.

"Do you feel sick?"

"More confused . . ."

The kitchens smelled differently when they arrived. It wasn't the smell of burning, but it was enough to cause Amy to check the stove, sniff the air, search for fire. John sat at the table and found that his thoughts were still uncommonly slow. His face was hot and dry. The warmth in the kitchen didn't feel like a normal sort of heat. With the outside cold and the size of the house it was impossible, he reasoned, to raise the temperature in the kitchens much above sixty degrees. But if the quality of an X-ray could be translated into heat it might feel exactly this way. He touched his face, touched sweat, yet his fingers were dry when he drew them away.

"Do you feel it?" he said, turning to Amy who was opening a can.

"Yes." Her voice was low. Her fingers fumbled the opener.

"Have you felt it before?" Surely she would have said something.

"Not nearly as much before." She dropped the can, stooped like an old woman to pick it up.

"I'm afraid again." His mind was moving slow as oil on ice. He knew he wouldn't have said a thing like that if his mind were quick. He'd have considered it and held it back.

"Someone's out there, I hear someone." Amy did not move.

Tracker listened, and heard nothing. "I'll go see." As he stood his knees ached so that he nearly stumbled. He did not want to go.

"Gone now," Amy said.

"I'll still look." He left the kitchens, walked through three rooms and felt as though he had stepped from the middle of a desert onto a cold plain. The internal feeling of dryness and intense heat left. He reentered the room and the heat returned. He went to the kitchens, took Amy's hand and led her back through the rooms. When she stepped clear of the zone of heat she gasped, then began breathing slowly.

"I feel better."

She doesn't look better, he thought as he watched her face, and knew that confusion must also show on his. He was getting a sliding-away feeling that she had two faces. He couldn't see the second one but felt it lay right behind the face he was watching. Illusion caused by tension, he supposed, but he had the distinct feeling that Amy's smiling face was like a rubber mask that could be peeled away.

"I think we should leave." He was sure they should.

"I do feel a little better."

"Let's go," he said. "I think I activated some kind of electronics in the kitchen. I don't know much about electricity."

"We can't."

"Why not?" He was tired, found a chair, sat down.

"Honey, I feel bad. I feel better, but I still feel bad." Her voice quavered. She'd never called him anything but John. "Something *is* happening to me and I don't know what."

"We'll leave now."

"I don't think we can." The mask was smiling, but her words were hesitant, almost stammering. "I feel like you must feel when you get old . . . I don't want . . . I can't *stand* to be old. I'm afraid if we leave I'll be old."

Tracker would never know how long they stayed in the room just beyond the zone of heat. Now they heard slow footsteps approaching.

"It must be Vera." Amy's voice sounded husky. "If it is, she couldn't have been the one who was screaming."

"Let me handle it." John didn't know what he was going to do, but he knew that the confrontation was his. He got up from the chair. The footsteps stopped. He looked around. They were in the middle of a central room where doors led to different corridors of the house. The room was an intersection for one side of the house. You didn't always follow the natural, direct routes from door to door; you imagined two isosceles triangles, one laid crosswise over the other, their tallest points in the two far corners of the room. You walked in the space covered by those triangles.

Behind him a door slowly began to swing open. He turned to face it, motioning Amy to stand behind him. The door pushed toward him. He waited for Vera to step through.

The open doorway was empty.

"Over there," said Amy.

He turned to see another door opening, knowing as he watched that it would stand before another empty passage.

"Tricks," he said, and made his voice as bored as possible, determined not to show anger or fear. "And," he said to the second empty doorway, "we were naturally worried, I always worry when the old folks get childish."

A third door began to open. This time he walked toward it, intending to pull it quick and perhaps bring Vera with it. He took three steps and was staggered by a wall of heat. He stepped back and the cold returned. "It's Theophilus," he told Amy. "Vera's not this good. Vera's just good with her mouth." He turned. The fourth and last door was opening.

It too was empty.

"Show yourself, old man."

They were surrounded by heat, yet it wasn't touching them. A time shift began, alternating waves of energy and weakness went through him. It was like, he thought, being bombarded with time. For a moment he felt like a child, in the next moment like an old man. He reached out and felt heat, behind him, more heat. Tracker wondered how long he could hold his composure. He remembered the screams and was afraid that this was no trick at all.

How did you kill a witch? A warlock? He did not know what he was facing, but now, with his knees like unoiled hasps, and with that rubbermask smile of Amy's, he knew he must act.

The heat increased at their backs as he felt it move away from their faces. He took a step, the heat followed. He stood firm. The heat pressed, burning inside, like it would scorch bone while leaving flesh unharmed. He led Amy another step forward. They were being driven toward the kitchens, driven deeper back into the house.

"The kitchens," he said. "That far and no farther until you show yourself, damn you."

The heat disappeared before them as the Red Sea must have parted in front of Moses, and they walked on the retreating edge of the heat.

It could not happen. Just because it was happening didn't really mean it could happen. But, oh yes, it *was* happening.

How to kill a warlock? Moving before the heat, he thought of Justice. A man wasn't mad if he spent his life on real things, and this heat and this house were real.

He squeezed Amy's hand, she looked at him.

"I love you. I do."

Loving someone ought to be real. His words did not touch the heat, which was steady and inexorable. As they approached the kitchens the sound of footsteps returned. Someone, Vera or Theophilus, walked in that kitchen.

Without some quick action he knew he was lost, but didn't know if lost meant dead. Lost. Well, he would not go into that kitchen. The heat gathered at their backs. Through the open doorway the sound of footsteps was heavy, the angle hiding a view of the walker.

The heat at their backs was not touching them, but it was intensifying. Amy was trembling, the mask smiled, lips moved . . . ". . . us sinners now and at the hour of our death, amen, Hail Mary. . . ." For a moment Tracker almost saw through Amy's mask, then the heat gathered again, and evil seemed to gather around them like a sound-dampening cloak.

Think, think quick about an answering decency. The first real job he'd ever had was picking the tassels from corn when he was eight. He could remember the fields, the paper feel of the leaves and the softness of the tassel if he pulled in the right direction, the roughness if his hand moved against the grain. The cultivated earth had a thin rain crust about the base of the stalks, the wind moved low and easy through the rows, indifferent to the heat and sweat of a kid earning his first thirty cents an hour . . . and another job once when there was a big forest fire and he was fifteen and he worked all summer against the far bank of that wide river planting seedling pine; the burnt smell of the dead forest, the young smell of the loamy rooted seedlings, he remembered . . . And the smooth roll of the Ohio River, mud-colored, catfish home, where the fish hovered like black indolent spirits under the cuts in the bank, the sun riding orange on the mud color of the slowly rolling river . . . and when Theophilus had first heard the dog get into the chickens he'd kicked that panel over there and grabbed a shotgun and yes, maybe you could kill a warlock if you used his own tools . . .

Tracker jumped through the doorway, kicked the panel, grabbed blindly, came up with a thirty-thirty that had a broken stock; wheeled, pointed—neither Vera nor Theophilus was anywhere to be seen.

Their masks came down then. When he turned back with the broken rifle like a clumsy oversized tackhammer in his hands, he saw the aging face of Amy, and her silent, numbed reaction when she looked at him.

He dropped the rifle and reached for her as she slumped, brought her back to consciousness by rubbing her hands, her wrinkled face, managed to kiss her when she started to come around. She looked at him, and he thought he could see her making a resolution, willing herself to act. And then she touched his face. And they knew, even if by an unknown force, that they were irrevocably bound together.

154

CHAPTER 15

John Smith was John Tracker's great great grandfather on his mother's father's mother's side. Smith died late in the nineteenth century, so old he did not know his age. It was said that he served as a seaman, a ship's boy, in the slave trade. The Importation of Slaves Act took hold in 1808, the same year that Andover Theological Seminary was established.

Before the Civil War, Smith lived along the Cincinnati waterfront, though his wife, Mary Blessing, was not with him. During the Civil War he trafficked westward as a scout. After a ranging life, Smith returned to Cincinnati and died of old age. His only accomplishment was a hundred years of life. He was buried beside the Ohio River and the grave has since been washed away. Among his many failures was the fact that he managed to live so long, and never learned a thing.

Understand or die. Tracker's knees hurt, there was rheum at his eyes. His confusion felt greater, if that were possible, than his fear. Understand or die, he instructed himself. He had lived all these years, scouting the angles and making the deals, yet had learned nothing that he was even reasonably sure could help him now.

He looked at Amy. Wrinkles now clustered about her eyes. Her high cheeks were undercut by emaciation.

Pursed wrinkles were on her upper lip. Amy looked a tired woman of sixty. Tracker checked the backs of his hands where thin veins stood beneath thinner skin. If his shoulders and elbows ached it was surely because the habit patterns of a forty-year-old were being forced on a body that must be a worn seventy.

They must leave, or failing that he must understand the forces that were operating on them. There was no logical explanation to lead him to that knowledge, only acknowledged feeling. If only they could leave with their essential selves intact, even the age would have to be considered not too great a cost.

He was unconsciously jerking on his belt. His clothes were too big. Understand or die. Or maybe it was understand and die anyway, but he still had to understand.

He doubted if Amy would, could leave. This shock, on top of the others, must have her unbalanced. She was certainly standing quietly, eyes like those of a frightened patient or a prisoner. Try to renew her hope. "I think we should try to get outside," he said. "Come with me."

She stood still, then shook her head.

"We need to try to go outside and see if we're still old. The power of this thing may not work outside."

A flicker of hope. She walked toward the doorway, her manner not quite so mechanical.

"Wait," he said, "I have to get something."

The heat and presence disappeared when he grabbed up a gun. Which made no sense, but he walked to the still open panel and took out a large pistol, a .45 Colt on a Smith frame. A blunderbuss. It made him feel ridiculous. It also provided a foolish sense of security. The loads looked useable, but the pistol could kill nothing in this house, except maybe Vera or Theophilus. The pistol certainly could not kill unseeables like force or heat.

Through rooms, around traps, past hidden doors that might open at their backs Tracker walked beside Amy so slowly that he sensed her impatience. He was nearly doddering, the pistol feeling as heavy as his steps. They were in one of the oldest parts of the house. Kids had played here. *He* had played here. He stopped to listen. Another time shift was beginning? The pistol felt lighter, the voices he'd first heard in the house returned, less distant this time, more pronounced . . . a child laughed, then another, and then the two voices were giggling together. Somewhere two women seemed to be arguing, a man cursed and footsteps that did not approach Tracker and Amy seemed to approach the women's voices. The voices stopped, there came a tinkling run of piano music, and then he and Amy were again enclosed by silence.

"You look a little better," she said.

He felt better. He looked at her. "So do you." As they went further toward the outside, it might be that the power of it weakened. He was still sore, his shoulders still hurt, but at least he had a little more strength.

The voices. They couldn't be attached to living beings, yet he was also prepared to believe that they were more than illusion. And Tracker . . . a man convincing himself that time did not shift, that the only world was now, now accepted the fact that it did. Of course he didn't know how or why it shifted, but he figured that maybe he'd be on the way to figuring it out once he accepted the fact that it actually happened.

He tried to think of all the old, old people he had ever met. He wondered if any of *them* could explain about time. How it was that age had come to them. How many times had he heard someone say they couldn't understand where the years had gone . . . how time *flies,* surely a fanciful notion. Except perhaps not. Time it seemed, had a life of its own. All of time, and its history, that had ever been in this house seemed still to *be* in this house. It was more than memory. If he hadn't been so smug in his success, he would have paid more attention to the few old people he had known. The wisest children of time. No wonder the ancients venerated age, believed it housed superior or supernatural wisdom.

Through the last part of the house it felt to him as though the walls were breathing in the past tense. He wondered if he was going to die when he stepped outside. He felt a little stronger as they neared the door. He looked at his hands; they seemed unchanged. He was not getting younger, but he felt better.

Into the hall now, past the coffin that held the bones of Johan. "Stay here," he told Amy. "I'll try it first."

She stood, passive, as he pushed the door open and began to lean forward to check the trap door.

He stopped.

The dog sat in front of him on the porch, mouth open, tongue lolling, the mouth like a laughing rose.

Tracker felt the unheard snarl. Savage. His own. A confrontation.

The dog's fur was thick, silvery gray, the feet heavy. It made no sound, no panting, whining or tail thumping. It seemed to consider the situation with amusement. Tracker raised the pistol and fired into the open, rose-colored maw. The shock of the heavy weapon banged hard against his thin wrist as the boom of the gun rolled through the rooms and passages behind him.

The dog tumbled, rolled, absorbed the blow in a sprawl through the blowing snow, to lay panting. Tracker moved forward, his mind blank as the darkness of a cave, as the black abyss of long-denied memory. His hand held the pistol steady, and the well of his rage erupted as he fired again.

The dog should have been knocked howling, spurting blood. Instead it raised a bloodless mouth, panted, snarled and came to its feet. Tracker answered the snarl with another shot. The dog broke sideways and fled across the gray light of the blowing snow, zig-zagged, tail high, and ran like a buoyant spirit cavorting with its own power. Then it made a wide sweep, turned a circle without zig-zagging, and pointed back toward the porch. Tracker threw the pistol onto the porch, crouched. There was no rose in the dog's mouth now, it was running easy, and making a straight line for the porch. Tracker leaned in his crouch, nearly went off balance and fell backward as Amy pulled him with such force that he fell through the doorway, panting. She slammed the door. A moment later came a thump as the dog's body skidded across the porch, and a panting came from beyond the door. Tracker stood up, breathing heavily, returning to sanity. He was incredulous and disoriented, but he also felt somehow proud. He turned to Amy, saw her backing away from him.

"I almost had it beat."

"What? You acted like an animal. I don't understand." She was looking at him indignantly. "You're younger than me."

He looked at his hands. It was true. They weren't exactly a healthy forty but they were no longer thin and brown-splotched with feeble veins rising through paper-like skin.

He stood there quietly, feeling weak from his departing rage. But he understood something now. Part of him was healed. And he understood something else. This house was so intermixed with himself that he could never leave until those parts of himself and the house were separated. He felt that he would have to walk the house, exploring and meeting and disowning those parts. Maybe Amy could leave, but the house was in him. Even if he was allowed to leave he would carry the house with him.

"Let's go back to Justice's room," he said. "If I can explain, I will."

Worn out, still fearfull of him, she didn't seem interested, so he cut the story down to the facts of Theophilus and the dog and the well. They didn't sound like much, even to him. Trouble was, he did not know how to tell her of a small boy's fright. When they got to the kitchens he asked her if she wanted something to eat.

"Please leave me alone." Amy could be contentious sometimes, he thought, and then told himself that he was an ignorant spoiled fool who was putting a loved woman through hell.

When they arrived in Justice's room she went immediately to the bed, lay down and closed her eyes, as though what she could not see was not real.

"I'll be right here," he told her. "I've got to figure something out."

He went to the bookshelves, where there were sermons, essays, other men's journals and philosophies. What he wanted was something that would explain such things as witchcraft and its accessories. There was nothing. The ancient books, some bound in new covers, some cracked and yellow, all dealt with religion and history.

All right, then, his father's journals. Reluctantly he picked up the last journal and began to read, telling himself that his father was dead and that he might just as well accept *that* fact.

He started at the front of the journal, skimming.

"Late now," ran one entry. "After a hectic and depressing day. If it were only my soul at stake, but this force is building beyond us."

John flipped more pages.

"Saw Sara Lily Tracker (plus whatever her name is now) today in Indianapolis. She is so beautiful. I stood on a street corner as watchful as any country bumpkin as she swept by like a lady. I loved her. Still do. Damned fool."

John remembered his mother, shook his head, continued to skim.

"Evil can imitate, it cannot create. It is only as powerful as ignorance. In this house, it displays itself as a force that grows from history. But while it grows from history, it is created by the people of this house. No, it cannot create, but people can. Here, it deals in time. But at least a man's thoughts are his own."

That was a relief. At least, John thought, whatever he was up against couldn't read minds.

"In this house, Einstein has special meaning."

John knew nothing of Einstein except the name of his theory, relativity, and that it was about time . . .

"Time is conceptual. If time/space curves, then all of time exists all the time. Time in this house is no different than time elsewhere, but the collective force of this house allows it to be experienced more acutely."

And so the time shifts? At least, he told himself, he was dealing with *intensity* and not just illusion.

"In this house, generations have combined to create a force far greater than all of them. One need not apologize for naming what it is. It has documented and given credence to itself through all the dark ages of our history. We are its creators. Evil."

John quickly flipped pages. The entry ended. "Evil in this house threatens to get beyond its creators. It threatens to become independent in its struggle for control."

So there it was. Exactly what John Tracker feared, exactly what he faced. Maybe Theophilus was no longer in control. Vera was not in control. Could that be? John flipped pages:

"Vera (Rothstein) Tracker died this morning. She was aged 74. Cause of death was probably a burst artery in the throat. There was a lot of blood coming from the mouth. I am only going to record a little of this, although her apoplexy lasted 74 years."

John sat there, stunned, wordless. All of his hope, his optimistic belief in rationality; all of his logic and profoundest emotions were suddenly fatuous and shallow. His dreams were the dreams of a self-deluded fool. He was like an unbaptised child being introduced to Hell.

161

"She was my mother. I owe her something. If this journal is ever read I trust that the reader will be respectful enough to read it all. I am 49 years old, have lived through a great deal of Hell, and it seems likely that I am almost ready to get beyond Hell. If I am lucky and strong, then this house will fall in defeat.

"Vera Tracker was not only a creature of this century but its living illustration. That is a long story. I'm tired. Father is drunk, which has seldom happened in these last years. Vera is sitting dead with blood caking the grooves between her teeth."

In a way the shocking disclosure was a kind of relief. At least matters couldn't get any worse. He read on, almost dispassionately.

"Somewhere I have read—ah, Michelet, that compassionate and angry man. He says that a woman may call and call on the Devil and the Devil will not answer because the woman is not yet fit. One does not become a witch by denying God. One must learn to hate God. Vera learned that early. I want to get drunk, but a word or two, anyway.

"Dear reader of the future, this is a crazy century I live in and a crazier century that it derived from. My mother sits dead in a chair with a snarl frozen on her mouth and with blood staining the front of her dress. It is only a little blood if it has to signify so many years of hate.

"I have this much figured out. Good and evil have nothing to do with each other. Good and evil are forces in this world, but nature is a power. Nature is life, egg and sperm. Now I'm going to get swizzled."

Tracker turned to the next page, which was covered with illegible scrawls. So was the next and the next. Then:

"May 3rd, she's been dead three days. The old man is crazy, and I'm still drunk, lord, lord, he won't move the body. Got to leave this place, the walls are hot . . . get sober, leave this place."

"May 5th, no entry yesterday. Tried to get him to move

her. He sat there staring. He has the body propped up, and they sit there staring at each other. Ate this morning, then resumed drinking. Trembly. Giddy. Got to write the summary, it's all coming apart, who would have ever thought she had this kind of hold?"

"May 7th, drunk and crazy, the old man has rearranged the body."

"May 10th. Our Father who art in heaven now is the time for all good men to come to the aid of their summary I'm crazy now tomorrow I wont be—tomorrow I'll start for sure."

John was surprised by the orderliness of the next entry.

"June 1. Today is the day to begin, but first a record of what has happened and the puzzle that greets me. There has been no entry for a long time. I was drunk for a while, crazy for a while, and then believed I was hallucinating. Now I know that was not true. Forces in this house, I keep feeling them ready to pounce. I know what stays them. Me. Through half a lifetime of work I have evolved into the counter force in this house. As long as I am alive the forces may pounce but they can never grow into a single, massive force.

"Dear reader of the future: I have a son. I had a wife. I have lost both because of this house. If you think ill of me, consider this: Rightly or wrongly I have stayed in this house when any sane man would have left years ago. I stayed because my grandfather and my parents (for ignorant and mistaken motives) created evil, though they would have claimed, especially Johan, that they created this house to trap and destroy it. Through enormous concentration and ingenious work they unconsciously gave voice to this force. They have become its creatures, just as it is theirs. At present neither they nor the force are in control. But as long as the force remains in their house it makes little difference. They would never admit that this force of evil has grown beyond their control. I have stayed

163

and fought so that it would not get *beyond* this house. If it ever comes to full strenth through the acquiescence, and the cooperation of Trackers, the countryside will be helplessly ravaged."

Tracker stopped reading. The phrase, "through the acquiescence and cooperation of Trackers" rang in his mind. He still wasn't sure whether Justice was a courageous man or a fool.

He sat back for a moment. All right, he could accept that Justice was right about the force of evil. After all, he had seen Vera walk. So had Amy. If it was Theophilus' doing, with his perverse illusions, then it was Theophilus doing the work of something that had gotten beyond him. All of them. Justice was no fool.

Not all he had learned from business was a loss. His decision-making, business mind began to sort facts. If the evil that Justice described actually existed, then surely it could have killed John and Amy at any time. Which must mean that it wanted them alive, or at least one of them. And if it wanted them alive, then they were needed for something . . . "through the acquiescence and cooperation of Trackers." Of course. They were to be its carriers, as Theophilus and Vera had been . . .

Even as he heard Amy move, even before he heard her first word, he knew she was a hostage to insure the "acquiescence and cooperation" of the Trackers.

"Father?"

He turned and looked. Her body was tensed, becoming rigid. Her voice changed, it had the sound of a contrite, frightened seven-year-old. Her face was being moved, pulled, molded, the skin tightening as she assumed the posturing of a defenseless child.

"Father?" Her eyes opened, although she didn't move. "Father?"

She half-rose from the bed, as if to get closer to what she was seeing. It was as though she were trying to see

164

movement in some far-off darkness, but her concentration continued to be fixed less than a foot from her eyes. Now her face was rapidly taking on the youth of a child. The wrinkles were gone, the lips were a soft and definite line, even with the slightly protruded look that one saw on babies.

"You are not my father." In a compulsive burst of movement she rolled from the bed and stood. Her eyes still searched close in. "Who are you?" She turned in a half circle, backed away, stood quiet. "It's dark here and I can't see you, why can't I see you . . . I can fly . . . " She bounded on the bed, jumped high, fell back, jumped again; bouncing as on a trampoline. Her shirt was pulled and torn and disarranged. She stopped, stood staring, rubbed her groin, tentatively at first, then faster.

Tracker crossed the room, moving like a young man, and fell against her.

She bounced against the wall. "I don't want to be *old* . . ."

He covered her body with his own. She tried to cross her legs, heaved against his weight and began crying as her body tightened. And then suddenly she relaxed and he rolled away from her, watching the child face deepen and age, mature through a range of young beauty and finally into the beginning decay of a woman of sixty.

She woke up, and he held her close until she could talk.

"I had a dream."

"You were attacked." He edited the account, no good reason for her to know how bad it looked. He told her just enough so that she could understand about the aging.

"Was I *really* young?" Her enthusiasm returned, it was as if nothing bad had ever happened to her.

"Yes."

"Tell me again."

He told her. She touched herself all over, lowered her eyes like a small girl hiding a secret.

"I'm not sure what you're thinking," he told her, "but before you do anything else I have something to tell you." And he told her about Vera, and once more she was listening and not hearing.

"What did you see when you were attacked?"

"Nothing. No, that isn't right. I saw shadows."

"You were *attacked.*"

"I wanted it, at the very last I wanted it." She was matter of fact, almost like she was describing the problems of combining splits between two inventories. Her face looked good, considering the age.

"You look pretty terrible," she said, "but I think I love you."

That stopped him. Fear or not, he could still feel pain.

"Go ahead and read," she told him. "I have to figure something out, just like you." She sat on the bed, and when he tried to talk to her she only shook her head impishly, like a naughty child.

He'd better finish that journal, find out what to do when she was attacked again. He returned to the desk, picked up the journal, flipped pages:

"Fire can be the important enemy here. I wonder if I have built well enough. Vera, my mother, has been dead for a month today. She still sits, undecayed and lifelike in a chair in one of the downstairs rooms. The old man, in a continuing state of drunkenness, has given order to that room in a way that could only be given by the builder's mind. Nothing is out of place so much as a fraction. In this great house with all its space and contrivance for evading, there is no consolation for him. He remains beside her, talks crazily sometimes, rationally at others. They argue, because he listens and then answers. They fight with their tongues just as they always have. If it is all in his head it is no less real in that room. I've watched for a length of time at various times. I know that Vera is dead, yet I know the old man hears her. The body does not decay, although

166

it does seem to be fading, becoming thinner, as if it were being drawn together from inside itself. Can't always be sure what their argument is about. At least three times—and each time his protest was weaker—I heard the old man claim that he is not God. Vera, or *something*... maybe Theophilus hallucinating . . . is convincing Theophilus that he is Jehovah. His mind is antique beyond its age, not greatly advanced from a mind of the Middle Ages . . ."

Tracker stopped reading and leafed pages. The entry for June 1 was long, the script in a disciplined hand. It marched for page after page. He continued flipping until he arrived at the entry for June 10:

"Don't know what is happening. Been working hard every day but have not visited the room where Vera sits. Suppose I should have made certain that the old man was eating, but experience shows that when you booze, the body has a way of cramming food at various times. This morning I awake, attempt to go to the kitchens, and find the door locked. The by-pass system from inside the room is blocked. I'm in prison. I wonder for how long. Later. It is twenty-four hours since I found myself imprisoned. Is it to be fatal? The old man may be crazy, but is anyone that crazy? Will continue work. Pretty thirsty. Have four bottles of beer. Ration them. I find that I stomp on the floor a good deal. I fear that my father Theophilus locked that door and then died or got hurt . . . The Devil entered the middlewest in 1801 riding on a horse. At least we know that the first preacher arrived then, and *he* was riding on a horse."

Another long entry. John skipped quickly:

"I am afraid now. No sound can intrude here. Sometimes I get the feeling that great activity is going on around me. In an excess I drank the second bottle of beer. I'm resigned. I pray for a miracle, but doubt if any miracles are reserved for me. Will die here of that I'm sure. The mind is still clear, and while it remains so my job is to reconstruct everything I know of this room to see if there is a way out. I fear I've designed too well. I'll not be the first man who dug his own grave. Will spend three hours on the job. Failing, I will return to work.

"Later. Simple physics has me beaten. Father, if you are alive I hope your mind is clear. I would not like for you to be enjoying this."

Tracker balanced the journal in his hands and felt something of the sadness he'd felt when he discovered himself drawing a sketch of his father. He turned to the next entry:

"Getting weak, only a sip or two of the beer left. Imagination swirls. Time, time . . . imagine yourself a visitor in the Tower of London. You dwell among knightly armor, crown jewels, ancient battle flags, stone axes, portraits of kings. Step from those museums into the busy streets filled with taxis and wedged traffic. You would temporarily be unsure which world was past, which present. And you would understand that there was only mechanical, not spiritual, difference between them. Time slides in this house. A moment in the thirteenth century is a little different than a moment in the twentieth. . . ."

The next entry showed an unsteady hand, although the entry was not scrawled:

"June 25. Again I imagine movement around me. Terribly weak. Dehydrating. Last few hours listening to the radio, which tried to sell me soft drinks. If you get to this house, if this house is still standing when you find this room and journal, the key to staying alive here is to keep walking and doing. . . ."

John was nearly at the end of the journal. "Keep walking." Could he still trust Justice?

"June 26 the whole thing is to tell the truth. Weak."

"June 27 laugh like flower, you should not have left Sarah I tried to be a good man messed up though."

One entry was left, one John had already read, but he

glanced at the last words of Justice Tracker:

"dying, dying father father burn, burn it, burn."

He put down the journal and looked at Amy at the far end of the room. He found that he liked to look at her, even though she no longer looked young.

"You're ugly, you're old and ugly and you brought me here. I hate you, hate you." Her voice was tinged with hysteria, her hands slowly rose until they covered her face, then fell as slowly away, sliding down her cheeks and wrinkled neck.

"Look at what you've *done.*" She stood, then slowly moved toward him. He backed away, almost stumbled. What was happening? Amy didn't talk this way. Her voice was a sing-song of hatred . . . Vera's voice . . . She advanced toward him slowly. As she came she began picking slowly at her skirt, hoisting it up her leg. Her motion was exact, careful.

The silence, the muffled feeling was returning. Force and heat were again at his back. He turned, and it still was at his back. His legs were weak, his hands trembled.

"I love you so much, I can explain it easy." Amy's voice was suddenly not only natural and sounded like her at her best, but it was full of relief that she finally understood, even if he did not. And with understanding she seemed to have reclaimed herself. She was smiling—not the mask smile—although she looked a little older. The muffled feeling was beginning to disperse as she walked to him, took his hand. "Let's get something to eat, I think I've figured something out."

"I've something for you to read—"

"You can tell me about it. Come *on.*"

CHAPTER 16

It was Theophilus Tracker, John Tracker's grandfather on his father's side, who uttered the dying screams when John entered Justice's room. Until that time Theophilus had been alive. His death was real. Theophilus, having created evil, was sustained by it. He tramped like a lead-footed soldier in its service. His destruction came when the force of the evil he created became ascendent.

What killed him is conjectural. Certainly, Theophilus could have killed himself. He was sufficiently clever to rig even that macabre death. Still, though one might have expected such a display from Vera, Theophilus seemed capable of too much fear.

More likely he was destroyed by his self-created force of evil, which ironically took the form of Vera Tracker.

Had John Tracker not lived for years in revulsion because of his youthful memories, he would have realized that Theophilus was not quite the low and simple man he seemed. Theophilus was, after all, the son of Johan.

In the Tracker family there was rebellion of son against father. John rebelled against the intellect of Justice. Justice rebelled against the seeming perverse attitude of Theophilus. But the most important rebellion was of Theophilus against Johan.

Johan built to defend against the Devil.

Theophilus built in an attempt to exceed, and thereby subdue, evil, by becoming the master of its power. And for years he was the master, until it exceeded him.

All seem guilty, all seem innocent. Like Vera, Theophilus fought against what he considered a cheapening world. Like Vera, he fought by rendering a diabolic order, out of which emerged the house of the Trackers, clean-lined and sane, given that less than sane premise.

While Johan was a holdover from the Middle Ages, Theophilus was a modern product; which was why in fundamental matters they seemed much the same. The difference between the work of Johan and Theophilus was only the difference in style. In the house of the Trackers, time was like the repeating octaves on a piano. The executioner of 1650 stood in exact and definable reference to the executioners of the 20th century.

The house of the Trackers rose as a work of satanic art in opposition to centuries of dogma, and in the end it was more Theophilus' creation than it was Johan's. Theophilus was not superficial, although his life made him seem so. When he was young he was known as a tomcat. As he grew older he would launch into tales of exploits with women. Some of the tales were recorded in Justice's journal, and were intended to announce Theophilus' independence from Vera. They bolstered his ego, and they aroused the perversities of Vera. Theophilus lived a life of drinking and violence and sex, and building.

When his grandson John Tracker returned to the house, Theophilus was still in marginal control of the evil. When it became known that the house was threatened, Theophilus was destroyed as power consolidated for its stand, for its survival. John Tracker would henceforth become the focus of power, its embodiment. That was the plan.

During the years after Vera's death, Theophilus' madness culminated as the power sustained and informed him. The abilities of a man in his nineties could not cover what had happened.

Theophilus built in a frenzy that paid no attention to approaching sightlessness, to weak hands, to a worn body. No doubt he finally became weary beneath the self-created forces that got beyond

171

him. He was surely tired of life, and terrified of death. Justice's journal shows Theophilus' desperation at the time of Vera's death. He had built on that house for more than seventy years with innovative genius, and his work did not save him. Because it was not, ultimately, his own.

The house of the Trackers seems little different from other great houses begun in the 19th century and completed in the 20th. Some of the architects, such as J. P. Morgan, died commending their souls to their makers. With his dying screams, Theophilus did the same.

As they walked to the kitchens slow footsteps followed. The footsteps did not speed up when theirs did, but they also didn't fall behind. Tracker prepared for another confrontation.

Hard to believe, harder not to believe. Had Theophilus somehow been able to contrive a Vera who was half corpse and half robot? Even that nonsensical notion seemed more acceptable than the *proof* of the detached force of evil Justice had described.

Theophilus had first created evil. Then he collaborated with it. Now, the instrument of his creation was loose in this house, and it spoke through Vera. Evil had even gone *beyond* Vera.

What Justice feared had come to pass. John Tracker was sure that evil was manifested in the gray dog, if it was the same dog; and he had seen that dog for the first time when it was several miles from here. That same dog had come back to confront him, impervious to his bullets, as it had been impervious to Theophilus' bullets all those years ago.

When they got to the kitchens he left Amy and went further into the huge dining hall to look onto the snow-covered terrace. The snow was still falling heavily, though not so bad as before. It seemed the storm was beginning to blow itself out. He checked his watch. Hard to believe they'd been in this house only a little over a day. It was Wednesday now, early afternoon. The cold and empty terrace beyond the leaded windows was unmarked by tracks or wind. The dining hall was cold. Antique furniture sat austerely in the otherwise plush surroundings of heavy purple drapes, thick red carpet, plaster-crumbling walls from which paper peeled like husks. Chandeliers above the long table provided small reflecting surfaces in the gloom.

Vera. He knew he would still have to confront her. It occurred to him that the only time he'd felt really good in this house was when he was prepared to take that dog by the throat and throttle it. The awful heat had disappeared when he'd grabbed the rifle. He walked to one end of the dining hall, picked up an ornate Victorian lamp and threw it through the leaded windows. Glass shattered, a cold draft poured in as he watched the broken lamp disappear into the snow of the courtyard.

Shouldn't have left Amy for a minute, but he'd needed a few moments with himself, needed also to be away from Justice's presence that rose up from those journals. Besides, his best decisions were always made alone. Now he was grateful to find the cold, business part of his mind still in some working order. Until now they'd been running, confused and frightened. All right, he was still frightened. He and Amy were trapped, quite literally, but even if you were trapped you could fight back. He had made some discoveries, he had more knowledge, however unwanted, even unacceptable, it might be. This house manifested the enemy. Tracker decided to disable the house.

The first step was to knock out the current that ran this place. The force of evil didn't survive from electricity, but taking current from some of the traps would be a start. Not a great one, though, he realized. It might plunge them in darkness, but half the time they were in darkness anyway, and at least a part of the house would still operate on the electricity that came from outside.

Amy was opening cans when he returned to the kitchens, her aged fingers moving slowly.

"Something broke," she said.

"I tossed a lamp through a window. I got mad and fed up."

"Good. I think that's the right thing to do, but a lamp isn't what broke."

"The window sure did."

"So did something else. Far off. Maybe even outside."

"Like the truck?"

"It was heavy like a truck, but I don't think you could hear the truck being torn up this far away."

He figured you could. If there was a force in this house that played the scale of time, then who was to say it couldn't foreshorten sound distances too? Not him. Not anyone.

"We'll see," he said. "If it's a scrap you want, then it's a scrap you get." He crossed the kitchen to the weapons cabinet. Rifles, a shotgun, two police .38s. He picked up an old center fire .32. "Hold your ears," he told Amy, and pointed the pistol through the open doorway and fired. The far wall of the next room was punctured, and a small stream of chalky plaster ran out.

"Just checking your work," he yelled into the house. He grabbed a .38 and emptied it into the next room. More plaster. Silence.

From far off came the sound of steel crumpling, like a truck being picked off the ground and dropped.

Amy was crying, and looked even older.

"You lost your temper," Tracker said. "Why can't I lose mine?"

"I didn't."

174

"You raised some hell with me in Justice's room."

"I was just acting."

"It was a damn sweet act." His heart and lungs felt like they were working harder than they could, but that might be because of his frustration and anger.

"Don't you see. I was trying to understand and now I do." Her voice rose in a near wail.

"Okay, you said that before. Now if you explain it we'll both understand. Let's hear it."

"You're letting it in. You're letting it *in.*"

She really did seem to understand something.

"When we're confused, or weak, or when we have trouble between us this *thing* gets bigger. When I attacked you, there was serious trouble."

"You were acting?"

"Of course."

"Then you fooled it."

"In a way. Anyone who acts works themself up to what they're acting. It comes out false, otherwise." She almost smiled, then turned back to her work. "You have to eat a lot when the food's ready. You need strength. I need your strength."

He started to tell her that he at least had a plan, then decided that something, someone, might hear. "I love you, he said."

She turned to him. "I love you too, but look at me. I can't help how I feel about how I look." Her forehead was wrinkled, and the shadows that undercut her high cheeks were deeper. Her hands were thin.

He went to her. "It will be all right, we'll get through this—"

"I tried to tell you earlier," he said. "Vera is dead. I found out about it in Justice's journal."

You don't dare lose control again," she said, "Now come and eat."

"It's true," he told her. "Vera is dead, and somehow

175

animated." He tried to explain what he had read in the journal. She listened seriously, and seemed trying to make up her mind about whether he, John Tracker, had lost control.

Half an hour later, when he began to pull blueprints from Justice's room, Amy pretended to read the journal entry. He watched her, and believed that he was once more denying the evidence of her senses.

John studied blueprints, and hated to think of what they must do. He spent more time than he wanted, because he had to be sure that Amy knew how to read a blueprint. It was like buying insurance, he thought. You never really expected to die, but you still bought insurance.

When he was satisfied he located the easiest entry to the cellar. He had left the .38 in the kitchen but kept the .32 in his belt. He wasn't sure why he bothered to carry the thing. When the force he was up against had appeared as the dog, a .45 had barely slowed it down. He supposed he carried it because it represented an opposing force, even if one that probably wouldn't do any good.

He thought of the well at the center of the house, the wellspring of all that had happened.

He checked the flashlight and turned to Amy. "I'm afraid this is going to be bad, I wish I could protect you better." He was surprised to hear the genuine warmth in his voice; what he'd mostly intended was an apology. More than warmth . . . the sensibility of love, which didn't seem to care that Amy was old and frail. He put his arm around her, drew her to him. It was all he could do.

She looked at him, smiled. "I can act, and I can tell when someone else is acting. You aren't."

She was right, but his emotions still surprised him a little.

They descended normal stairs, which held no traps but were slick with ground water and slime. He flashed the light on the steps. No one had passed this way in a long time, the scummy slime was a thin, untracked layer. On down, carefully, slowly, to arrive at the bottom of the steps.

The cellar was a musty, lime-smelling place that oozed water. They were on a wet dark plain above the dark well that the blueprints showed to be in the subcellar. The well lay at the very heart of the house. Sulphur seemed to float in invisible streams through the blackness. Tracker figured what they really smelled was sulphuric acid released when the limestone was shot for the freeway.

The cellar seemed endless, appropriate for the fantastic structure that rose so high above them. Lights were small naked bulbs that were activated by the pressure of John's feet as he led the way, then went off when John and Amy passed into the arc of the next light. It was impossible to gain any perspective, or comprehend the vastness of the cellar.

At each light they checked blueprints, read descriptions and thereby avoided the traps. So the main route was safe, though without the blueprints to help his memory he was certain they would soon be dead. Water was sluggish at their feet, making the going slick underfoot. This was the ooze of sour water through limestone, the lime and sulphur like a fundament of the house.

It was warmer in the cellar. The dark crawled after them. The cellar was a soundless, deep night. The silence was only interrupted by their footsteps and the drip of water. He smelled another odor that was a long time past the state of vital decay. Thick air cloaked them and lay on their tongues, and John felt like he was chewing on soggy paper.

"I don't believe all this." Amy was trying to scoff, and not being very successful at it.

Tracker's flashlight beam was swallowed up as he swept it back and forth across the vastness to reveal gigantic supporting timbers, nothing more. It was with the flashlight out, in the dark, that he sensed a not so far off presence. No choice but to go on, confront it in the darkness. He could not find it with the light.

"Do you feel it?" he asked.

"Yes. Not as bad as in the kitchens when it tried to burn us."

Tracker stopped underneath a small light and again unfolded the blueprint. He knew the right way, but if there was going to be trouble he wanted to know what traps might lie in the stifling darkness.

The light on the blueprint faded, like a streetlight suddenly surrounded by blowing fog. He looked up. The light shone lower, like a black cloth had been thrown over it. The feeling of a presence grew, distinct now, becoming isolated. It no longer seemed diffused through the darkness, it was off to the right, not far from the route they had to travel.

The light blanked out. He flipped on the flashlight, pointed it. The beam was swallowed at a distance of ten feet, and the darkness continued to encroach, gnawing at the foreshortened length of the flashlight beam.

He took the pistol from his belt, turned the flashlight off. And listened. And waited.

Quiet. Blackness. The sense of presence grew. The slow drip of ground water pervaded, then seemed hushed by the blackness. His senses fingered the darkness as though it possessed texture, like a blind person skilled at reading the invisible. He hunted for the exact spot. He found it. He snapped on the light and fired between the outstretched arms and into the open, silently screaming mouth of his dead grandmother Vera Tracker.

Amy grabbed him, but not before he fired again. The report of the pistol echoed and died. Running footsteps sounded. He traced the sound and pointed the gun. He listened and the footsteps slowed, faltered, and stopped.

He searched with the light, followed the last of the

sound, thought he saw movement hanging off in the distance at the edge of light. He fired. In the darkness the bullet *zinged,* richocheted, and the sound of a falling blade thumped in the dark. He searched back and forth with the light. Nothing. The light above was bright again. The sense of presence was gone.

"It apparently can't be killed," he said. "I can't figure why it runs."

"Vera?"

"It isn't Vera."

"I know . . . but it is, too."

"Vera was taken over, call it possessed," he said. "She won't be back. What possessed her will use something else because Vera is no longer useful." He was reacting to shock, which was when memory seemed to get a good hold on the mind. Possession of a corpse? His father never taught such things, and yet he knew something about them. Forbidden reading when he was a boy? Some odd or additional reading in college? A name . . . Jean Bodin. A baby killer. 1580 or thereabouts. Bodin wrote about possession. "In possession of the dead," he told Amy, "the possession has to occur before the soul leaves the body. Anyway, you're right. It isn't Vera, but it is Vera."

"Was."

"Yes. It was Vera."

"You sound very sure, like you really *know* it—"

"I'm afraid I know a good deal more than that, if I can only remember. I spent a lot of years trying to forget things I didn't like."

They had arrived at a damp passage that went through the foundation, took a long loop and then reversed. Here the lime and sulphur hung like a wet curtain in front of their faces. The lime-encrusted walls seemed to glow. The walls were rought-cut, rough-laid stone, but soft-edged now by the coating of lime, beneath which mortar crumbled to lie loose pebbly beneath their feet as they descended the spiral further and further into the subcellar.

Around the last curve a dim blue light appeared above a door. John stopped, checked the blueprints. They were coming from the south side. In the northeast corner was the generator room. In the center of the subcellar was the well.

Suddenly his legs felt tired, his shoulders drooped, and in his mind a gentle voice echoed. No evil force had slowed him. He was a frightened child listening to a gentle-voiced psychiatrist trying to explain about reality to a child who mistrusted that there was such a thing. This was time passed out of repressed memory. This was the child, John Tracker, reluctant to move forward.

"Is something wrong?"

"You remember I told you about the well? I'm having a hard time going in there." He did not want his voice to sound apologetic, but he knew it did.

Her sympathy was evident, but so was her practical side. Amy might not be able to deal with all of the events of the house, but she was practical about problems she thought she understood. "There is nothing in that well, and especially you are not in that well. You were a little boy, now you're grown up—"

"A part of me doesn't seem to know it."

"You were ready to fight some crazy dog. Fight this."

That made sense.

"If you can do it," she said, "I know you'll beat it."

"I'll try." He looked at the blueprint, which revealed a room that would have been appropriate for the Inquisition. Yes, in its way the house made terrible sense . . . There was a trap just inside the door. Taking a deep breath, he opened the door—and stepped back to watch a halberd slice down from the wall. He stepped over the blade and into the subcellar, to be assaulted by the dry heat.

It was not the heat of the kitchens. This blast was the

180

essence of heat, like midday in a desert. He could *feel* it sucking the moisture from his face. And as his eyes adjusted to the near-darkness, it seemed to him that the heat came from the center of the room. From the well.

He resisted, and tried rationally to test the feel of the heat. Feeling it there in near-darkness, it could be heat blown from regular oil furnaces. He instructed himself that this made sense.

In this place even the possibility of the rational, the easily explainable, was of value. All around him were shadowy forms in dim blue light. Shapes of ancient machines were crowded together. A walkway ran between the machines like a black path through a mechanical forest. He heard the hum of machinery in the distance. The subcellar could be no more than a hundred and fifty feet by a hundred, but the machinery seemed more distant than that. Fans circulated the dry air. The blue light flickered so rapidly that you would miss the flicker if you did not look carefully.

He directed the beam of the flashlight into the subcellar, and it was promptly swallowed, diffused, made impotent. It was like a bright light in dense fog. He turned it off.

"Why are we here?" Amy whispered.

"Because we're at the very center of the house."

"Vera?"

"Whatever animated her is surely here."

"There's nothing in the well," she said. "At least remember that. You were a child when—"

"If there's nothing in the well, it's only because it's walking around out here." It sounded entirely reasonable to him. His eyes were adjusting. He could see the black furrows in Amy's wrinkled face. "I want to take a look at something."

The dark pathway between machines branched, and he chose to follow the branch running along the wall, circling the subcellar. He did not even look at the branch that ran to the center, and the well. The heat was intense. Even in the diminished light he could see that the wood of the machines was dry and worthless. A touch would turn some of them to powder.

Still, they stood there. Straps of iron designed to fit around skulls hung pebbled and beaten, with tightening screws that when applied to the skull would make it bulge before the brain popped through the thin temples. A seat of spikes. Iron tongs. Stakes to be thrust upward through living bodies. Racks to pull and fracture and draw muscles to the cracking limit. Choking pears to expand throats. His mind felt centuries of torment, and he recalled from old reading that around 1650 an executioner in Germany had used clay ovens like these to roast over a thousand people, including children, alive. He wished he did not understand what he was seeing.

The path turned now in the direction he wanted, and they followed it to a heavy concrete door set in the rock. He turned the knob, pushed the door open and was nearly blinded by normal electric light. It was cooler in this generator room. As Amy stepped in beside him, he remembered the fate of his father. Carefully he left the door open, searched and found a heavy wrench to jam between door and frame.

The generator room, which was slightly above the subcellar, was concrete and treated against seepage. The floor was dry. Fuel storage sat behind the generators in two two-hundred-gallon tanks. Both were full, and Tracker figured they were connected to feeder tanks outside the house.

One generator was round-headed and old-fashioned, the other fairly modern. Both ran off of two diesel engines, one a base unit and the other a back-up. Theophilus certainly wanted to be sure the current did not go off. Tracker took tools from a board on the wall, searched for the oil drains on the engines. He opened them, stuck the plugs in his pocket, and watched oil spill over the painted concrete floor. He considered the risk of fire, shrugged, and opened the drain petcocks on the fuel tanks. Then he beat on them with a wrench until they broke, and watched diesel fuel run in a thin stream across the concrete and make light waves on the spreading puddle of dark engine oil.

First objective accomplished.

"We'll have light for a while," he told Amy. "If the lube is good, it will still take those things a half hour to burn out."

"This was what you couldn't tell me."

"Sabotage."

"I hope you're right."

"We have to take the offensive."

Even with the spreading puddle of oil and fuel the generator room seemed a relatively safe place. Still, the stench of diesel rose in the air, and he knew they had to get out.

Amy left the room and stood in the blue light. Through the frame of electric light her face seemed to fade and take on the aspect of a skull. The sight got him moving. Illusion. The well, he told himself, was also illusion, the haunt that plagued a child. He told himself that but did not believe it. His lie got him through the doorway and into the blue light. He shut the generator room door behind him. The puddle spread gradually. It would back up against that door, he figured, and then at least a little of it would seep through. He wondered about the source of the blue light. He wondered about the force, its strength, what was left of his truck. He was sure that the destruction of the truck had caused the sounds of steel crumpling. He'd fired a pistol in the kitchen, and it seemed to have increased the force against them. He hoped he hadn't made a mistake in disabling the generators.

He stood waiting for his eyes to adjust to the blue light. "I have to get oriented," he told Amy, who was moving a slight distance from him.

"It's safe here?"

"As long as you stay on the paths," he told her.

"I'm not afraid of any well. I never fell down any well. This way," Amy said.

Her voice seemed abrupt and alien. Tracker's knees were rigid as welded joints. He willed them to bend, to raise his feet, to propel him beyond the fear that blanketed his mind. He began to move, heavy-footed, back in the direction they had come.

"This way, this way . . . oh, this way, this . . ." The sing-song voice of Amy was moving from him, further off. Amy was walking in the opposite direction—to the north wall, to the next branch that led to the well.

"I like coffee, I like tea, I like the boys and the boys like me." The spirit voice of a mindless child who skipped through a quiet park.

Tracker stood frozen, not able to move toward her, not able to move toward the well. Both seemed almost in the same direction.

"I'm waiting, waiting, waiting . . ."

Darkness flooded, the voices of Justice and Vera and Theophilus, warning, threatening. He thought he heard splashing, saw the dark mouth of a well opening, beckoning. In a moment he would be into the well, falling, twisting, grasping, the hands clawing—

Tracker staggered backward, turned, and stumbled after the voice of Amy that was not the voice of Amy. "Please," he said. His legs would not work. He staggered against a press designed to crush bodies. Time shifted. The empty machines were once more vibrant with death screams, and a Gregorian chant underlay them. An infant died. A man stood staked. John stumbled to escape, and fell on the path.

184

"It's interesting," Amy said. "It's kind of dirty, if you know what I mean, but it's interesting." She was bending over him, and her voice was far away.

He could not even get to his knees, his face lay in oil.

"I never knew there were so many positions," Amy was saying in her new voice. "I always heard there were. Why don't we ever try anything new?"

"Help me to stand . . ."

"Fifteen minutes, ten minutes, spring is here, school's out, school's out," she was sing-songing, her voice moving further and further away.

"Help me, Amy."

"Teacher let the fools out." She appeared beside him, reached down, and helped him stand. "Teacher let the mules out."

"Help me out of here." He staggered.

"There's this," she said, holding an object that was dull in the bluish light. He grasped with uncoordinated hands at her, at the object, and missed. He looked closely. It was a twenty dollar gold piece.

"There's a lot of them scattered around the well," she said. "Come see."

"Throw it *away.*"

"What?"

"Please, throw it now." His arms shook, he was afraid he would fall again.

"Welcome to hard times," she said. "I'm sure it's perfectly good."

"Oh God, throw it."

Impish like a little girl, she stood on her toes and threw the gold piece, laughing like an excited, teasing six-year-old. The gold piece pinged against the metal of one of the machines.

"It's fun, it's fun, I'll do some more." Her voice was distant again, disappearing, moving toward the center of the house, toward the well.

"Come, and see, and play with me—hey, nonny, nonny . . ." The elfin voice was diminishing.

He had to get out, had to follow along the wall, stay on the path. He couldn't help her now. Maybe not himself either. He staggered forward, stumbling from the path into mouths of contraptions that vibrated, cracked with his weight. Blades were stopped in their arc. Knives did not spring forward. He did not know why, but his sensibilities warned him, forced him to walk the path. Step at a time, half-step at a time. His legs were rubbery, his feet heavy as concrete blocks.

He tried to warn her to get out, to save herself. Turning to call back to her he heard her muffled scream, and then she was running down the path from the direction he'd struggled, and she fell against him.

"Ahead, up there . . . oh, Mother, Mother Mary, oh, our Father . . ." Her eyes were wide, shocked. It was a human reaction to something near-inhuman. It was Amy's face, not a cunning surrogate. Amy was restored.

Still, she was stronger than he, and younger. She clutched him now so tightly he was surprised at her strength. "What is it?"

She shook her head, not yet able to speak.

"What is it?"

She shook her head back and forth, as if she tried to cast madness.

"Stay here." He moved forward, and as he did the blue light intensified, became nearly electric, and he became conscious that a few feet away a figure stood by the path. At first it was blurred, vague. He moved closer. It was tall, shadowed, as though brooding between those infernal machines; a figure like a man, but this man had incredible arms stretching high, arms that were too long by a third.

Tracker stopped and waited for movement. There was none. Was it some sort of mock-up? The figure remained motionless. No doubt it was frightening, but after all the other frights in this place it shouldn't have affected Amy so terribly. Tracker breathed deeply as his constricted lungs would allow, and stepped forward.

Now the light diffused around him in a pale glow, and as it shifted it concentrated on the brooding figure, pushing away shadows, glinting on sharp blades, coating long decayed wood with a soft velvety glow. It touched the brooding features, uncovered the face slowly, until Tracker stood looking into the dead face of Theophilus Tracker.

Without dreams, now; without plans.

The white hair was luminous and changed to soft blue. The face in its last constriction was contoured like a blue mask. The eyes stared at Tracker so intensely as to claim that death itself was vital. The face hovered above him, a dead moon circling, staring down, while the once muscular arms of Theophilus were raised high enclosing his face.

Tracker tried to back away but felt compelled to confront what he was certain must be the final outrage of the house of the Trackers.

Theophilus was strappadoed. That accounted for the ungainly long arms, the grotesque position of the head. Theophilus' hands were tied behind him. He had then been hoisted by the wrists.

In times past, the strappadoed victim was dropped or yanked on, causing immeasurable pain. The force of the drop popped shoulders from sockets, tore at the neck and chest, ripped muscles in the back.

Theophilus had suffered worse. Whatever force had brought him here, and had raised him had also pulled him down. The shoulders were reversed. The joints of the arms were cracked. Rolled sleeves drooped to show sharp fragments of bone thrusting through flesh. Theophilus hung connected only by muscles and flesh. In the drying heat he would shrivel; the water sucked from the body until paper-thin skin could no longer support even the lessened weight.

The force that had brought him here, bound him high, and bore him down could have been no less than, in effect, hydraulic. No mere set of hands, no matter the power of their owner, could so wrench apart living joints, bones, cartilage. A force like a suction of darkness, like the pull of evil into a well; a force that could shatter steel or toss aside the doors of the house—oaken, heavy.

The light dimmed, and the features of Theophilus became more vivid with shadow. The eyes took on a new aspect; they seemed knowledgeable, wise. As the light dimmed, the eyes centered with darkness, dulled as the blue light moved down the long frame of Theophilus Tracker, and pulled John Tracker's gaze down, downward.

The gray dog was silvery blue in the light as it lay at Theophilus' feet, as if protecting its former enemy. Tracker backed away, braced on uncertain legs and tried to call out to Amy to run.

The dog remained silent. It did not pant in the heavy heat. The thick fur did not raise; rather it lay rich, nearly luxurious. It was not until Tracker approached with two hesitant steps that he saw that the fur seemed slightly ruffled in places. Another step.

The dog was an assemblage. Flayed chunks leaned their weight against each other. The loose head rested as if sleeping on legs and paws that were ungainly, torn and then tucked lifelike beneath the carcass. The dog was an aggregate, an approximation, lying silently before the strung corpse of Theophilus Tracker. The light faded. His last sight of the pair was of a flash of silver gray, and the black of a lolling tongue.

CHAPTER

17

Light and darkness crosshatch Tracker history. Figures struggle, looking as if they stand on a stage and before a curiously illuminated grid. When they fail to struggle, or even when they fail to pay attention, they are taken over by the enmeshing force of a darkness that seems preordained.

Tidings Snider was John Tracker's great grandfather on his mother's mother's side, and he was a farmer. He married Ruth Miller, who had been sired by a preacher and birthed by an idiot.

As a child, Ruth had been passed from one family to another. The stigma of bastardy followed each move. She was not happy until at age fourteen she took up with a family of Creek Indians, who, having fled their lands during the Removals of 1836–37, fished along the Ohio River.

After their marriage Tidings Snider, who as a boy had witnessed the murder of his father by his mother, isolated himself and Ruth on eighty acres and was rarely seen off his place. This suited Ruth, who knew the value of solitude.

Their daughter, Amy, was married. Ruth disappeared into the Kentucky hills after Tidings was killed in a freak accident at age fifty-seven.

Tidings died painfully. He was in the haymow guiding the carrier rope as hay was plucked from a wagon by hooks and carried aloft. He glanced away for a moment, stumbled and fell, impaled by a pitchfork.

The darkness that lay in Tidings' history seemed much like the darkness in the history of John Tracker. Tidings was caught in a moment of total inattention. John Tracker faced capture in his moment of revolt against his history.

As he walked he became stronger, but his mind was filled with questions he couldn't name, questions between himself and Amy, even more than about what he'd seen —what he'd been forewarned of, in a sense, by Justice's journals.

By the time he reached Amy he felt as strong as he'd ever been. He felt sure, capable. He looked down at Amy as she crouched. She looked at him, at his normal forty-year-old face, and began to recover. When she was sufficiently in control they left without hindrance, walking through the shadow-making blue light.

Tracker stumbled, slid on the slick stairs and felt himself clumsy again. He began to manage better as they progressed, and Amy walked ahead. Her narrow shoulders and long, tapering back were like lines of good sense. Her hair moved gently across her shoulders.

Tracker was still confused about her actions in the sub-cellar. He felt he should tell her about her strange voice. Instead, watching, he wanted to tell her how important she was, wanted to say that if he was decent, human, it was because of her. A moment before the generators died, and the lights went out, he moved to her side and put his arm around her waist.

"I think we at least have a temporary stalemate. We can leave now, I think."

She smiled. "There go the lights. We have this thing on the run." She seemed eager, restless. She whirled away from him and began climbing. He shot the beam of light ahead of her, and they soon emerged from the cellar.

"Part of the house will still have light"—he didn't know how much time they had. He wanted to hurry.

"We don't have to leave now," she said.

190

"We do. I want to get Justice's journals to the truck, if it's still driveable. Otherwise I just want to get out."

"I have to figure something out, I have some questions—"

"So do I," he said, "but I'm willing to ask them after we get out of here."

When they got to the kitchens Amy wouldn't go on. Instead, she began to make coffee. They were still reacting to the awfulness of the subcellar; he felt they were not talking well to each other. Any delay seemed like a wanton waste of opportunity, and he said so.

Amy was behaving the way she dealt with scheduling when they made a business trip. Her competence, or at least her attitude, worked to put him slightly at ease. He went to one of the sinks to clean himself. The pistol was lost. It had been just luck or a good defensive reaction that had allowed him to retain the flashlight.

"What did we see?" she asked.

"We saw a man dead of incredible force. We've got to leave. Now. It's not farfetched to say we are in the presence of possession."

"What does that mean?" He suspected she was stalling for time.

"I've already told you."

"You've changed, how do you know all that?"

"I know a lot more . . . for a long time I forgot I knew it, I wanted to forget." He walked to the table, sat down and tried to figure out his next move. "One cup of coffee and we leave."

Amy poured coffee, pursed her lips, leaned against a counter. She seemed distant, away in her thoughts. "What else did we see?"

"Unreason, the absence of the rational," he said. "I wasn't able to move. You were twittering around like a six-year-old—"

"What?" She seemed shocked, but her beginning anger

seemed larger than any shock. She flushed, but he thought it came more from confusion than anger.

He told her what he'd experienced.

"It wasn't like that at all," she said. "I tried to lead you, you couldn't move." She was angry, but the anger was stitched with something else. John Tracker had been in too many business situations to miss what he was hearing. Amy was defensive, she was defensive because she was lying. Either that or she wasn't telling all that had happened. He flipped it through his mind. She had seen the corpse of Theophilus first. She had screamed and returned. Amy had been leaving. *She had been leaving him.*

He had been leaving her, thinking he couldn't help her.

Betrayal. Both of them.

He felt sick. His hand trembled. The coffee scorched his mouth. He scarcely felt it. She was watching him, looking puzzled.

"You told me to go find the lights," she said. "You said, 'Amy, turn on the lights.' "

Maybe it was better not to know. "You went to the well? You found money?"

"No."

"Could you have hallucinated?"

"Honey, you were stopped. You couldn't move. I don't know what was going on with you." She sounded neither unfriendly nor friendly. "John, you were not in control. I was desperate, but I was in control."

It would have to do. He could see her revising as she went along, and believing her revision.

The house of the Trackers.

"Horrible, horrible." He sat looking into the empty coffee cup. He didn't know whether to remain sitting or to stand. He didn't know whether to stay or try to escape.

The heat that began to gather at his back was like all the pressure he had ever known or imagined.

"You have to be young," she said, "you have to be young to act—"

"You're the same as you were, the same as when you came here."

"Yes."

It was shock on shock. Now she thought of becoming younger.

"I had it all going for me . . ." The words were full of regret.

"Can I help you?"

"No," she said. "This is private, this isn't your business."

"You can't be younger than you are—"

"*I was,* you said I was. I could be again."

"I'm going to go now," he said, not wanting to argue with her. "I'm going outside and touch the snow, taste it, hold it in my hands and watch it melt." He stood, and it was not age that made him dizzy. He went to her. Stopped. "For the record. To keep it straight"—he felt himself choking on guilt—"for the record, I have to tell you that in these kitchens when we were attacked by this heat . . . I thought of trading you . . . it was terrible and I'd die before I did it, but I did think about it." He passed by her, determined not to look at her face, or her brown eyes in which tears were beginning to gather. He walked through the empty dining room, looked through the leaded windows, and saw the light fading. His watch said it was five o'clock.

He walked across the dining hall. In the center of the wall of windows a door led onto the terrace. Cold air poured through the window that was broken. He opened the door, stepped onto the first floor terrace, which lay like the bottom of a well between the enclosing sides of the house. This whole house was a well. Snow was piled higher in the center because there was no wind. He leaned over, picked up a handful, compressed it in his hand and felt the melt begin to trickle down his wrist. Snow over-topped his shoes.

If she was such a good actress, why hadn't she acted? Why hadn't she lied without hesitation? Instead she'd put on an act, pretending she'd not been running away from him. He could have easily handled the truth, understood it. He'd been doing the same thing to her . . . To save himself, he'd told himself. As though everything he did—or she did—was totally voluntary, not influenced by what had possessed this house. As if the house was not trying to manipulate him, and her, playing on, exploiting old weaknesses and desires. He thought he was so rational, did he? She wanted to be young again to act, to be inno-cent and never rejected, did she? Well, *it* would show them no doubt. Above him was the huge breath of the sky; wind blowing and churning and expressing the mouth and fury of storm.

But the storm was decreasing, wasn't it? He no longer remembered.

He remembered when she said she loved him. It was true then, only a little over a day ago. Maybe it was still true. Maybe, at least, it *could* be true—if they could survive intact.

He turned back and walked through the dining hall. She was not in the kitchens. He decided she would either be in Justice's room or struggling on that grade, rushing from this thing that had risen up between them.

He went to the front door through rooms so familiar he didn't even need the light. He checked the trapdoor as automatically as he would put his car in gear or stub a check. He went through and looked into the tunnel of blowing snow. The storm *was* diminishing, but it still blew. There were no footprints on the porch. He looked at the grade, where dark pieces of steel lay fractured, rapidly being covered by the blowing snow.

Those things had once been a truck.

Amy would be in Justice's room poring over blueprints. If she was set to track down the evil in this house, then she would go about it methodically, efficiently, just as she did a problem or task in his business. She would find her problem all right. Unless it found her first.

The freeway ran in front of the house toward an invisible horizon. In another year cars would be running there. The dead spruce stood in front of him. A spruce depended on a long tap root, you had to get pretty close with a bulldozer to root-cut enough to kill it. In a year cars would hammer along the top of that grade. They would whistle across the bridged river, disappear over that invisible horizon, and occasionally end torn and burning in a brake-squealing, tire-burning crash that would cure their driver's frustration.

He turned, went back into the house.

The business-efficient part of his mind ran like a calculator. It told him that now was the time to leave, to trudge through that snow and climb that blown and feathery grade and walk away from this place as he had twenty years ago. Apparently, this side of his mind was not going to cooperate in trying to save Amy. It wasn't pressing, would make no decisions. It lay on idle, giving advice.

All right, then. He'd look into John Tracker, and what he saw, felt, was a spark of encouraging warmth. It got him going.

Through empty rooms there was no immediate feeling of presence, no outrageous heat even in the kitchens. He knew it was hovering, though. The house surrounded him. Still, it was familiar now, unspectacular, he passed around traps as easily as a man taught to wait on red lights, go on green.

His mind began running like a computer, fed information and he listened. It was figuring the meaning of events, juggling weights and balances, projecting the deal to be constructed, just as he might figure the intent when a wholesale distributor dropped inventory at cut-rate. First, you thought of fraud, second that you might be party to an act of bankruptcy. You judged all the information, checked the distributor's money and supply sources—if you could. You calculated the percent of risk. You made a decision. Yes, that's what you did in the real world, and just now he felt this house was in the real world. It was so familiar.

The truck was torn up. Before, it had only turned sideways on the grade. He chewed on the implications of that. Vera had taken on strength from the force of his hatred and fear of her. The force in the house had directed Vera, he suspected, into the cellar so that he would destroy her. It had made no attempt to keep him from knocking out the generators. He had helped build force against them; and force had destroyed Theophilus because destruction fed its need and eliminated the competition of its creator.

Even when the deal was setting up against you there was the thrill of knowing you were going into it armed, smart. His calculating mind told him that Amy was safe, for the time being. He turned back to the kitchens, went to the stove and heated the coffee. When he sipped at it his scalded throat hurt momentarily, but the coffee tasted good.

Of course, he had to admit the deal looked lousy. But it was also the only game in town. If Amy was a hostage, then she was safer when they were not strong. This force had attacked her with the obvious intent of pressing them apart, and he had to admit that it was doing a good job. But this force of evil did not want him dead. Otherwise it would have had him dead. It would not allow them to leave, which meant he was needed for something.

Which brought him right back to Vera and Theophilus. They were destroyed because they were no longer needed. They were shifted to the debit side of the ledger. He stood to go to the stove and pour more coffee.

"Through the acquiescence and cooperation of Trackers . . ." The words from his father's journal seemed to form in the air around him, to imprint on his brain.

And John Tracker knew why he was needed.

Of course, damn fool. He had not been needed for as long as the house was not attacked. It was self-sufficient. The force, evil, even tried to run him away on his first visit. Now it needed him . . . it needed a different kind of Tracker. It needed John Tracker, the expert in the world outside. He sipped at the coffee and looked at the deal. It wasn't promising, not for him. He was needed as a creature that was equal to legislatures and boards of directors. A creature, as Vera and Theophilus had become. And then victims, when they'd become no longer operational. Think on *that,* John Tracker.

He sat drinking the coffee, trying to figure which way to jump. He was, as people in his world put it, caught by the short hair. He remembered a retailer once saying that whorehouses were like banks. You hated to go there, but sometimes you just had to. In a manner of speaking, he had to go to the bank.

He sat there, drinking his coffee. The house was silent, waiting; as if it too had taken a breather to reckon its moves.

CHAPTER

18

Tracker women have dealt with sex, and with gender, almost as poorly as have Tracker men. Few people in the family's history have been happy in their acceptance of either. They have been trapped by illusion.

John Tracker's great great grandfather on his mother's father's father's side was Alexander Lily, who thought all women were ladies.

While she lived, his wife Mary enjoyed what few New England women were allowed to enjoy; loving respect and complete, devoted loyalty. After her funeral, scandal had it that Alex was in a Boston whorehouse attempting to bed every worker in the place. It was deemed blasphemous, but even slight knowledge of Alex concludes that it was his way of mourning. As a sometime artist he later tried to do a nude portrait of Mary on his bedroom wall, but his imagination distorted his subject into a sort of Madonna.

If Mary had not died the story would have been different. She was an overweight, intensely active woman from Sudbury who laughed as a habit and made most people happy. It took three years for tuberculosis to kill her.

The offspring of Alex Lily and Mary Chambless was Alex Lily, Jr., who grew up in a house peopled by a series of women, none of whom stayed more than a year. It was said of Alex, Sr., that during one six-month period he bedded with four women daily. Not surprisingly this had an effect on Alex, Jr. Prudery and the built-in

constraints of gender once more entered Tracker history. With this
tradition of confusion, it was not surprising that John Tracker had
chosen a woman who could not keep sex and gender separate.

She should not have lost control and run, Amy thought. She should not have gone to that ghastly well, kneeling like a novice to examine figures cut in the huge block of black marble that sat flush in the floor and covered the well.

She should not have disturbed the small piles of coin that lay on the marble, like eyes; or seen the heavy black steel cover of the well, tossed aside like an enormous coin. She should not have done any of that, and she should have admitted it right off instead of trying to keep it hidden. Amy sat before Justice's desk. She thought it was like she was two people down there . . . one a little girl, and the little girl started to talk but did not make sense. How could she admit that?

John was a good man, and now they were apart. If only he knew how much a second chance meant to her he would not be so harsh. If only he knew how much *he* meant to her, he would be here right now.

Journals and blueprints were pushed randomly about the desk. The answer to their personal problems might not be in there, and on the other hand they might. If you knew a man's father, you would surely know more about the man . . .

"People get what they want," she read. "If they really wanted peace and freedom and love and beauty they would have it."

Anyone who had lived half a life, as she already had, could tell how wrong that was.

In her life events and circumstances were exactly ten years out of place. When it was time to go to high school it was also when everyone had to have nice clothes and money and clubs. The religious school at least made everyone dress alike. After school, though, you changed clothes and the competition began. Ten years too late. You had to have a great figure, nice sweaters and bobbity hair. If she were twenty now, it would be all different. She would not be poor because she had learned so much. She could have a good man . . . she leaned back and thought of Jim Randall. But John was a good man too, and her saying she loved him made him more a man, which was good. She meant it too.

Amy flipped more pages of Justice's journal.

If you knew a woman's father, you should be able to know more about the woman. Amy's father, Jefferson Griffith, was a good man. He just had had no opportunities. He was just as smart, though, as this Justice Tracker, if the truth be known. Well, almost . . . Jefferson Griffith drank, so did Justice. Except . . . she had to be truthful . . . except for drinking there were really no grounds for comparing the men.

She studied the handwriting in the journal—measured, steady, confident and smart. "In Salem of 1692 we see the same thing," Justice had written, "young women and pubescent girls danced and accused. In that spring and summer the Devil walked. Salem *created* the Devil. In Salem village, and now here in this house, evil stopped being an abstraction."

Of course, blame it on the woman. At least Jefferson Griffith didn't go out of his way to attack women like that. It was hard to be a woman, especially if you were not very young and pretty . . . this man Justice had a dirty mind, no matter how wise and knowing he talked, wrote . . . It was exciting, this notion of another chance. John would see that a second chance was important. For her, it could be the theater, where she could make a real contribution. Which was the most important thing that anyone could do. It had nothing to do with priests, though, or with religion or faith or the Devil. She nudged the journal across the desk. Religion was pretty easy. You believed what worked and ignored the rest.

Silence. John would surely be back soon. He would pout some and then he would return. They would make up. Oh, she hoped that was true.

They'd been in and out of this room a lot, but there had been no time for a full investigation. Desk, files, bookshelves were all pried into. That accounted for only half of the room. There was a closet with suits, a bureau, drawers in nightstands.

If you really wanted to know about somebody you could tell a lot from what they wore.

The bureau was uninteresting, though like all the furniture it looked heavy and expensive. Clean and folded underwear. Folded shirts with yellowing paper bands. Socks and a pair of cuff-links. The drawers slid smoothly, and then one stuck. The bottom drawer opened halfway, there was pressure, then it stopped. Amy felt beneath the drawer. An envelope was stuck there by aging tape that was cracked and peeling. She worked it free, held it up, opened it.

A ring and a woman's picture. The remnants of Justice's marriage. She felt like an intruder, but she was intrigued. Plain ring. She put it aside. The picture had no writing on the back. She flipped it over. It was hard to tell about the age, but it was easy to tell about the beauty. The face was broad, high-cheeked, the hair coiled. It was an aristocratic, even severe face. Strong . . . the woman didn't look like her, yet she had most of her features, including the thin, aristocratic nose. Slightly broader forehead—that made a difference. The mouth was full. Looking at the picture, Amy knew what the woman must have felt when she looked in a mirror. She replaced the ring and picture in the drawer.

The standing wardrobe was as large as an old Victorian

piece. This one was plain, though, just a large piece constructed of unornamented wood.

Suits, jackets, pants. Justice had dressed well, conservatively. The colors were mostly dark blue and brown. Shoes were in the bottom of the wardrobe. A couple of hat boxes were on the shelf.

She pulled one forward. It came easily and contained a hat. She pulled the next. It was heavy and nearly fell through her hands. She carried it across the room to the desk, opened the box. A conglomeration. At first she thought it was jewelry, and saw that some of it was—a lot of medallions and a strange mix of pins and rings. She lifted a handful. The shapes matched a lot of the symbols on the stained glass in front of the house. Thunderbirds, Mayan suns, Stars of David, curious little fertility figures in clay. It looked like Justice collected religious symbols like some people collected stamps. A crucifix dangled, twisted in with strings and leather thongs. The little cross and its figure of silver and gold was tangled around the string of a pierced, ancient coin.

Amy plucked and separated, finally got it free. She kissed it, hung it around her neck. Familiar feel in her fingers as she touched it. Her hand fell away from the crucifix, then came back. Such a small thing to give such tranquility.

All right, she could stop being superficial now. She could quit thinking easy thoughts about people. Now that she was safe she could face the truth.

A force had led her to that well and made her kneel. It didn't feel unfriendly, although it was certainly compelling. Abruptly she felt for the familiar contours of the crucifix, which she believed stood between her and this house. When she went to the well she was under so much stress that she really could not blame herself. John would not blame her. When she was compelled to kneel, compelled to look, she also felt youth wash over her. She felt the possibility of youth. A quiet assurance of dreams coming true. It was like this force was making a promise to her.

She shrugged. Only the promise of a promise. She wasn't sure how she felt about it now, but she understood her reasons and feelings then.

She fondled the crucifix. Listened. Only silence. The experience in the subcellar had been beyond belief, except so much in this house was beyond belief, old-time belief, that the incredible got to be almost the normal. It was upside down, and it wore a person out just to think about it. She stood and stretched. You had to trust somebody, or something—and this small emblem was something to trust.

She lay on the bed with the crucifix lying openly on her shirt front. No evil would come past that. None could. She'd learned that, at least.

Yet, as she eased into sleep in this small place that had been designed as a sanctuary, it seemed in either dream or memory or imagination that there was a flurry, a rushing outside the vault that surrounded Justice's room.

Above the room the house rose towering into scudding snow clouds, and lay foundationed and rooted in the substrata of rock. Wrapped in arctic cold, its weather-beaten symbols scowled into the wind. . . .

A murmur, a mist. Grayness hung in the halls. Whispers, like cold breath, were in the rooms. Slight movement puzzled its way through the house. A small, silent explosion of dislodged dust fell from dark rafters, invisible in the darkness. Scurrying feet, their sounds tumbling toward the center of the house—the well.

Confrontation. Of force against force. Faint blue light and green light coalesced, grew more brilliant, finally luminous. The light pulsed, was charged as it first drifted toward the center of the house, flowed slowly and then more quickly through the halls and down the staircases, flowed by the infernal machinery like a surreal brook running across a battlefield. The light built in the cellar, flowed to the subcellar, past the corpse of Theophilus, which hung like por-

traiture. The darkness increased as the light arrived, the merely dark from the dead generators—the natural darkness—gave way to black before the merged green and blue light, which now gave over its pulsating force to the low throb that built around the central well, the growing well of darkness.

Hear it come. Smell it come. Movement through hours and days, and centuries. Into the pit. Through all the halls and rooms, carrying in airy hands the remains of Vera Tracker, skull pierced, bones dry, mouth lankly open as if for a last curse. Past generations of ritual death, of symbolistic murder in the service of greed and superstition . . . the last rites chanted over intelligence.

It rose slowly from the pit, at first all but formless, gathering strength as it gathered substance. A half-blown image, like broken volcanic slag. The form increased, faded, then concentrated . . . to the accompaniment of the heavy clunk of gold, or the tossing curls of a thousand flags, a raised fist above them, and oil slicks and burning bodies on a torpedo-roiled sea; the splash of man-thrown fire against green hillsides; the whoosh of rockets and the tatting of drums . . .

It shaped, formed, reshaped. It grew wings and beat the blackness, then sunk into a coil and hissed. It became a rat, erupting from the coil to climb a supporting beam, darting in the blackness, tumbling in pain, becoming a many-legged thing that descended on a web. The form faded, grew stronger.

It emerged. At first it was compact, cold like frozen tundra, so intensely black that it suctioned the natural dark. It stood in the dark, a radiance of black. It struggled for form, got it, held it vaguely. It grew. It was launched. A pale mouth and pale, washed blue eyes. A mist that might be hair. The figure appeared above the constructing forces of the pit, seemed to shrug misshapen shoulders, tested awkward legs, and walked.

CHAPTER

19

On the crosshatched grid of light and darkness that is Tracker history, there are occasional streams of pure light.

Justice Tracker, John's father, died of dehydration in his sanctuary. Theophilus sealed Justice in that sanctuary because, after Vera's death, Theophilus was profoundly afraid. He spoke to Vera's corpse, and its animating force, the force of the evil of this house, and beyond, answered. Or perhaps Theophilus' crazed fear caused him to answer himself. But if so, what of John Tracker and Amy? They too imagined
—were made to imagine?

The important work of Justice's life was not his summary, on which he spent his last days and which was too hastily written. His masterwork is the sum of his journals. Because they still exist, his life is almost completely known; his sorrows are recorded, as are his appreciation of the tracery of sunlight through arbors. He writes of music heard and not forgotten, of the intimate and knowing smile of a beloved woman. Failing in life to succeed with the mind and spirits of others, he left his own mind and spirit standing like an intricately worked and beautiful tower. The tower has weak masonry in places, but it is still the sanest production of the house of the Trackers.

Raised in a tradition of violence, Justice became the antithesis of it. Rebellion for him amounted to silent study. He early learned to tell the difference between truths that were told as lies, lies told as truths, and truths told as truths. He developed perfect pitch for lies, which would keep him quiet and working for years.

The failure of his marriage caused sorrow that turned to romantic sadness. Justice was not original in his view of women; was, in fact, a fool about the matter, and there is every indication that he knew it. During the few years when he was teacher to his young son John he was overprotective on all but one occasion. Considering where they lived, and who with, protectiveness was understandable.

To go, or to stay? That question occupies his early middle years. The growing anti-human presence that dwelled in the house of the Trackers was also silent and subtle in its beginnings. Justice, so interested in his own theories, was shocked when he finally understood what was happening.

He did want to leave, and could not. He gets no name for bravery because of this. It appears (being who he was) that he had no choice. It would always be his lot to have peaceable yearnings while living through one battle after another. The evil that grew in the house of the Trackers found its opposition in him, and finally grew beyond him. It was strong enough, because of his death, to make incursions into the countryside.

Justice's conclusions are unremarkable. He believed that good and evil are not in active conflict. Sometimes when in motion they collide. He believed that time is eternal, but not linear, that it moved back and forth and overlapped itself. He believed that power was different from force, and that the one ruling power in the universe was nature. Hell, and its various replicas, distorted nature, and the world he knew detested nature. Justice believed there were only two real sins: pride and ignorance. He did not believe in original sin. He believed in the possibility of original good.

It was not a matter of cutting losses, it was a matter of consolidating his position. He had to get Amy away from the house. As long as she was a hostage they were both vulnerable. As long as he had to deal with another opinion, another physical presence, another set of movements, he could not control the action on his own end. His only chance was to make this situation one to one. He and Amy could not leave together.

He knew what he had learned. Parts of this house, its tradition, were a part of him. He was bound as surely to this house as was Justice, as was the dangling corpse of Theophilus.

He felt the texture of silence in the house, remembered the muffled silence in Justice's room, then that first silence when he first encountered Vera.

Vera. When he was little, Vera did not have much time for him. Still, thinking back on it, he could remember no act of Vera's that actually tried to hurt him. There were plenty of painful words, which was a special kind of hurt. She was a master of the spirit but she had not, like Theophilus, dumped him down a well, or killed his dog, or done anything else that would be terrible in the world of a child.

He sat wondering if Vera was all right. He did not know if in shooting her he had committed a kind of murder, done nothing, or had done her a favor by making her seeming living death, death only.

He was tired, and it was not the good fatigue from action. It was the fatigue of confronting the unspeakable, the unanswerable. It was the fatigue from walking the mile you had to walk that went beyond the mile you could walk.

His mind, he decided, was telling him that it was time to act. "You want something. Stop sparring." This deal was going to be bad enough. He had to open strong.

He yawned, stood, and went for more coffee. He opened a can of fruit juice, some tinned meat, and searched on the shelves for crackers, then returned to the table and sat chewing the tasteless food.

When the answer came it was from some far recess of the house. It trilled with the quality of an echo. It was, he thought, the kind of sound that the blue light in the subcellar would make if light were translated to sound.

Silence. He stood, left the kitchens and walked through empty rooms, probing for the chink or cranny the trilling came from. He was drifting toward an entry he hoped would eventually bring him to the fourth floor.

In this house, with its outrageous contrivances, what he hated only a little less than the well were the stairways. Stairways were tunnels that ran up or down. So they were not much different from wells. He stopped, listened, walked on. He found an entry and climbed to the second floor. This stairway truly was like a tunnel, running as it did beneath the broad set of carpeted steps, which were wide and open like an invitation. You could actually look up and see the underside of the main staircase. You also had to avoid what made the main staircase deadly. Not even Theophilus had ever used that main staircase.

On the second floor the rooms were orderly, and for the most part furnished. No supporting beams appeared, no uncovered rafters. Smooth, bending surfaces and plain fronts on furniture were Edwardian, Empire. On parts of the second floor the styles blended to the stainless steel arcs of Art Deco. The second floor was a floor of bedrooms.

It was also a floor of bizarre faces, of impressionist carving and sculpture and collage. It was profuse with distortion in paint. He stopped, as if weighing facts. He found an entry and climbed to the third floor. This passage wound in circles, dropped lower, rose. He passed by traps he was only partly aware of. Even if he tripped them, the traps did not spring.

As he emerged onto the third floor he again paused. "Put it to the test."

Off-white walls and a ceiling without apparent fixtures surrounded him. Light came from recessed fixtures in the walls, ceiling and occasionally from the floor. The third floor had half-walls that ran like solid fences, like a

208

maze, beneath lighting arranged so that there were no shadows. He could see over the tops of walls but at a distance he could not see between them. Full walls stood only where they concealed supporting timbers. In the distance was a huge octagonal column that must conceal one of the towers. At first impression the third floor was light and airy, like well-designed museums, or open mental wards. The low walls also ran like a maze, but here the maze was different. Here there were no furnishings, except as the floor was a furnishing. The floor ran in a continuously changing pattern of lines and symbols and colors, like a three-dimensional chessboard. Eventually the floor captured the eye, and then the captured, challenged intelligence would twist the senses into confusion, as was intended. The low walls faded to background and the sky was white and the floors became the sky—the world turned upside down.

He searched for an entry to the fourth floor, moved toward the octagonal column that concealed the tower. There was a pause in the trilling, so slight that it was almost unnoticeable. Time to make his play.

"Let her go away young," he said. "I get twenty-four hours grace in which there's no influence. If I can't deliver by then, I deserve the bath."

Silence. Then a roar behind him, he turned to see a bank of low walls rising from their seatings in the floor, wood and plaster cracking about him like shrapnel, bouncing from walls and defacing shapes on the floors. Debris lifted, hung in the air, dropped.

"Eighteen hours, then." He knew the deal would get worse. He paused, the trilling seemed to concentrate, become louder. "Twelve hours then." He checked his watch. It was a little after seven P.M.

"All right. It's started." He turned to retrace his steps, moved as quickly as he could. He had no more time to spend on Amy. He could not afford emotion clouding his thoughts.

When he got to the sanctuary, he was surprised to find her asleep. When he sat beside her he saw the crucifix and thought he understood. It meant nothing to him, but maybe it worked magic for her.

"I did go to the well," she said when he awakened her. "I was running away, but I was looking too." Her eyes were puffy with sleep, and now they also held tears. She rubbed at them like a child. When she stood her body was slightly stooped like a child about to be chastised.

"I didn't help you either," he said. She was younger, her hair was even thicker. Sadness seemed never to have pursed that mouth. There was no gray in her hair, her face was as smooth as a child's.

"You're a lot younger," he said. "We have to talk and act, and we haven't much time." It was difficult to make your voice kindly and businesslike at the same time.

"We haven't failed," she said, "anybody else would have been beaten by now—"

"Still, we have to talk. I'm afraid you must leave, and I'm afraid it's dark."

She was feeling herself all over, looking at the backs of her hands, pinching at her arms. "I can still act," she said, "with the best of them—"

"You'll be no kind of actress at all if we don't get you out of here." He explained what he wanted, with neither the time nor the heart to explain why. He could see her misunderstanding.

"Put on your coat."

She stood, her hand went to the crucifix. The tears that had collected in her eyes were now on her cheeks. Later he would feel badly for having inflicted this pain. Later he would have time for the luxury of feelings. He hoped.

"Amy, when you get over the grade, follow the road that runs by the freeway. There's a town three miles to the

210

right. It's still early evening. Chances are someone will come driving along and pick you up. Go to the hotel in Indianapolis and wait."

"Why?"

The whole truth would slow things. Maybe part of it would speed them up. "While you were sleeping I had a sort of confrontation. You have to leave. I'll follow you, tomorrow. Something still has to be accomplished here, and time literally is of the essence. I can't explain any more. I'm sorry."

She looked at him, trying to decipher how much of what he said was true, and then her eyes widened. "You can't talk, like in the subcellar."

"Yes . . . Now go to the hotel, wait, do nothing else."

"You love me?"

He was on the verge of losing control. He reached for it, clamped onto a tonelessness. "Always, of course, let's go now." He reached for her coat.

"I know what to do—"

"Just get the hell out of here," he said. "Don't come back."

She was shocked. She shrugged into the coat, turned without speaking and began to walk.

"I'll lead," he told her.

It was in the kitchens, it drifted behind them. He walked, trying not to show he was aware of it.

"Look straight ahead," he told her. "Put your hand on my belt. If anything happens close your eyes and let me lead you." He did not want her to see what he knew was forming out there. They arrived at the front door.

How to tell someone you loved and might never see again just how much she was to you, had been, could be?

"Before you cross the top of the grade feel yourself all over," he said. "If you're okay . . . I mean like always, unchanged, then wave. If not, go anyway. Don't wave."

Tracker watched her go—the wind-blown hair, the long

and youthful form. She was on her way, and suddenly he realized she was gone. Even if he succeeded here she was gone. He could visualize the long letter that would be waiting in the hotel room. He tried hard to push back the reaction of his emotions to that.

Amy struggled in the snow, slid back three times, and then reached the top of the grade. She felt under her coat, reached into her sleeves. She peered at her hands in the dark. She was a dark silhouette as she waved, and then slid out of sight.

CHAPTER 20

Movement in a family's history sometimes stops. When it does, inertia descends like a weight of stones. Evil is content to wait. Eventually one small stone will shift. The weight begins to slide. The force rides the momentum.

Alexander Lily, Jr., was John Tracker's great grandfather on his mother's father's side, and he was a deacon. His wife, Faith Smith, was a religious fanatic, transplanted from the midwest to the west; and then returned east after her mother's disappearance. Faith had more than "a touch of the paint brush." She passed for white by claiming to be Spanish.

They were penurious people, clever and hard-working. They raised one son and so tired him with cant that he became a questioner all his life. They never missed a church service and contributed almost regularly one-tenth of their income to build steeples. They thanked heaven for everything, although the record suggests that except for money they had next to nothing. They were buried in waterproof coffins encased in waterproof vaults deep in the cold New England soil. It seems safe to say that except for their son Samuel, they neither added nor subtracted one jot from the life of the earth. This static condition in Tracker's history waited to be faced. John Tracker had to face it, to act.

He had to get moving. Had to. He checked his watch. A few minutes before eight. He took a dozen steps, felt himself losing control, and stood fighting to regain it. This time he lost . . . "What's in the well?" "Nothin' in that one, boy. Don't go anywhere near that other'n." "What's in the well?" "Water." "What's in the well?" "Fall in there and you'll see. Look in there and it'll grab you." Slow falling, slow, like the descent of the newly drowned into fathoms of water; turning, legs locked, then bent with knees held into his face, arms at first flailing and then rigid and then limp. Hands clasped in claws, fists, loosed, clutching, hooked, and then immobile and stiff as rusted hinges.

"When you are raised with crazy people, then you're crazy." His father's voice once more seemed present. His father's voice brought him slowly to awareness. He had not expected this. He stood there, weaving, as the gaping well closed over, shimmered and disappeared. He had no time for this, he had very little time at all. He didn't know whether this was a manifestation of the house, or of his own mind. Two lights, like blue sparks seen through fog, like eyes, dwelled in the far corner of the hallways beside the coffin. The door was still open at his back. Wind whirled snow into the hall.

It seemed he had been running for the hall and the doorway, because when Amy had left he remembered taking several steps back into the house.

He turned to the doorway, saw the trap door yawning open. This was his mind doing this.

The deal was still on.

He looked at his watch. In a little under eleven hours, he would leave this house. If he did not succeed in his purpose, he would leave as a creature of this house.

His rewards would be unlimited money, power, sex and youth. He would be a thing incarnate; also success incarnate, strength flowing from this house and independent of this house. It would no longer make any difference whether the house stood or not. What made the house special, demented, would be loose in the world. It would wear the form of John Tracker.

But that was if he did not succeed. He'd purchased a dozen precious hours. One was already gone. The force of this house was ironic, sporting, willing to grant time on the promise of Tracker's capitulation if he did not succeed in discovering the key, the power that would set him free. Of course, to the force inhabiting this house he must have seemed like a pathetic creature, easily ruled, easily captured. He must seem less than Vera, less than Theophilus. So the proposition was really not so sporting.

"Evil is weak because it is evil."

His father had written that the way to survive was to keep doing, to keep walking. So that was the general scheme Tracker had in mind. It was impossible to walk the entire house in twelve—no, now less than eleven—hours. But it was still possible to walk much of it. To take action? He was less sure about that.

He stood unsteadily before the open doorway and open trap door. In the corner the blue lights faded, and with the fading it seemed there was a movement, like a wisp of mist. He didn't have to be frightened now, he told himself. He knew what he was up against. He didn't care how it showed itself, even as Vera.

He worried about how he was going to stay awake through the night, but in the kitchens it at least ought to be possible to rest and plan.

Except for the sanctuary, which was not safe after all, he wondered what else his father had built. Thoughts of Justice accompanied his trudging advance to the kitchens. Maybe he could get wired on coffee. In the kitchens he leaned against a door frame while waiting for the coffee to perk. He drowsed, standing. When the coffee perked he inhaled its aroma, took it from the heat, and leaned back against the door frame, his mind rapidly filling with dreams . . . drifting, going away into sleep—and it was the dreamed-of voice of Justice Tracker urgently calling that awakened him.

He shook his head, opened his eyes and reached for the coffee pot. It was warm. He checked his watch. Ten hours left. He'd stood there drowsing for at least a half hour.

No time for regret. He reheated the coffee, then sat at the table determined to drink the whole pot. He wished Justice had made an index to those journals. They might lead him to more information, maybe to the answer, but there was no time to do that much reading. It was John Tracker who must pull this off.

Tracker stood, checked his flashlight, and began to walk.

Before the main staircase, which ran over the hidden staircase, there was a concealed entry that also led to the second floor. If you pushed the door the wrong way you got shot. Tracker nudged the door the wrong way. It did not move. He stood to one side and pushed harder. It did not move. He pushed as hard as he could and the door remained solid. This was a mechanical trap; it did not depend on current. So he was not going to have to avoid traps. Apparently he was needed alive.

Since the generators went off, nothing but the cellar seemed affected, and you didn't need those generators to run the few small lights in the cellar.

He wished there were blueprints for the fourth floor. If he failed he would try to fling himself from one of the towers into the river. At least he would die *outside* this house. It was not much of an option, though. For one thing, it was not likely that it could be done. He would no doubt be stopped. Besides, he didn't want to die. What was worse than death? He was afraid he knew.

He climbed to the third floor and decided it came down to: what did he want? He could have money, power, youth, sex. Before coming to this house he had money, limited power, limited sex, and the knowledge that he would get old. Not so bad, but were they enough?

Amy.

He shrugged, tried to make himself ignore his feelings for her. He'd taken losses before.

The third floor was where the terraces were built, and he walked now in the direction of the large one. As he did so he concentrated on the movement of his hands, looked at his watch, looked at his legs moving . . . he couldn't afford to be drawn into the world of shifting currents beneath his feet. He looked again at his hands. Maybe hands were like the two sides of your mind.

The terrace was a broad expanse of flagstones, in the middle of which sat a fountain, decorated with concrete turtles. If you twisted one of them a chute opened that led to the cell where the skeleton lay. He didn't want to see more death and wondered if the skeleton was the same as before, lying there as though dreaming.

A cold wind across the terrace chilled him, and he walked to the edge, leaned over. A three floor drop. He would bounce off of at least one railing. It might be worth the attempt, but something was sure to break, and you could not get over that grade with a broken limb.

He turned and looked up into the dark sky. The house rose above him. Even from the third floor there was another floor to view; ornamented, threatening. Above that floor rose the towers and turret. Wind whipped and swept the terrace. He looked into the dark at the winter landscape. It seemed that nothing was alive out there. The thought struck him as even more oppressive than the house at his back. With the towers behind him, he felt as though he stood on the bridge of a great ship. Out there in the darkness was the snow-covered landscape and the hump-backed mound of freeway that vanished like a thread into darkness.

The wind whistled, moaned.

The dead spruce towered from the ground. Nothing alive out there. The world seemed dead.

Not true, he instructed himself. It was snow-covered. Dormant. The promise of growth and life lay beneath the snow. It was a renewing promise that needed the protective mantle of snow.

Sex and money and power and youth . . . Could you also have love?

He tried to clear his head. There was one decent thing in this place, and Justice had built it. He remembered now. There was a greenhouse up here. He walked toward it, eager, confident that he could cross the entire third floor and not be captured in its illusion.

He walked faster. He felt almost spiritlike, moving through the airy-feeling third floor. The greenhouse was on a small terrace, not hard to reach.

It was a good place to build a greenhouse, catching as it would the afternoon and evening sun. He walked faster still, went onto the terrace and broke into a run. The greenhouse was not large, no more than twenty-by-forty, but it was a good one. He could remember shades that could be pulled against the hottest afternoons; you had to do that for trees in order to prevent scald.

The greenhouse was almost intact, without much broken glass. Tracker opened the door, found light switches, stepped inside.

Crumbling woody plants, leafless stands of skeletal tiny branches, soil dry except under the occasional panes of broken glass where it lay frozen, light puffs of snow scattered about. Planting flats were stacked to the right of the door. Overhead irrigation was rigged from fine spray nozzles. Tracker turned a faucet, found it frozen, and checked the spray heads. They were green with corrosion now, caked about the freckling of holes that directed the mist, but it was a good rig at one time, professional. At the far end of the greenhouse was a large door, which was a rig for trees as well as plant flats.

Tools were stacked to the left of the door—reaching tools, small tools, pruners, old cord and burlap for root balls. He looked at the center section. There was probably three-and-a-half feet of soil. You could go with pretty big trees. The dead ones still standing looked like small maple.

A hand pruner, a nice tool. Tracker picked one from a rack and walked down the line. He scraped bark. Dead. He snipped top branches, went low, scraped low branches. It was all dead, no green in any of the trees, the wood brittle and turning gray. He went to the plant beds on one side. The soil was dry and cold except where moisture came through broken glass. He stirred a little of the soil with the tips of the pruners, and went for a hand rake.

One thing you learned early in this game was the tenacity of life. Even in the middle of the most arid and terrible desert, seeds lay dormant and waiting. He'd read that wheat seeds had been uncovered in a two-thousand-year-old tomb, and some of them germinated. He didn't know if that story was true, but he did know that seeds seven hundred years old had sprouted. Life was always just beneath the soil.

Tracker checked his watch, sure that time was faulting against him in the same way that it had faulted against Theophilus and Vera. He should be about other business, he should be walking, trying to understand.

He felt for the flashlight in his back pocket. One more minute or maybe two could make no difference. Rake the soil. Root with fingers at the base of plants. His hands felt like dull stumps in the freezing soil. But there was always beginning yellow or green somewhere—beneath frozen tundra, underneath salt water, flowers blooming on the edge of glaciers. Plants were the most tenacious life in the world. They had only one job, and that was to seed.

The soil was crusted. Where it was dry the loam beneath

the soil was loose. A thousand, a million webs of roots from small plants. Dead. But somewhere, surely, he would find green. He raked out ten feet of bed along one side. He checked his watch. Almost half an hour had passed. A couple more pulls with the rake and he must quit. The light was different, or else the darkness was. Was time faulting?

The best seed, he knew, held weeds. You could never get rid of weed seed, as evidenced by the skeletal remains among the tiny jungle here. Grass, dill, as many uncultivated plants as desirable ones. He'd seen enough varieties: tangles of green and red and purple attacked with hoes, flame throwers, chemicals.

He tasted the soil. There was no oil or chemical. Besides, no matter what the manufacturers said, the sprays never got full kill. A lot of times they did no better than ten percent.

The grass was dead, but there was a clump he was saving back. It was gray and dead on top. Grass could survive anywhere, though, in the cracks and crevices of twenty-story buildings, in the back of pickup trucks, even once in the trunk of his car when a coiled hose had drained on seed. He raked now all around the clump, dug with clumsy fingers, reached under the soil and felt crumbling roots, then pulled it free. It came with a puff of dust. No white, no green, no yellow. The roots fell to powder as he looked past lights and through broken glass to the sky that was like ancient night. Break loose frozen soil, pound it apart, crumble it. You could see germination that water started even if it later froze. He spit on it, rolled cold and muddy particles between cold fingers.

He frantically raked out the rest of the plant bed. He dropped the rake, turned, and thought of one last hope.

Afternoon sun would have been more on the western bed. As he raked his breath came in an almost animal-like pant. He returned to raked-over areas, crumbled soil, dug deeper, and his breath froze in bursts against the glass panes. The soil humped and hollowed and furrowed. It remained gray, dead. He finished with the bed, wheeled and walked along all the bads, and found no life. Pressure crescendoed, flowed all over him, punished him.

He was *tired.* Tired of being strong, of enduring. He wanted to give up. He sat on the edge of the plant bed, shoulders hunched and finally gave way to tears of grief and remorse. Death was failure, and failure was horror. There would be no job for him in Council Bluffs. Some other man would do that job, but it would not be the same. Who else would try the alder? Who would argue with that architect? Or argue for the right trees. He could see them already, the sweep of the dark leaves, the liquid motion and feel of alder; the straight insistence of alder that made order and sense. He was not going to get to do that job.

He checked his watch and was furious. He was not done yet. Let time whirl, let the sky color or contort. Let the wind suck dust from the terrace to cloud an ancient cathedral sky.

The dust around the roots had puffed. The roots themselves went up in tiny puffs. Dust. Death. Well, he was not dead, not yet, and he resolved that he would die before he would give up.

Time to get inside. He could not feel his fingers. He shuddered and crossed the terrace as quickly as he could. Inside it was not much warmer, but at least there was no wind.

He walked, and as he walked he searched for signs of his father.

But keep walking. If the evil of this house wanted John Tracker alive then it meant that evil could not exist without him.

In this house evil could be, but was not yet, John Tracker himself.

CHAPTER

21

A second stream of light appears in Tracker history. Sarah Heidiger was John Tracker's great grandmother on his father's father's side. Tracker legend says she was a saint, but Sarah, who was quiet, had a revolutionary source as did her daughter-in-law Vera.

Justice, himself quiet, missed the essence of his mother and grandmother. He thought Vera was only in a line of transmission for power in the house, and he was murdered too soon after Vera's death to rethink that.

In those old centuries when the sky was low and there were few sounds except for the lowing of cattle and the clank of the church bell, a second revolutionary figure captured the minds of noble and peasant alike. That figure was the Virgin Mary.

Vera rose from the revolutionary tradition of satanic rebellion. Sara rose from the revolutionary tradition of the Virgin, the last great goddess of the west.

The patriarchy assigned the best human qualities to women. Where the Virgin was the symbol of love, fireside, kindness, intelligence, good and the power of compassion; governance by men turned to greed, exploitation and war. Noble and peasant celebrated war, but they loved the Virgin.

Sarah's Catholic parents died when she was young, and she became town property in Matamorris, Ohio. From the age of two she was raised in the kitchens of a dozen wives. In that boisterous

town, families sought stability in family activity. Families over-
lapped. It is easy to see how Sarah thought that all children were
her brothers or sisters, and that all adults were in some way her
relatives.

At age twelve she was sent to a city school run by nuns. In
Presbyterian Matamorris, this caused a town feud that lasted two
generations, but the dead parents had authority in the sentiments
of most people. John and Anna Heidiger had seemed decent in spite
of their Pope.

At sixteen Sarah was teaching in her first one-room schoolhouse
near the site of present-day Rome, Indiana.

At eighteen she met Johan, and did not find him peculiar because
in his day he was not.

Sarah lived as a peacemaker in the house of the Trackers until
her death from diabetes at age forty-five. (Insulin would not be
developed until after World War I.) Sarah bore two sons—Jude,
whom she buried; Theophilus, whom she saw begin to fight for
control of the house.

There is no record of Theophilus' reaction to Sarah's death, but
local legend says that for more than two years Johan was often
found wandering in remote places. Sometimes he was sober. Some-
times he was seen working his place at three A.M. by moon and
lantern light.

Less than six hours now. John Tracker was trying to find
an entry to the fourth floor, as he had been trying for
nearly an hour. He opened doors and found them leading
through walls to empty him back again on the second or
third floor. He checked casings on the tower and found no
entry. He walked, head tilted backward, trying to find the
slightest crack in the ceiling that would show a trap door.
He had been to the very heart of this house. Now he felt
that there was no chance for him unless he went to its
highest point.

Time was passing, the minutes jumping away. Think

like a Tracker. If there was any good in this house it would be cleverly hidden. It would need to be. If any shred of mercy or rightness remained, he would only find it if he found his father. Justice must be concealed somewhere, among the tricks and the traps.

You could look at the floors if you had some object in the periphery of your vision, something to keep you in balance so that the sky of off-white did not descend. Maybe you could look at the floors if you crawled along them, cutting down on the patterns and whirling shapes.

It had to be in the floors. It took him only fifteen minutes more to find the entry.

He kicked on the floor and a trap door swung open to reveal stairs. The stairs ran down, then moved in a long, gradually rising loop. They brought him to the fourth floor, where, so far as he knew, no man but Theophilus had ever been. The long well of stairs had him breathless. The deep well of his memory would not allow him to be free of his fear. He supposed it never would.

He stepped through a doorway.

It took several moments before he comprehended the theme of the fourth floor. He was looking at himself, and, through the shock, he was realizing how badly he looked. Oil from the subcellar was caked on his clothing; his hair was stiff with oil; his face was drawn, wrinkled not with age but anxiety and fear. He turned in a complete circle three times before he accepted where he was, and what it was. And then he froze, could make no movement for minutes. This floor, seemingly stretching beyond limits, was a chorus of mirrors, of crystal and murk. It was clear, shadowed, gray, blue, red and green; it was a symphony of reflecting surfaces where waterfalls ran down sheets of polished metal. Thawing ice floated on some pools, while other pools lay deep and silently reflecting. Cold mist drifted slowly. Ice mounted in crystal spires, dripping, rolling thin layers of water toward drains.

It was the generators that had supported all this.

Ceilings were mirrored in the high distance, reflecting, refracting, writing hugely perverse images of the walker below. The walls were mirrors. The floors were overlaid with thin sheets of polished steel, aluminum, bronze, copper. Water and metal, ice and glass. Here was the weight of the house; here was what justified the enormous supporting pillars, the heavy beams, the double walls. In this place steel was a plaything.

He moved, and movement surrounded him. It danced, jigged, as mirrored surfaces reflected not only his movement but amplified ten thousand pictures of his movement. Behind him was John Tracker, before and over and beneath and beside him was John Tracker. John Tracker was being swallowed into himself.

Light, reflected, amplified, lay against the towering ceiling. There was a breath as cold as ancient winds. Sound was like the voice of a mirror. Somewhere high and thin it seemed that the wind blew a chant. Tracker, who had never been in a medieval church, believed that he was in one now . . . a cathedral of glass with steel and aluminum bones. It was new as extruded metal forms, as old as the manifest echoes of lost centuries. A cathedral that held movement even when his stopped. A fleeting something was moving; quick and light, running mirthful, flicked like a shadow in the mirrors, a creature of the mirrors.

In the center of the room an altar stood. Black reflecting glass, it towered toward other mirrors, cast fragments of black reflected like numberless eyes in the high ceilings. Around the altar the floors were etched and lay slab-like in duplicating polished surfaces, like slates that covered graves in ancient churches, shielding those with wealth who could afford burial in the stronghold against witches and demons.

It was to the altar that the insubstantial creature fled like a sardonic imp. It was toward the altar that Tracker stumbled, trying to grab the throat of the invisible, clasping in darkness, falling against the altar to see no one but himself. Dazed and disoriented, he was captured by image, by illusion.

He raised his head and looked at the dark altar, rising all the way to the high arc of ceiling. This had to be a cover, a façade, a shield that concealed one of the towers. Get inside, away from illusion. Enter the safe darkness of towers that hid you from light and its trickery. He searched, keeping his eyes close to the altar so that his impressions would be restricted. He knelt as if in prayer, hands searching. A section of the altar swung aside, a small trickle of water ran onto the reflecting floor and spread like a gloss.

It was silent and dark in the tower. He stepped inside, rested. His legs were so weak he thought he would fall. He leaned against the cold stone wall and flicked on his flashlight, which threw only a dull, orange beam. He shook it and it brightened, then went to dull orange again. There was supposed to be no influence, but why should he have expected his adversary to be guilty of honor, of holding to a promise? The darkness became luminous, and then faded.

The low orange beam of the flashlight shone on the wet steps. Tracker turned it off and slowly, reluctantly began to climb into darkness. His watch showed its luminous face, and he thought the time was up. Then he steadied his mind, added, saw that that was not yet so.

The steps corkscrewed through a midnight dark. His steps were dragging, twice he failed to raise one foot high enough and stumbled on the edge of a step, terrified of tottering backward into the gulf. His hands could barely clasp the handrail.

A whisper and rustle in the dark. The backs of his legs twitched. Muscular spasms worked his arms. He felt ready to black out, to tumble into the dark, circular well of stairs.

Take a chance. He eased down, caught a step with his hand, wedged himself against the step and the wall while one hand dangled over and wedged around a bannister.

He thought dully of Amy. He had to go on. After all, a man did not have to walk, it was not safe to walk. His hand reached the next step, clawing but tentative. Feeling with his knees, he began to crawl upward. The waterslick stairs were a cold treachery under his hands. Before him they wound into darkness. Behind him they wound like a descent into a pit.

"Help me," he said, and he did not know whether he was talking to Amy, or to his father. He felt the sharp edges of steps against his knees. It was becoming colder as he ascended. Slivers of ice crackled under his nails, and he reached further back into the sheltered corners of the steps, where the water was not yet frozen. A wind stirred in the stairwell. He remembered the tower. This must be the one that was a turret, and a huge tower rose from it.

His fingers felt like the near-senseless stubs they'd been in the greenhouse. He moved them carefully, with great concentration, like the last expression of his will. They grasped, slid, clutched and found grips as the breeze changed to wind that diminished to a low howl, washed the sides of the stairwell in a whirlpool of numbing cold. It whirled under his arms to strike his sweat cold. It pressed him down as he pressed forward. Three steps from the top he broke through the vortex and the wind became a lifting force as it plucked at him, made him feel lighter, denied his weight against the now completely iced steps across which water ran in a slow trickle.

He fought upward, gripped wall and bannister, half-raised his head like a blind and groping creature.

And then he attained the top, fell forward. Light and wind poured over him. Moonlight, broken by clouds, touched him, departed. His mind searched for sleep, refusing to go further. But this was the turret, and there was still the tower. He struggled to get up, fell, struggled again. He was still on all fours as he crawled toward an open, wind-swept wall and hooked his frozen hands over the rimmed brickwork and pulled himself up.

He was looking onto the river, which wound far and dark below to the horizon. It elbowed, fishhooked, made black patterns across the land; and on each side of the river were dark forests that in daylight would show the winter green of conifer. He had planted some of those trees when he was fifteen. He remembered the loamy smell of the seedlings as they were unpacked from wet burlap. Perhaps it did not matter, but surely he had planted at least some of those trees. He looked up and down the river, which here and there was lighted under a glimpse of moon. His eyes watered from the wind, but his body was regaining strength and his perceptions seemed cleared by the wind.

Over the bluff and down, he must be four hundred feet above the river. He had planted on the other side, and guessed at the once burned areas where he'd worked twenty-five years ago. The river ran around a bend. You could get away with pine on the lee side, but he would have been tempted to experiment with cypress, which could take a hell of a lot of wind and some cold.

Cold. It was so cold. He turned back, slipped on the ice and fell. The door to the tower was straight ahead. It stood slightly open, like an invitation. He crawled to the door, reached to pull it open. He climbed through over a sill of ice, raised himself, knelt back in a squat and looked into moonlight . . . knelt there looking at the final, terrible human sacrifice that had not been a sufficient offering to save Theophilus Tracker.

John Tracker looked up into the dead and at last tranquil face of his own father—Justice dead by *his* own father's hand.

CHAPTER

22

John Heideger, John Tracker's great great grandfather on his father's father's mother's side, died young. Both he and his wife Anna Schmidt are an enigma. Records reveal nothing of when John and Anna appeared in Matamorris, Ohio, except that it was shortly before the Civil War. Sarah Heideger was their only offspring. Anna died of "milk fever," infection of the uterus and womb, shortly after giving birth. She was about nineteen.

John, still in his early twenties, was killed two years later. A group of men loading logs on a barge stacked the load too high and a man was pinned by a sudden shift. Heideger rushed forward. Both were crushed when the load tumbled. John Heideger, like Justice Tracker, showed that when some Trackers die, it is not always without purpose.

Consciousness, a feeble ebb, touched him, departed, returned. Tracker tried first to flex his freezing fingers. Though cold, it was not as cold in the tower, so that he found himself lying in water and not on ice.

Slowly he remembered where he was, and what he had seen. It was incredible, perverse, and because it was, Tracker knew that it was the work of Theophilus—the furious closing statement that transcended the endless halls and rooms of the house of the Trackers.

No doubt his nemesis was certain this sight would assure his destruction as well. He clutched with stiff, trembling hands and found that he was clawing up sodden handfuls of money. In truth, he lay face down on a carpet of money. Slowly he scrabbled an area of the floor clear so that his hands could get purchase, and came to a kneeling posture and looked about before raising his head. Money lay like a sacrifice around the room, a circular room not more than fifteen feet across. The shaft rose in the center, and at its base was a great stack of cash. It was too much to simply pick up and count. Impossible to step without wading in cash, kicking it like sodden, rotting leaves. It was scattered, tumbled, stacked, piled—green and gray and gold and silver. Water festered at the bottom of the piles, covered the floors, plastered the bills against each other.

Blowers from refrigeration machinery were spaced along otherwise smooth walls of stainless steel that gleamed dull in the moonlight. It was the silent blower units that told Tracker he was in the middle of an enormous freezer; a freezer that cut when the generators died. It explained the water, the refrigerator smell. The walls were otherwise round and smooth, and moonlight filtered through sets of heavy, double-paned and vacuum-sealed glass. Far above, a variable, cloud-scudding light fell softly along the base of the thick wooden shaft.

The shaft was a cross upon which Justice Tracker hung. The feet were lashed to the wood six feet above the floor, and money was piled to an inch beneath the toes. The naked body was cinched to the shaft by a rope tied around its middle. The arms were spread and bound, and one was disjointed where Theophilus had broken it in order to attain the position. The head slumped slightly forward, but it did not fall as far as a dead man's head should fall. John crawled across the money, looked up, was not surprised to find that the head was wired with a padeye that entered the wood; another padeye was screwed into the skull.

John tried to rise, slipped and fell. He hooked his hands in the grating of a blower and pulled himself to his feet. Strength was returning to his legs, his heart was thumping like a sledge on set-stakes. Slowly he walked the perimeter of the room, kicked sodden cash before him as he walked.

He thought of Theophilus, staggering, after he had opened the sanctuary and drawn forth the corpse. He thought of the long walk as Theophilus bore his son's body to this tower, of Theophilus returning to whatever treasury he owned, bearing load after load of wealth in hopes of further appeasing the destroyer that had taken him over.

Tracker kicked wet cash before him as he walked, at last stopped to stand in front of his dead father. Where the weight fell against the rope that cinched the middle, flesh rolled and puffed. A nail secured one hand. The other hand was not nailed and dangled from the lashed arm. Light from high windows touched the fingertips and turned them lifelike. Perhaps an hour of sunlight had warmed the upper air of the shaft, and the partly thawed body of Justice Tracker was colored in moving streaks of white and gray and ash in the flooding winter moonlight.

The face looked dry, the hair slack but dry and still retaining the thick mat and curl around the ears. There was a light beard.

Tracker stood looking at his father, a portrait more masterful, in its terrible way, than the one in stained glass at the front of the house. With a difference. The face of Justice Tracker now was calm. There was no dying despair from belated wisdom. The face was at peace. Above it the tower reached twenty feet higher into the scudding mist, and the gray and ashen light shifted gently across the face, again suggesting life.

Remembrance. Words that for half his lifetime had

been discounted. The voice of his father . . . "I hope you'll understand this, but please remember until you do understand." "I'll remember," John had said. "But, I've got homework, and I have to clean my room." "A minute more. Stay just a minute more and give me your attention. It wanders." "Yes, sir." "Hope you'll care enough to remember this. Those who have the most owe the most, and it can't be paid with money."

"We have a lot, sir."

"Of everything. You'll understand that later. You've got your mother's eye, her hands, her feeling for the form and shape of things. Maybe that's part of what you owe."

He had not, of course, understood, nor had he tried to remember. But now he stood looking at the face of his father, felt the returning movement of his own fingers, felt strength pouring into his arms, his legs. Now, for him, was the time to search, to discover, even to feel grief. He gazed at the face of his dead father, felt his own life reach out.

His voice choked, turned against him, and his mind faltered as he searched for a statement. "Good-bye, sir," he said.

Tracker turned, pushed open the door which had been so carefully left ajar. He stepped onto the windswept turret, felt for the presence and knew it was there, hovering like a question. He looked at the river and the scudding clouds. He saw his old planting of trees. He turned back to the stairs and descended into darkness. Grief for his father was mixed with a celebration for his father's success. He held the feelings closely, felt their warmth but disclosed no emotion.

The traps were real. The presence hovered about him, questioning if it had won. When it answered its question he would have to be careful. He wound down circling stairs and saved his dying batteries for moments when only light could assure his decision.

The mind of Theophilus, the mind of Vera, of Johan;

the mind of the entire Tracker past was in these halls and rooms and darkness. It was a mechanical, and at the same time, superstitious mind. Tracker could respect it, he could no longer fear it. He could, he must, face it and control it.

The mind of the past had sense and form, it had control and structure, and it was bankrupt. In his mind were the firm tones of his father.

". . . who have the most owe the most . . ."

Tracker did not know precisely what he had, so he could not know precisely what he owed. That was in the future. It had to be pursued, its full nature discovered. He did, though, know what he owed Justice Tracker. First, right now, it was to outstride this house. Later, it might be that what he owed would kill him, as Justice's search and understanding had killed him. But for now he had a single purpose, and he believed he had the strength for it.

Evil was weakened once one understood its corrupt premise, but it was like a trapped animal . . . it could rend and tear and kill in the throes of its own extinction.

He did not know how long it took him to go down to the first floor. It made no difference. Only his actions counted. He entered the old part of the house, turned off feeble electric lights as he moved. He walked through the kitchens with the kind of deliberation of a man about to say good-bye to this house. He felt a kind of tranquility in his obligation to Justice. He walked to his father's room, entered the sanctuary, went to the desk, flipped through the pages of the summary, then laid the book down. He turned back, leaned against the great doors to close them, then turned and walked toward the kitchens. He rattled his flashlight. The orange beacon of his flashlight was even dimmer now as Tracker deliberately began to make his way to the center of the house, to the pit—to the well.

As he started downward the heat was like a blow as he entered the subcellar. He smelled oil. He walked forward to the well, to the huge slab of ornamented black marble, slick with oil at this lowest spot in the house. His shoes seemed to suck up the oil. The brooding figure of Theophilus hung in that midnight path that ran between the machines of destruction.

He found what he wanted. Dry fragile timbers from the press designed to break bodies came apart and splintered with a single kick. He picked up a timber, then another, and he returned to the well. He felt the presence, questioning.

He laid the timbers beside the well, and they absorbed oil like sponges. Kneeling, he lit a match.

Thus, he thought in a biblical fashion that was at once alien and yet natural, once blazed the torches of Gideon.

Held upright, the torch burned in a black-smoking flame from the top. It would burn downward like a candle as it was held upright. He lit both of them and threw one. He pressed the second torch into the face of blackness. Once again he heard the scream of Theophilus that had torn the house, and out of the well the dessicated corpse of Vera rose and turned to flame.

But these were merely artifacts of the house. Already destroyed. He had a larger purpose. Now. He pressed forward, pushing the torch in front of him, and entered the passageway. Behind him there was flame.

And the attack came, as he knew it must. His legs weakened. Time shifted as he climbed the passage, and he felt as though he were falling through space against a background of blue stars . . .

Somehow he steadied himself. The torch threw shadows and dull light. Smoke lay in his lungs like acid. He moved forward and age crept over him. He turned forward, then back, then forward again, fighting the past and its pain with fire.

234

Next to the top of the passage, across the broad plain of the cellar until he found the stairs. The torch flickered. His breathing was shallow. Behind him, in the heart of the house, a murmur sounded, a roar dulled by distance like steam blowing from a drowning vessel. He reached the top of the stairs, and with his last strength threw the torch forward and lay in a near stupor as he watched dusty, dry fabric of drapes and cracked rugs ignite. The room came alive with fire.

He did not move, could not move, until the house shuddered, the sound like an enormous sigh. Now he began to struggle to his feet. In the distance, the floor raised, the explosion welled and boomed and threw fire into the kitchens. Fire burst through the rooms as fuel and trapped gas lying deep in the well reached into the house.

The fire surrounded John Tracker. He stood victorious and burning.

His shoes were aflame, and his hair. He turned and ran, a torch that ran and staggered to the front door, spreading sparks as he rolled across the porch into the snow, face burned, hair gone, feet cooked.

The snow smothered the fire and saved him. His pain was severe but the snow covered it. He got up on legs that flashed with pain but managed to carry him to the grade, which he clambered like a desperate beast, mindless in flight. When he made the top of the grade he fell in the snow, squirmed around to face the house.

The light began slowly, flickering from the inner parts of the house. Drafts and crosscurrents in those endless and winding halls were sucking the fire. For a long time in the darkness there was no more than a faint red and yellow glow.

Tracker lay panting, waiting for control.

The light moved here and there, shifting, growing, steadily becoming a force in itself. Yet for a long time as he lay in the deep snow there was no visible smoke or flame.

Then a tendril of smoke appeared as fire sucked up from some unknown shaft. A puff then of smoke through a partly open window. The drafts moved the fire, fanned the fire, spread the fire. Flame was appearing from the depths of the house as a door fell open and the angel took a last walk through the snow of the front porch, presented the upside down cross like a salute, turned mechanically on its tracks and disappeared through a door into the growing flame. Its final exit was complete, no trick.

Now the fire took firm hold as windows on the second floor heated and shattered, the winter air pouring in, feeding the growing combustion.

On the third floor an explosion threw phosphorus to break windows and bring a draft. A fiery trap, the house was broken.

Sounds of the fire swirled, crackling and popping. The stained glass window on the front of the house came alive, illuminated by fire. Flame burst from the window on the fourth floor, danced through the skylights. Reflected brilliance sparkled against clouds of dark smoke. Fire reached now toward the tower of Justice. Fire bloomed now above the construction of Theophilus, broadcasting its brilliant color into the night sky. John saw headlights in the distance and knew that he would soon be joined by men from the towns, the streets. He turned to look at the country road, and then at the empty expanse of freeway. The night winds moved about him. It must be nearly dawn.

The tower where Justice hung was now aflame, the fire high and dancing in the winter wind. Tracker turned back to the house to see the pyre of Justice burning like a beacon.

The fire searched. It was finished in the bowels of the house, stretching out and transmitting heat along pipes, telegraphing itself. The front rooms were in rapid destruction, and as John looked at the melting stained glass, the figure of the sorrowful face began to move forward, smoking, disintegrating as the melting lead lost form and it crashed forward. A spray of flame followed, reached across the snow toward the dead spruce, which ignited slowly at first, and then the fire climbed quickly among the brown needles, and Tracker recoiled as the dead tree turned into a monument of flame.

A sound of collapsing timbers as part of the second floor caved in, and it was then that the screams began. They would live with him as long as there was time. They seemed to rise with the smoke, sounding through the night like souls battering to get to the sanctuary of an ancient church.

From deep in the heart of the house the explosion built, gained form in the center of the fire, rose like a grounding wave as a deep pocket of gas in the substrata inflamed, expanded, ignited. The explosion grew and boiled up through the sinking house and collapsing tower. Fire and exploding timbers rose in the air on the heavy sound of thunder as Tracker stumbled down the grade, falling, sliding, past what he thought was the face of Amy, the faces of police, and into the outstretched arms of a black-suited black-cloaked figure.

EPILOGUE *John Tracker's family faltered in the third and fourth generations. John would understand that Johan, Theophilus, Vera and others of his ancestors may have been hideous, but few of them had any doubt about who they were. That question was reserved for his parents and himself.*

The black loam shone dark and rich in the sunlight as it cascaded from the yellow dump trucks. Behind him the continual rising and falling roar of a D6 Cat was a stacatto across the raw land as it knifed the soil, hit rough grades, a small flame at its stack. The backhoes were already chopping trenches for irrigation pipe.

Tracker stood on a small rise, in his mind already seeing the sweep of alder. He checked his watch. Her plane was not due yet.

In a way he still had hope. Amy was coming back from Europe. This man John Tracker who would meet her was not the same man as before. He was pretty sure that Amy was also changed. Her voice on the phone told him part of what she felt and thought. He needed to hear it all.

He leaned on the new, yellowish cane that he would be using for a while. Intending to think of Amy, he instead thought of other women who had touched his life . . . his grandmother Vera. His mother Sarah.

Then he thought of still other women in his experience, women who had sometimes touched him, tried to love him, or who were attracted by his business success. He hoped all was all right with those women. He hoped they had dismissed his failings, but he especially hoped they had forgiven themselves their own. These were new thoughts for him.

Amy had gone to see that man in Europe, and Tracker understood that she either had to enliven or bury the past. Coming from a hospital bed as he had—and facing the job of liquidating the business—put work in front of some other new feelings that were difficult to handle. If the future presented him a condition that did not include Amy, there would be time enough to feel pain. If the future presented Amy, there would be time enough to feel other emotions. He smiled, shrugged and turned to the small man who approached him in such a hurry.

"You can see how it will be," Tracker said, pointing to the curving sweep of grade that would lie graceful as the easily moving river. "It isn't just the pull-off of the darker color."

The architect was well-dressed. He moved efficiently and had an efficient mouth. "It's your baby," he said. "I only point out that you've doubled your cost on those trees."

"It won't break me."

"Like I said, it's your baby." The man turned to head for his car, stopped for a moment. It seemed that his eyes were also registering invisible trees, then he shrugged, checked his watch and nearly ran to his car.

Tracker thought then of the men. His grandfather Theophilus, his father Justice. He thought of men with whom he had done business, and of the auctioneer who had trained him. He hoped those men were all right. Even his grandfather.

A different river ran low in the background. In Council Bluffs the land rose gradually in a deceptive grade at this point. It was going to require a cut to bedrock. He did not think he'd have to blast, though. From the nearby road a string of dumps were coming on the job. Across the job, machinery moved in a purposeful, intricate counterpoint.

Amy must surely have questions. Perhaps he could help answer some of them. He could tell her how he had once tried so hard to explain too much of the inexplicable in the house of the Trackers with his grandfather's tricks and his great grandfather's constructions against the devil. How his superficial need for rational, worldly explanations had nearly kept him from recognizing the reality of the under-lying force that had been loose in the house, the well-spring of all that was time-warping him, and her; indeed, for centuries the world—the deadly, too long transcen-dent reality of evil incarnate. And shunning sufficient rec-ognition of it for so long, he had very nearly let them both be destroyed by it. Yes, he could try to tell her something of this, and hope she would understand. She had, after all, as he had, been exposed to it, fought it and survived. If she wanted to try, and he did—and he somehow felt they both would—then she could count on him for whatever support one human being could give another. Only, he couldn't act for her, he couldn't make her less than thirty . . . He could guess her terror and exhaustion during that walk into the night and the snow. He could understand how the farm family who picked her up believed she was out of her mind. He knew what kind of argument—and acting—from a hospital bed must have gone into the final persuasion that brought her back with police and a priest.

Laborers with grade rakes were already hitting some of the contours. The sight of men carefully making accurate forms with a rake made him feel that he was watching something very old which was also exciting and new. It was a feeling that continually came to him these days. He

241

rubbed the side of his face, automatically touched the scar that lay like a permanent burn, and knew that this was his last landscaping job. There was more to trees than planting them.

He smiled, nearly laughed and turned to look over the great run of land. High cumulus floated in blue air. The spring rains had been heavy. The grass was waist high in the countryside. Upstate, the deer would be crossing the highways. There was sense to it all, power in it all. Tracker tested the air, tested the force of his mind, and felt renewed.